The Greek Coins Affair

Rick Adelmann

Mysteries by Rick Adelmann

2020 New Titles:

The Greek Coins Affair
The Hilltop Ranch Affair
The Blue Sky Affair
The San Carlos Business Guild Affair
The Forgotten Murder Affair
The Irish Manor House Affair

The Greek Coins Affair

MG&M Detective Agency Mysteries, Book 1

Rick Adelmann

Secret Staircase Books

The Greek Coins Affair
Published by Secret Staircase Books, an imprint of
Columbine Publishing Group, LLC
PO Box 416, Angel Fire, NM 87710

Book layout and design by Secret Staircase Books
Cover images © alaver, Alona Stepaniuk

First trade paperback edition: April, 2020
First e-book edition: April, 2020

* * *

Publisher's Cataloging-in-Publication Data

Adelmann, Rick
The Greek Coins Affair / by Rick Adelmann.
p. cm.
ISBN 978-1649140050 (paperback)
ISBN 978-1649140043 (e-book)

1. MG&M Detective Agency (Fictitious). 2. Jazz Age—Fiction. 3. Roaring '20s—Fiction. 4. Major James Mallory (Fictitious character)--Fiction. 5. Sherwood Garth (Fictitious character)
6. Private investigators—Fiction. I. Title

MG&M Detective Agency Mystery Series : Book 1.
Adelmann, Rick, MG&M Detective Agency mysteries.

BISAC : FICTION / Mystery & Detective.

813/.54

I would like to thank those who provided valuable input and fair criticism into my writing. For my fellow writers in my critiquing group Writer's Round Table, thank you for putting up with me over the last five years. There are many friends in this group and I don't want to leave any names out. So, thank you all for your help.

Chapter One

It Begins With the Stones

The trip up the west coast of Africa and around the Iberian Peninsula had taken four days. Henry Spellman stood at the bow, staring out to sea. "We're almost home, Chadwick," he said to the slightly built, older man clinging to the railing next to him. "Well, your home anyway. I could tell by the dirty, brown skies ahead."

"Must you always be so caustic, my good man?" Sir Holdsworth responded. He gazed out to sea, his small eyes searching the surface of the water.

"What the hell ya looking for, Chadie? You seem as nervous as a dogged squirrel."

"Periscopes," he answered, his white hair flapping in the cold wind. "Those devils are out there, waiting for us to cross their paths."

Spellman started to laugh heartily, then shook his head. "You're not gonna see no periscopes, ya fool. The Kaiser is a man of his word. He said he wouldn't torpedo any ships in the south Atlantic. Quit your squirming and enjoy the trip."

HMS Aquitania passed by the White Cliffs of Dover as the two passengers stood on the lower deck, watching the shoreline of England draw close.

"I say, do you think they've discovered our deception yet?" Holdsworth asked.

Spellman stared down at the dirty foam along the hull. "I told Douglas we needed to go to Pretoria to renew our mining permit. He was more than happy to scrape up as many diamonds as he could while we were gone. The greedy bastard. The round trip to Pretoria and back to the Kimberley River would have taken a week or better."

"So, he won't suspect anything until sometime next week. And, Steven Jackson is too addlebrained to know that we're gone."

"Relax, old fellow, I've got it all covered." Spellman made a crooked grin as he slapped the older man's shoulder. "As long as you've got everything set up in London."

Holdsworth gazed up into the dark clouds. "Yes, he'll be there. Miserable day, don't you think? Inopportune time of year to travel."

"It'll be fine," Spellman answered, but a shadow of gloom seemed to fall over him. "I like it dark. It covers my thoughts like a cold blanket."

On this voyage, along with these two men, the commandeered *Aquitania* held fifteen hundred soldiers of the Rhodesian Regiment. Their next stop was Southampton, then to a training camp in the north of Wales. After that, the miserable trenches of France and Belgium to face the Germans.

The two civilians had paid the captain's mate a considerable sum to share an officer's quarters. No questions asked, and no explanation offered for their immediate departure from Africa.

Sir Holdsworth had spent almost all of the voyage on the flush deck, pacing nervously as he stared out to sea, his face drawn, his skin chalky. He hadn't slept well for some time.

Henry Spellman, the American, was more adventurous. He spent a lot of time below deck playing cards with the crew and soldiers, where he had a talent for getting the winning cards. He took a great deal of money as well as the ire of his opponents.

The two noticeably different men held the same secret. One feared capture, the other, ostensibly, dared the authorities to catch him.

They arrived at Southampton on Monday, January seventh. Sir Holdsworth wired ahead for his driver, Malcolm, to pick them up at the port. He arrived in Holdsworth's 1909 Rolls-Royce Silver Ghost. Outside of Holdsworth Manor, the auto was his last possession of value.

Malcolm loaded the luggage into the Silver Ghost and drove toward London. "Will you be going to the manor house, sir?"

"Not today," Holdsworth said from the back seat. "We will stay at the Rosewood Hotel tonight, taking the train to Leeds in the morning. We'll be at the house by nightfall."

"You know that you were not expected until the eighteenth, sir. None of the staff will be there."

"I understand that, Malcolm. Once we're settled at the hotel, you can take the auto up. Contact Noreen and have her supply us with enough food for a couple of days and prepare the boiler with hot water. The two of you may then resume your holiday as planned," Holdsworth added, retrieving his gold watch from his vest pocket. "We'll all meet at the manor house on the eighteenth."

"Very good, sir."

Sir Holdsworth stepped into the hotel's lobby as Malcolm placed the luggage on the sidewalk. Returning to the auto, Spellman walked up to the driver's side. "Hey buddy, make sure you and Noreen aren't at the house when we get there Wednesday night. We've got a confidential business matter to deal with." He slapped Malcolm on the forearm, giving a wink. "You can go now."

"We're checked in," Holdsworth said as he returned to the sidewalk. Porters had already picked up the luggage and were on their way to the room. "I say, where's Malcolm? I wanted to give him some last-minute instructions."

"He told me he had something to do, and left," Spellman lied. "He said he'd see you on the eighteenth.'"

"Dash it all! He knows better than to run off like that."

"Go easy on the guy, Chadie. After all, he's on holiday." Spellman grinned.

"We have an appointment with Rupert Shepperson at ten tomorrow morning," Holdsworth said, still upset with Malcolm.

"The man from the British History Museum?" Spellman asked, hoping there were no prying ears.

"Indeed. He'll bring the 'items' with him." Holdsworth felt equally cautious. "Rupert wants to conclude the trade as soon as possible."

"As I do," Spellman said, walking up to the hotel entrance. Once inside, Spellman took Holdsworth's arm and led him to a quiet corner of the lobby. "How do we know we can trust this chap of yours?"

"I explained before," Holdsworth snapped, shaking his arm free of Spellman's hold. "Rupert is an expert in Greek antiquities. I've known him for years; he's bloody good to his friends."

"I'll take your word for it. I'm going to the bar to get rid of my sea legs."

* * *

Tuesday morning came with a hangover for Spellman and another sleepless night for Holdsworth. The Englishman didn't like being in the middle of this. However, if he didn't follow through on his end, he would lose everything.

It appeared Shepperson was also in a hurry to make the exchange. Holdsworth and Spellman arrived at the Sweetings Restaurant just after nine o'clock, carrying a brown leather valise. The restaurant owner met them as they entered, "Mr. Shepperson is waiting at your table, gentlemen."

Only a sliver of light came through the front window blinds. Holdsworth gazed about the dining room. "Where is everyone?"

"We don't open until two this afternoon, sir," the owner answered. "I am a friend and confidant of Shep. I allowed him the use of the booth in the back for your meeting."

"Did he tell you why we're here?" Spellman asked.

"No, sir. He said I didn't need to know."

"Then, let's keep it that way," Spellman advised, with a hard glare at the owner. "You can go about your business as long as you don't listen to our conversation."

"I was about to do that, sir," The owner answered, pulling back the curtain to the booth. He glowered at Spellman and walked to the kitchen.

The short, plump Rupert Shepperson sat with his back to the wall. He eyed Spellman suspiciously when the two men entered.

Holdsworth saw the doubt on his friend's face. "It's okay, Shep. He is trustworthy. I've been in the fields of Africa with him for quite a long time."

"Sorry, old chap. I'm a bit put out about this whole affair. Sit down and pour yourselves some tea," Shepperson offered, pointing to the teapot and cups on the table.

"Ain't no time for tea," Spellman said, as he straddled his chair backward. "Show him what we got, Chadie."

Holdsworth glared at the uncouth American whom he was beginning to loathe. "You must do something about your rude demeanor, old boy," he said as Spellman slid a plate toward him. "It's not good for business."

"Never mind about my demeanor, Chadie," Spellman growled. "Here, dump the rocks on this plate so he can see them."

Spellman moved the valise across the floor to Holdsworth with his foot. The older man opened the bag, pried the false bottom open, and retrieved a black cloth pouch from a secret compartment. He poured its contents, clattering, onto the plate, then slipped the plateful of diamonds to Shepperson. The antiquities expert held onto a small, oblong wooden box with brace hinges that sat in front of him.

"Allow me to examine these stones." Shepperson brought out his tools and gave a sigh as he appraised the diamonds. He held each stone up to the light, gazing through his loupe at it. Spellman and Holdsworth remained silent, noting that Rupert smiled and nodded as he went through them meticulously. "Quite exquisite. I am satisfied with the quality of the diamonds. Here are the coins." He slid the small oblong box across the table to Spellman's eager hands.

Squinting at the eight small objects inside, Spellman asked, "How do I know these are the real McCoy?" He leaned back in his chair.

"I'm the curator of Greek antiquities," Shepperson exclaimed, his chin up. "I can guarantee their authenticity. If you don't trust me, we can stop this transaction right now."

"I've never known Shep to cheat a friend," Holdsworth said.

"You can take the coins or leave them." Shepperson appeared angry with Spellman's attitude. "There are others who would give anything for them."

"It's a shame you can't sell these coins yourself. They're worth a fortune."

"Yes, Mr. Spellman, I know their value. However, if I were to sell them, the world of coin brokers would know at once who sold them. Remember, I'm the curator, I'm responsible for the coins. However, I can go to Stockholm and sell these gems without being caught. So, I will accept your offer." He bagged the diamonds, then slipped them into his overcoat pocket. "The coins are yours."

"We'll keep them in the same box," Spellman said, handing it to Holdsworth. "And divide them once we get to Holdsworth Manor."

"It's a bloody shame we have to break up the set," Holdsworth muttered as he gazed fondly into the open box. "My buyer in Scotland would be quite jolly to have them all."

"Yeah, it's a bloody shame, all right," Spellman replied under his breath.

"Oh, so you're staying in London a bit longer?" Shepperson asked, rising from the table.

"Only another day. I have reservations on a ship that will depart Liverpool in a week. I thought Leeds would be a good out-of-the-way spot to lay low until the ship leaves."

* * *

They arrived in Leeds, County Yorkshire, the next afternoon. The train carried them through open lands and hills, giving Spellman a view he had never seen before. But he wasn't at all interested in sightseeing. His mind was on the coins and the fortune he would make in Chicago. They summoned a cab for the trip from the train station to Holdsworth Manor and arrived just before sundown.

At first sight, Spellman was impressed at the size of Holdsworth Manor and its ornate architecture. But, as they drew closer, he saw why Chadwick needed money. The building was in terrible disrepair. Upon entering, the shabbiness of the interior stood out to Spellman as well.

Noreen had provided a platter of cold cuts, bread, and cheese for them. The two men ate heartily then retired to the front parlor. Holdsworth filled the air with the scent of strong Turkish tobacco as he smoked one of his pipes. Spellman pulled out a pack of cigarettes.

"So, you've got your buyer lined up, Chadie?" Spellman asked, watching the rings of smoke he blew.

"But, of course, young man. Always be prepared, that's what I say," Holdsworth answered, puffing contentedly on his pipe. "I told you in London, he's a man with money, up in Edinburgh. Always on the prowl for coins to add to his collection."

"He'd certainly like all eight of them."

"Indeed, he would, but he'll have to be satisfied with the four I have," he said, tapping the ashes from his pipe. "I think I'll go upstairs and bathe. I feel quite fatigued from our trip."

"Good idea. I'll go change into something comfortable." As Holdsworth left the parlor and went to the staircase, Spellman rose and walked around the house. He explored the servants' quarters and found it empty. Next, he stepped outside into the cold night air and trod through the snow. Opening the side door of the garage, he saw only Holdsworth's automobile. They were surely alone.

Spellman went to his assigned room, but not to relax. He had other plans. Down the hall was the master bedroom. He listened to water flow into the bathtub. He continued to listen while removing his socks and shoes. He listened as he rolled up his pant legs and shirt cuffs.

Down the hallway, he stood quietly, his ear to Holdsworth's door. He waited until he heard Holdsworth turn off the water, a sigh escaping the old man's lips as he slipped into the tub.

Spellman opened the door, swiftly walked through Holdsworth's bedroom, and into the bath.

"Dash it all, Spellman, can't a man have some privacy?"

In one quick movement, Spellman reached into the

water and grabbed Holdsworth's ankles, jerking them up, forcing his victim's head below the water. He stepped into the tub and planted his right foot firmly against Holdsworth's neck.

Holdsworth squirmed, struggling desperately to push himself up, but Spellman was too strong for him. The old man grabbed the leg holding him down but was unable to budge it.

Spellman clenched his ankles firmly. "You're giving me one hell of a fight, you old codger. Did you think I would let you have all eight of the coins?" He laughed as his victim writhed in agony under him. "Go ahead, keep trying to kick free," Spellman said through gritted teeth. Finally, Holdsworth became still. Spellman continued to hold him, another full two minutes.

Finally, he stepped from the tub, removed the shower curtain, and wrapped the body in it. In his own room he dried off and redressed. Putting on his overcoat, he returned to the bath and dragged Holdsworth down the stairs to the back entrance. He peered outside once more, gazing around the grounds. Malcolm wasn't lying; no one was on or around the property.

Spellman felt elated. He'd just committed the perfect murder and knew he would get away with it. He laughed as he dragged the frail body across the frozen ground to the gazebo he'd seen when they'd arrived. Removing a few boards at the bottom of the gazebo was easy enough. Shoving the naked body of Holdsworth was just as simple. The skinny little runt slid right in, out of sight.

Spellman returned to the house. He rehung the bathroom curtain, emptied the tub, and cleaned up the excess water splashed about the room. His next step was to slide Sir Holdsworth's luggage under the gazebo as well. He then set the boards back in place.

His final step was to go to the study, find something written in Holdsworth's hand, and copy a note to the butler. The note stated that Holdsworth would stay in London indefinitely. Just in case the butler became curious, the note didn't say where Holdsworth would be staying.

He tacked the note to the butler's pantry door then went upstairs for his own luggage. He especially wanted to check on the small valise. All eight coins were present and accounted for. They sat in the hidden compartment, where the diamonds had been placed before the transaction.

"It's over." Spellman got into the Silver Ghost, which Malcolm had left for them, and drove toward Liverpool. He would soon board the *HMS Aquitania*; yes, he had lied about that too. He didn't have to wait even a few days. The *Aquitania* was leaving Liverpool tomorrow on its last leg of the trip to America. It was due to arrive in New York on the twenty-first.

Unless an iceberg blocked their way, he would be a free man with a fortune in ancient coins securely hidden in his valise.

Chapter Two

The Soldier Meets the Investigator

I waited anxiously for the arrival of Lieutenant Patrick Brady of the Cleveland Police Department. As I paced the floor, dispelling excess energy, I peered through the curved frosted windows of my library, searching with my one good eye for Brady's car.

I unfolded the slip of paper Brady had sent and reread it:

My old friend,

I have a special favor to ask of you. A distinguished young man is coming to live in Cleveland. He received the transfer notice with little warning and now needs a residence for a short time until he finds his own dwelling.

If you would be so kind as to consider this request, I will be dropping by with the gentleman tomorrow afternoon.

With my regards,
Lt. Patrick Brady

I looked around the library and adjacent hallway, thinking that this old, stone mansion has stood on Sumner Street for decades. It has too many empty bedrooms. So I agreed.

The only other information Brady had shared with me was that my guest had spent time with the New York Police Department as a detective. I trusted the lieutenant as a family friend and knew he wouldn't saddle me with a wayward wanderer. However, his description of the man as unusual and engaging bothered me. I waited anxiously to see what he meant by that. I have the unfortunate habit of being prematurely judgmental when I meet someone. First impressions are important to me. I say unfortunate, but a lot of the time, I pin the man for what he is right up front. If I don't like the guy, out he goes.

Little did I know, this stranger would alter my life in a way I never expected. If I had known it, at the time, I'm not sure I would have taken him in. As I write this down, I must say, I'm glad I did.

* * *

As usual, in early February, there was a foot of snow on the ground with the expectation of more. The snow softened the view of the cemetery across the road. The gravestones spent the winter of 1918 comfortably wrapped in a blanket of warm snow in anticipation of spring on its way to uncover them. My thoughts shifted to the poor souls huddled in the trenches of war-torn France. As a retired Army man, I understood the ugliness and devastation of war.

Thankfully, the weather didn't dampen the tenacity of the old policeman. I saw Brady's little 1914 Scripps-Booth

Rocket wobbling down Sumner Street at close to thirty miles an hour. I watched the automobile slide from one side of the street to the other. Fresh snow flew up the side of the vehicle like the wings of an angel. I smiled, watching Brady try to keep from sliding off the road. He drove up to the front of my house and slid to a sudden stop.

Brady, a tall, thin man, exited the driver's side. He wore a long wool overcoat with the collar turned up to protect his ears from the cold. A wide-brimmed Fedora was pulled snugly over his bald head.

I was more interested in his passenger. Brady pulled a couple of satchels from the trunk, while an average-sized man, who appeared to be about thirty-five, stepped out of the automobile. He covered his broad shoulders with a chocolate brown overcoat with a fur collar. He wore a Fedora as well, but his hat was black velvet with a felt band. The band held a few blue feathers.

What a dandy, I thought as I watched him. He walked through the snow to the back of the Rocket, picked up both satchels with ease, and tramped up to the front door. Brady trailed behind the energetic young man. I moved away from the window, walked to my mahogany desk, and pulled out another of my favorite, thin cigars. After stubbing out the first, I lit the new one. An energetic dandy, yet a dandy, I thought.

Frederick, my elderly butler, gardener, handyman, close friend, and confidant, answered the door. I didn't wait for Frederick to escort them to the library. Instead, I met them in the entry hall.

"Lieutenant Brady, sir," Frederick announced as if I didn't recognize Patrick. Frederick played the part of a faithful butler well. In reality, he and his dear wife Elizabeth were my guardians as I grew up.

"Thank you, Frederick. We'll leave the gentleman's bags here for the moment," I said, studying the young man who stood next to Brady.

My potential boarder removed his coat and hat and handed them to Frederick. He was what the ladies would call 'dashingly handsome.' His dark brown, almost black, hair was brushed back. He had short sideburns and no other facial hair. His prominent feature was his sky blue eyes, eyes that were all the more vivid in contrast with his olive complexion. My guest smiled at me and revealed a near perfect set of teeth. This guy's put together, I thought, as Brady pulled off his hat and overcoat. Brady had a stern, cold look in his eyes. However, the family has known him for years as a jovial man when not on duty.

"James, I'd like to introduce Mr. Sherwood Garth," Brady said, tilting his round, bald head toward Garth.

"You must be Major James Mallory." My visitor sharply extended his hand to me.

"Yes, Mr. Garth," I answered. "Won't you come into the library and warm yourselves at the fire?"

"Splendid." He rubbed his hands together. "Come on, Lieutenant; you must be as cold as I am."

The three of us entered the library and huddled around the fireplace. I watched as Garth gazed around the room at all of my memorabilia. I puffed on my cigar, then remembered my manners. "Patrick, Mr. Garth, would either of you care for a cigar?"

"That would be swell of you," Brady said. He knew where I kept the humidor and helped himself.

"None for me." Garth gazed up at the book covers that lined the shelves. "Smoking cigars, pipes, and those new cigarettes do a great deal of harm to your lungs."

"I'll have to remember that," I said. Wonderful— a know-it-all.

"Is that a bullet hole I see in Poncho Villa's sombrero on the wall?" Garth asked, pointing to one of my war trophies.

"Indeed it is, sir," I said, taken by surprise. "How did you know it was Villa's?"

"I recognized the Mexican bandito's sombrero from newsreels. I try to remember small details. You must have been with Pershing's expedition in 1916. How did you come by the sombrero?"

"My company was in a skirmish with Villa and a large band of his outlaws. One of Villa's men came at me with a bayonet," I answered. "He did a great deal of damage to my left eye, as you can see by my patch. However, not enough damage to remove me from the fight. After I had finished him off, I took a shot at their leader. My poor vision hampered my aim, and all I got was a souvenir, Villa's sombrero."

"I'm terribly sorry, Major. Is the injury what caused the end of your Army career?"

"It's not a pleasant subject for me." I angrily flicked ashes.

Garth continued to gaze around the room. "You haven't read many of these books, have you? That's evident by the accumulation of dust and the titles."

"I'll have to talk to Elizabeth about the dust. By the way, Elizabeth is Frederick's wife and a dear lady to me. Go on, Mr. Garth."

"There are a great many romance novels on this side of the room. I don't see you as a man who reads that genre."

"Those were my mother's books," I said, looking away. "Now and again, Elizabeth will read them."

"Your mother is no longer with us, then?"

"Nor my father. They were killed in a boating accident on Lake Erie when I was a child of ten, and Phillip was eight."

"Your father asked Frederick and Elizabeth to raise you?"

"Yes. Fred and Liz raised my brother, Phillip, and me as their own. It was left in Father's will that the Burmeisters were to be in charge of our upbringing, and money left to the estate would be provided to do it properly."

"I perceived by the smile you gave Frederick and your tone of voice that there was something different about your relationship with him. He is more to you than a butler."

"We're family, although we observe certain proprieties around visitors."

Garth continued to survey the room.

This man seemed to be a master of observation. "Why don't we continue this conversation as we have lunch?"

"I have much business at the precinct," Brady said, bowing out. "It appears you two have a lot to talk about."

Frederick came to the library door with the lieutenant's hat and coat. "Have a good day, gentlemen," Brady said as he flipped up his collar and walked out.

"That's another reason I knew there was something novel about your relationship with Frederick," Garth said. "The master of the house would not stand for the butler eavesdropping on a guest."

Frederick's broad, rugged face parted with a grin. "You got me nailed, Mr. Garth. How did you know I was listening?"

"I noticed a slight wheeze in your breath when you took our coats. I heard it while I stood by the fireplace as well," Garth said, his eyes on the hearth.

Frederick cleared his throat. "I've been under the weather lately, sir." He turned his attention toward me. "Elizabeth will have lunch on the dining room table momentarily, sir."

Lunch, it turned out, was my famed sweet-and-spicy chili recipe, courtesy of the kind Mexican family who had housed me during my war injury recuperation. Liz always made it to perfection and served it with huge slabs of buttered cornbread. The four of us sat down to eat.

Chapter Three

Getting to Know Garth

"You mentioned something about a case in San Antonio," Fred said, between bites. "What's your business, Mr. Garth?"

"Right now, I'm with the Pinkerton Agency."

"Oh, one of those strike busters," Fred muttered with disdain.

"No, not at all," Garth said, "In fact, when I took the position with Pinkerton, I insisted that I work outside the realm of the strike busters. My contract specifically stated that I would be an investigator for major crimes. I have a reputation for my skills as a sleuth, and I generally come up with the culprit."

"I beg your pardon. From what I heard about the Pinks… well, it's not very complimentary," Fred said, applying butter to his cornbread.

"I understand," Garth responded. "I hate what that branch of the company is involved in. They should stay out of union business."

"You're a young man," Fred said. "Did you spend any time in Europe?"

"No." Garth took a spoonful of his chili. "I served my country here in the States. I spent much of the past couple of years rooting out enemy spies and their American connections."

"Is that right?" Elizabeth asked. "Tell us more about it."

Garth gazed at Elizabeth with a warm smile. "Ah, dear lady, may I call you Liz? If I wrote a book about my exploits, it would fill volumes. But—, how can I say this?"

"You need to keep it secret," I said.

"Right you are, Major," Garth responded, with a nod and a salute. "If I told you, I would have to shoot you all."

I glanced down at the gullible Elizabeth. "He's made a joke, Liz."

Garth leaned back and wiped his mouth with his napkin. His blue eyes silently inspected the dark panels of the dining room. "I suppose it would do no harm to tell you about what happened last night in New York City."

"It may help us understand why you're here in Cleveland," I said.

"I can't tell you about what led up to last night. That would be revealing too much. However, about nine o'clock, I walked into the Top Hat Club. I was dressed in my snazzy white suit and wore a boater to melt into the crowd of young people."

"White, in February?" Liz exclaimed.

"Yes, dear lady, these jazz clubs and their patrons are quite the outlaws of fashion. And the girls— If their mothers saw how they dressed and danced the shimmy, they would have fainted."

"Oh, my." Elizabeth's eyes grew as big as an owl's. "I've heard about those girls, the flappers. Shame on them."

"I have no objection to dancing and music," Garth said with a slight shrug. "I've frequented the Top Hat Club myself. But, last night, I was there for business only."

Liz encouraged him to go on.

"I slipped through the crowd and went up to the bar to find Vinnie Russo, the bartender, and one of my informants. Earlier that evening, I made arrangements for Butch Avery and Heinrich Katz to meet in room two on the second floor of the club."

"I suppose you can't tell us who they are."

"Now that Avery is dead and Katz is in custody, there's no reason for secrecy. Butch Avery was a dockworker on the New York City Pier. He was about to sell information to Katz, a German spy, about the contents and the schedules of ships going to England. I can't give any more than that."

"We understand," I said, pulling a cigar from my vest pocket.

"So, Vinnie nodded to the second floor and says, take them out quietly, Garth. We want to keep the place respectable."

"I turned toward the stairs, then, wouldn't you know it, Louise comes over to me and starts to flirt."

"Louise?" Fred asked, with a sly grin.

"Yes, one of those rich, spoiled girls who loves to spend her daddy's money. I have to admit, she was a pretty little thing, a real skirt who loves to dance. In fact, I have spent a few evenings with her in the past. But last night I was on duty. Both Vinnie and I tried to convince her of that. She batted her long eyelashes and pouted at me. Fortunately, Vinnie distracted her long enough for me to slip away from the bar."

"You went after the spies?" Elizabeth rubbed her hands together in anticipation.

"Yes, I shuffled up the staircase, my eyes glued to room two. No one was on the balcony that ran past the door. I had a clear trail to my quarry." Garth spoke in a low, slow tone, his eyes scanning the three of us as we listened to every word.

"I reached the room and put my ear to the door. I heard two voices. One was the gravelly voice of Butch Avery. The other was the soft voice of a German. I put my left hand on the doorknob; the other grasped the handle of the .45 under my jacket." Garth stopped the narrative and gazed around the table. "What do you think happened next?" he asked.

We just stared at him. "Louise!"

"Louise?" I gasped.

"She snuck up behind me, just as I was about to storm through the door. 'Is this where your new vamp is?' she asked, far too loudly."

Before I could push her away, Avery opened the door with his revolver in hand. He grabbed Louise around her neck and aimed his gun at her head. She froze.

"Avery says to me, 'Move down those steps behind you or your girlfriend gets it.'"

"Oh, my," Elizabeth gasped.

Garth went on. "I assessed the situation. I refused to let Avery or the spy go, yet I couldn't let Louise take a bullet. I then noticed Avery's finger wasn't securely on the trigger, and he had failed to take the safety off."

"What did you do, confound it?" I asked, impatient to hear the conclusion.

"In a split second, I pulled my weapon from under my jacket, flicked off the safety on my .45, and put a bullet in Avery's forehead."

"You killed him?" Elizabeth asked.

"Of course, he did," I responded. "He had no choice."

"What about that young girl?" Liz asked, holding her hands to her mouth.

"When Avery fell backward Louise went down with him. She screamed hysterically, but was unhurt."

"Did you help her?" Elizabeth asked.

"I had a spy to catch. Heinrich Katz had heard the commotion and dashed for the fire escape. I went after him." Garth shrugged. "Other Pinkerton men were in the alleyway below and Katz was captured and taken to jail."

"This happened last night?" Fred asked.

"Yes, that's when I was told that Allen Pinkerton III, the founder's grandson, urgently wanted me transferred to the Cleveland office."

"That's odd," Fred said, as he leaned back. "Why at that time and place?"

"Your guess is as good as mine," Garth answered with a shrug.

"They may have had an informant who told them that your life was in danger," I speculated.

"Could be." Garth shrugged. "The agency bought my ticket under an assumed name. It appears like they're covering my tracks. The agent who put me on the train, said the agency would contact me."

"Very odd indeed," I said, stroking my goatee thoughtfully. "How long have you done police work?"

"I started with the New York P.D. as a beat cop at the age of eighteen, soon after leaving the orphanage. They recognized my talents and promoted me to a detective first class when I was only twenty-three."

"How exciting," Liz said.

"I thought so too until I had to deal with the corruption within the department. There was money changing hands so fast, I couldn't keep track of who paid whom."

"We've got the same problem here in Cleveland," I confessed, doling out more chili. "Brady is one of the good cops. By the way, Liz, you did a fine job with lunch today."

"Thank you, Jimmy. You were saying, Mr. Garth?"

"The corruption turned my stomach. I quit the department and found a position with the United States Secret Service."

"That would have been about the time I worked in the War Department."

Garth glanced over at me and said, "Yes, sir. It was. I heard about you. You did a great job helping to modernize the Army for TR."

"It wasn't easy dealing with those damned politicians. My usual way to handle thick-skulled fools like them was to … never mind." I'd known I couldn't knock heads together. "It was a great honor to serve my president and my country. That's when the Army promoted me to Major. However, before the end of his term, Roosevelt assigned me to the staff of Blackjack Pershing."

"They should not have cut you loose so early." Garth pointed his spoon at me. "A big strong man like yourself has plenty of years left in him. With one eye or two. What's your weight and height? If you don't mind the question."

"No problem at all," I said with a grin. "I'm six feet five inches, two hundred forty pounds. Last time I checked."

"All muscle, too," Elizabeth added.

"Any other injuries?" Garth asked.

"No," Fred chimed in. "He's fit as a fiddle, as they say. I trained him myself, ever since he was a little tyke. I taught him to box, wrestle, shoot, and fence. We work out with weights down in the basement." I felt a little embarrassment over the bluster Fred and Liz had poured out, but I felt the same pride and love for them as they did for me. "It was always my dream to be an officer in the U.S. military and defend my country. So, I prepared myself my own way. Now, Mr. Garth, it sounds like you're recruiting me for some task," I said, stroking my mustache and goatee.

I received a shrewd smile back from Garth. "One never knows what the future holds. I'm always prepared for whatever comes my way. I think you're much the same, Major."

We finished lunch, then Sherwood Garth allowed Frederick to carry his luggage, leading him up the wide staircase to the second floor and the bedchamber my brother had used before he moved across town.

Chapter Four

A Call From the Sisters

The Pinkerton office in Cleveland had promised to stay in touch with Garth during the time he roomed with us, but three days passed with no word, and I could tell our guest was becoming impatient. He and I were alike in our need to keep active.

The next day I suggested we get out in my Hudson for a tour of the city. Garth even turned the crank when we started the car, and we bundled up against the cold. For the next few days, we toured the historic locations, and in the evenings, we began to visit the local jazz clubs. Garth seemed right at home in these places, so reminiscent of his former haunts in New York. I enjoyed the jazz music but not the dances or excessive drinking the younger people indulged in.

As it turned out, one week of vacation was all Garth would get to enjoy.

Saturday evening, the four of us sat in the library, enjoying cakes and black tea with honey as we chatted. Fred and Liz soon decided to call it a night. After they left, Garth and I planned on a few rounds of billiards in my game room. We had just stepped out into the hallway when I was disturbed by the ring of a telephone. I jumped in surprise.

"Now, who's calling at nine o'clock at night," Fred mumbled, as he stomped down the stairs.

"I didn't know we had a telephone," I said to Fred. I felt slightly upset that I wasn't informed of the changes in my own home.

"I had it installed while you were on a hunt a couple of weeks ago."

"Welcome to the twentieth century, old man," Garth said, seeing my displeasure.

"I wonder who it is?" Elizabeth asked.

"Only way to find out is to answer it," Fred said, ducking under the staircase.

Fred joined us in the hallway in about two minutes with a frown on his face. "That was Margaret, one of the Spellman sisters from out in Medina. The sisters heard that a Pinkerton detective was a guest at our home."

"What did Margaret say, dear?" Liz asked.

"The old cow didn't say much except that she invited herself and her sister, Rachel, over here tomorrow. She wants to hire Mr. Garth."

"That's no way to talk about her, Frederick," Liz scolded.

"Liz, do you know the Spellman sisters?" Garth asked.

"They are social acquaintances," she answered.

"Margaret is an old spinster lady who inherited a fortune from their father. She's an overbearing bully. Not liked by anyone, and doesn't care."

"Rachel is the primary target of her sister's assaults," Fred added. "I feel so sorry for the younger girl. You'll see for yourself tomorrow."

"Did they tell you what they wanted to see us about?" Garth asked before Fred's wife scolded him again.

"No, just that they'd be here by tomorrow afternoon. I guess we'll find out then."

Garth sighed heavily. "I don't like to start a case this way. If she'd given you some information, we could get started on the preliminaries of the investigation. I suppose it can't be helped; we'll just wait 'til tomorrow."

"What did you mean by 'we'?" I asked, my right eyebrow arched.

"I insist that you be a part of the investigation, Major," Garth beckoned.

"You know, that's an exceptional idea, James," Fred said. "You've complained steadily about your languid lifestyle. You're bored, and time has wasted away in your forced retirement. This will give you a chance to do something useful and intriguing."

"I know little about the detective business." However, I gave it some thought, while the others watched me. "I suppose, if you need a skull cracked or an arm twisted, I may be useful."

"Excellent, old man," Garth exclaimed, a bright smile on his face.

I turned my gaze toward the staircase. "I'm curious, Liz. How did it become common knowledge that I had a detective in my home?"

"You know how she likes to brag, James." Fred laughed. "She tells everybody at her pinochle club, bingo parlor, and church socials about what her boy Jimmy is doing."

"The Spellman sisters are with what group?" I asked.

"The pinochle club," Liz said, sheepishly.

I smiled warmly at her, "It's okay, Liz."

"It's apparent that you two don't care for the Spellman sisters, Liz. Can you tell me more about them?" Garth asked.

"Well, Frederick is right; Margaret is quite a bore. Rachel, on the other hand, is hard to get to know. Her older sister has her in submission."

Garth shook his head. "I've known people like that; It's sad to see one sibling belittled by the other."

"Indeed, you have it. Rachel is a tiny thing only five feet tall with a girlish figure. If she applied herself, she'd be quite attractive. She has natural features that she tries to hide from others. You'll see how shy she is when you meet her tomorrow."

"I'll find something else to do tomorrow, away from home," Fred grumbled. "Good luck with the old cow."

* * *

We expected our visitors around three, so Garth and I went to my library. Garth stoked the fire to life as I lit a cigar.

"I see you were given an Indian peace pipe," Garth said, his eyes on the south wall at a display case. "What's the story behind that?"

"No big story. I was stationed at Fort Shoshone from 1902 to 1906. It was a peacetime position. My cavalry unit was patrolling the area to protect wildlife from poachers and watch for renegades from the various tribes in the area. Washakie, the leader of the Eastern Shoshone, was a wise chief. He made an honorable peace with the white man."

"He died in 1900," Garth reminded me. "What had you to do with him?"

"I didn't. Washakie's nephew, Wolf Dog, was a friend of mine. When I transferred away from Fort Shoshone, he gave me his uncle's peace pipe to remember them. I treasure it."

The Spellman sisters were late. However, we gave the ladies some leeway as I knew the roads could be icy. The expected mid-afternoon arrival stretched out to near our dinner hour.

"I believe I see them now," I said to Garth.

"Wonderful. Now, we can get this show on the road."

"Show on the road? Where did you pick up that jargon?" I asked, grinning at his statement.

"It comes from show business, old man," Garth answered. "When the play comes to an end in the New York theater, the actors and crew are eager to go on the road. Circus people use the term as well."

I turned my head, once again, to the street and saw a 1907 Packard limousine stopped at the curb. "Come here, Garth, you've got to see this," I said, with a grin, my earlier foul mood dispelled.

He rose, came to the window, and stood next to me, his hands placed on the windowsill. He leaned forward with his clean-shaven face almost touching the glass pane. He also began to grin as he witnessed the comical scene that took place on Sumner.

Out of the rear of the driver's side of the top-heavy

Packard limousine squeezed a fat, clumsy woman. They built the Packard for short in town travel. Unlike other motor cars, it wasn't comfortable for large people on extended trips. The driver, a tall young man, tried to aid the large, scowling woman, but she kicked him away as she stubbornly struggled with the half-opened door to the back seat.

To make matters worse, the strong wind blew her skirt up around her legs. Her large hat, which she wore on the side of her head, strained to fly away with its ostrich feathers flopping fiercely.

From the passenger side, scurried a petite woman. She grabbed her sister by the hands and dragged her out of the auto. The larger woman tried to recover her dignity by shoving the thin lady away. Still, at war with the wind, she tried to straighten her bustled skirt and re-pin her equally out-of-style hat as she marched to the door. The younger sister followed, her head down and hands folded in front of her. She reminded me of the Japanese Geisha girls I saw in Tokyo while on leave from the Philippines.

I turned to Garth, with a grin. "These ladies should offer us an interesting conversation if nothing else."

Garth, who still surveyed the automobile on the street, answered. "A rare taste these women have. That 1907 Packard is one of a kind."

"Like the clients themselves," I observed, walking over to the fireplace and stoking the fire.

Garth turned from the window. "The heavyset woman is presumably Margaret, judging by Frederick's accurate description."

"And, the other is Rachel."

We stood patiently by the fireplace when we heard the

heavy rap on the front door. An instant later, Elizabeth swung open the doors to the library.

"The Spellman sisters are here," she addressed Garth with a despairing glance. "Did you want to see them in here, sir?" Elizabeth asked, shifting her eyes from me to Garth.

"Of course," Garth said. "We've been greatly anticipating their visit."

Elizabeth walked to the doors but had no chance to introduce the visitors properly. Margaret brazenly walked past her. Rachel followed close behind. However, she turned her head toward Elizabeth and thanked her with a smile.

Garth and I stood erect and greeted our guests. "Good afternoon, I am Mr. Sherwood Garth. This gentleman, as I'm sure you know, is my friend Major James Mallory. Would you like to be seated?"

"Are you to be trusted?" the large woman asked, a frown on her round face.

"I should say we both can be trusted. Why would you insist on seeing us if you had any doubts?" I asked with a frosty glare.

"The Major and I have made an alliance of sorts that relies on mutual trust. Whatever you divulge to me can also be entrusted to the major and vice versa." Garth remained calm in the face of her rudeness. "You have failed to introduce yourselves, ladies."

"I'm Rachel Spellman," the thin lady said, extending her hand.

The heavyset woman held up her hand to silence Rachel. "That makes me Margaret Spellman. Now let's get down to business."

The Spellman sisters sat at a small oval table in the center of my library. I sat opposite Rachel to study the women closely. Margaret was overdressed to the point of absurdity in a dark blue dress that was popular in the 1880s. It did nothing to flatter her figure. Around her neck hung what appeared to be a silver fox stole. Her still-unsettled feathered hat was of black velvet. The ensemble was ostentatious enough but made worse by adding at least five necklaces of pearls, three bracelets on each wrist and one ring on each finger. Not since I passed through the back alleys of Cleveland had I seen such makeup. Her pale complexion and constant frown exaggerated the horror of it all.

On the other hand, younger and more attractive Rachel was demure in her attire. She wore a simple calf-length dress of amber with a black sash around her waist. A cloche of velvet sat on her head. Unlike her sister, she had applied very little makeup. She wore her age well. I ventured to guess, she was in her early thirties, with Margaret about twelve years her senior. I noticed Rachel's eyes fixed on Garth. She paid little attention to me.

"I don't wish to waste any time," Margaret demanded. "I want this business started, so don't offer any refreshments. I didn't drive through that horrible weather for a tea party." She held all three of her chins high.

Garth sat listening and watching. I saw by his steady eye he was sizing her up.

She continued, in her loud, high-pitched voice. "Three weeks ago, my younger brother, Henry, returned from a business venture in South Africa. He and three other gentlemen formed a partnership that dealt with South African diamonds."

"Do you know where this place was in South Africa?" Garth asked.

"Does it matter? He's here now."

"It was someplace close to Kimberley," Rachel offered, her voice soft and apologetic for interrupting her sister.

"Henry told me that Sir Chadwick Holdsworth, one of the partners, was given a tip by a man who worked for the Anglo-American Corporation," Margaret said, interrupting her sister. "Instead of receiving payment on a gambling debt he was owed, Lord Holdsworth took the tip. Henry told me about it before he left two months ago. I don't know the man's name at the corporation, Mr. Garth, so don't ask."

"Ah, the newly formed diamond mine company in South Africa," Garth said. "You've heard of it, Major, haven't you?"

"I've heard the name, the Anglo-American Corporation," I answered. "It has connections to the estate of Cecil Rhodes, I believe. You say that Chadwick Holdsworth is one of the partners?" I asked to clarify the issue.

"Yes, Major. An English count or something," Margaret said.

I turned to the newspaper rack that sat at arm's length and picked up today's *Plain Dealer*. I turned to the international news to find the article I had read earlier. I read it through once more, folded it, and tucked it under my seat.

"I hope I'm not boring you, Major," Margaret sneered.

"Oh, no, not at all. Please go on." Garth and I made eye contact.

Rachel added, "This man at Anglo-American told Sir

Holdsworth of a previously undiscovered tributary of the Orange River that had overflowed with diamonds. Please forgive the pun."

A sweet smile crossed her face. Garth smiled back with a wink.

"The three other partners trusted Henry with the diamonds. The fools," Margaret said, pulling the conversation back to herself. "He returned with the linings of his pockets filled with gems."

"Did you see them?" I asked.

"How impertinent." Margaret glared at me. "He is my brother. If he said he had the diamonds, he had the diamonds."

"Then you didn't see them?" Garth prompted.

"He rarely stayed home," Margaret replied. "He spent his short interludes at home lying about lazily, which he does quite well. Henry was always an incredibly lazy boy; now he's a lazy man. He is always in search of the big score, as he calls it. In the evening, he would go either to the clubs in Cleveland or, more often than not, the sleazy bars in Medina. He loves to spend my money indulging in his wanton ways."

"Well, that gives us an idea of his character, wouldn't you say?" Garth said.

"Indeed it does," I responded. "Have you a picture of Henry?"

"I'm afraid not," Margaret said. "However, he's a tall, lanky fellow with sandy hair. An altogether attractive man."

"He has sideburns below his ears and smooth skin," Rachel added. "As my sister said, a handsome man who would have made any debutant an ideal husband if he would settle down."

Garth and I listened pensively. I sat straight and made eye contact with whoever spoke. Garth, on the other hand, leaned back, his legs crossed at the ankles and his arms across his chest.

Margaret Spellman paused as she rummaged through her large, brown purse. "To cut the story short, Henry left us in the middle of the night. This note, we found on his pillow yesterday morning." She slapped a crumpled piece of paper down on the table and slid it across to Garth. "I never understood that boy. Even when I raised him, after Mother passed away, he would do whatever pleased him."

"As you can see by the note, he is not one for writing. Not a single complete sentence, not a single period or comma. What have I done to deserve this?" Margaret groaned, sighing deeply. I glanced at Rachel, and caught her scanning the ceiling and shaking her head.

Ignoring Margaret's dramatics, Garth reached over and picked up the sheet of paper. I scooted my chair closer to his and read along with him. The Spellman sisters remained quiet while we viewed the note. Indeed, Margaret was right about Henry's writing abilities, the basics of rudimentary English seemed to elude him. The letter was a series of lines that needed a bit of a re-read to follow.

Leaving on next train west
tomorrow night
Diamonds have been taken care of don't worry
Yours, until I return,
Henry

"May I keep this?" Garth asked.

"If you need it." She glared angrily at both of us. "I

just want those diamonds. If you find them with Henry, so be it."

"You don't want your only brother found or brought back?" Garth asked, astonished by her coldness.

"What did I just say?" she shrieked. "I don't care about that shiftless brother of mine. I was happy to be rid of him while he ran about Africa. What I want are the diamonds. Let me finish my story, and you'll understand. Early this morning, I received an anonymous telephone call. The caller said, and I quote, 'Those diamonds belong to me. I don't hold for thieves. I mean to have them. You can ask your dear little brother how he got them.' He then hung up."

"I won't shy from telling you, Mr. Garth, I was pallid with fear. You can't understand how two women, living alone, would react to such a message. When Elizabeth told me you were here, I thought it providential and called for help."

Garth interrupted. "You have no servants?"

"Yes, of course. Four people. Only two of them stay the night. A young scullery maid, Katy, and my lady-in-waiting Cynthia. They both stay in the servant's quarters on the third floor. Two others—a housemaid, Oda, and a gardener, Joseph—have their homes elsewhere. They leave at eight o'clock on most days. Joseph is also my driver. I don't pay him to sit idly around during the winter months."

"So you see, Mr. Garth, we have no protection if that caller wished to accost us," Rachel said.

"Yes, I understand how you must feel," he said, nodding at the younger sister. "Do you know if Henry received any phone calls while he was staying with you?"

"Yes, he did," Margaret replied. "Just about every

night, he would receive brief calls. Henry always sounded annoyed after hanging up the earpiece. When I asked about the calls, he wouldn't answer. I assumed the calls came from the tramp he associated with at the bars in Cleveland. I shrugged it off at the time. Now I regret not pressuring him for an answer."

"What's the name of this tramp Henry associates with?" I asked.

"Karen Bender," Rachel said. "She's actually a lovely lady. I met her once when—"

She stopped abruptly and pursed her lips. Big sister didn't seem to notice what Rachel had said. I did and made a mental note to remember it.

"Did you recognize the voice on the call?" Garth asked Margaret.

She frowned thoughtfully. "No, I don't believe I've heard the voice before."

Garth asked Rachel, "Did you ever receive a call like that?"

"No, Mr. Garth. I rarely answer the telephone. Only Margaret picks it up."

"Correct me if I'm wrong, Miss Spellman," Garth said, turning once more to the elder sister. "What you want from me is to recover the stones and then return them to the rightful owners?"

"Once we have the diamonds, we can determine who the rightful owners are." Margaret sighed heavily once more. "I want my share, of course; his partners can have the rest to fight over."

"Miss Rachel, do you have anything to add to the story Margaret has given us?"

The thin woman sheepishly peered at her sister for

permission to speak. Margaret nodded her head. "I think Margaret has stated the case well, except for one minor detail."

The older woman's head jerked at her sister's daring to correct her.

"The names, Margaret dear, don't you remember? Henry told us the names of his partners."

For an instant, I saw the surprise on the heavyset woman's face. She gritted her teeth and said, "I was just coming to that." Turning back to Garth, she slipped another piece of paper to him. He moved it across to me, and I read the names silently.

The partnership consisted of Sir Chadwick Holdsworth of Leeds in County Yorkshire, Allen Douglas of Washington DC, an aide to a United States senator, and Steven Jackson of San Francisco, and of course, Henry.

"It would be of interest to know how four men from such extreme geographic and social backgrounds got together to form this partnership," I mused, as I scanned the list once more. "Do you think the mysterious caller is one of these three men?"

"I would assume so," Margaret said, frowning at me. "After all, Henry took all the diamonds for himself. I can only imagine why the three of them haven't searched for him."

"Ah," Garth exclaimed. "Little brother is a thief. They'll come after him sooner or later. Did you want us to keep the dogs at bay while we search for the stones?"

"I honestly don't care. I just want this business done with."

"And so it shall be, my dear woman." Garth stood and ran his fingers through his black waves. "If you can accommodate us at your home tonight, I can delve into the problem more deeply."

"Of course," Margaret answered. "We have plenty of living quarters for the two of you."

"Stay as long as it takes to finish the job, gentlemen," Rachel added with a smile toward Garth. It did not go unnoticed by him.

Margaret added, "We'll deduct room and board from your fee, which I'll determine by how well you do your job."

"I'm afraid not, Miss Spellman. The company sets the rates when a customer hires a Pinkerton man. It will cost you five hundred dollars to begin the case. You can give me the fee tomorrow," Garth said.

"Why that's ridiculous . . ." Margaret began to say when Garth interrupted her.

"Let me show you to the door."

"I don't want the police involved unless absolutely necessary, so I suppose I don't have a choice, do I?"

"Then, you still wish to hire us?" Garth asked.

"Yes, Mr. Garth. There will be no need to show us to the door. We found our way in; we'll find our way out. Good day, gentlemen. I hope that lazy chauffeur of mine can drive safely in the dark." Margaret rose and waddled to the door.

Rachel gracefully followed her sister. Before she passed through the library door, Rachel glanced over her shoulder and smiled at Garth. "Don't let her ways discourage you. Thank you for your help and patience."

"Are you coming, Rachel?" an irritated voice called from the hallway.

"Yes, Margaret," Rachel scurried to the front door.

We heard the door slam as Garth turned to me. "It's best we eat before our trek. Please call Liz, ask her to prepare something for us?"

I pulled the cord to summon Liz, then held out the newspaper to Garth. "I remembered this article from this morning."

He unfolded the paper as I pointed to the article. His brow knitted as he read the short piece. "It seems that Sir Chadwick is not our caller. It says here that he was murdered two weeks ago. Dead men don't need jewels on the other side."

Chapter Five

Drive to Medina

We packed our bags hastily after we finished the leftovers from lunch. We each carried a mid-sized valise as we stepped down the front steps. Greeted by Frederick in my Hudson Super Six Town Car, I slid in behind the wheel. I had bought the enclosed Hudson precisely for this type of weather. The black hardtop with windows rolled up kept the winter winds outside the automobile.

Because of my intimacy with the area, I drove. We went westward, over the bridge that spanned the Cuyahoga River, and turned south onto 25th Street. Garth instructed me to find a telegraph office along the way. As we drove, he wrote a few notes on the pad of paper he always carried with him.

"Who are you sending a telegram to?" I asked.

Garth watched the business signs as the auto crept through the snow. "An acquaintance of mine in London. He's retired but spent years in the same business as we are. From what I've heard, he is now keeping bees in Sussex."

"What makes you think he'll know anything about Chadwick Holdsworth?"

"Excellent, Major," he said. "I never told you why I was sending a telegram to him. You're already part of the game."

"Well, it seemed obvious, Garth. If you contact a person in the UK, it would be about Holdsworth." I steered the Hudson with one hand and lit a cigar with the other.

"Nonetheless, you showed a quick mind. That's important in this business. To answer your question, this man never misses a chance to help in a case. I plan to ask him where Sir Holdsworth has been since he returned from South Africa and who he has kept company with. I will also send another telegram to the San Francisco Police Department. I'm hoping they have records on Steven Jackson."

"You're not having the telegrams returned to the Spellman place, are you?" I asked.

"Certainly not," he said, gazing through the darkness that now engulfed us as we looked for the telegraph office. "Just because Margaret Spellman trusts us, doesn't mean I trust her. Or Rachel, for that matter."

I thoughtfully blew a cloud of smoke toward the crack of my window. "I never gave a notion that Henry's sisters would be after his jack. Hell, they've got enough money of their own."

"The sisters can be tied up in this in some way or

another. I don't want the returning telegrams to fall into the wrong hands."

"You're right, Garth. Trust no one. So, you'll have them delivered to my Sumner Street house?"

"Right. I spoke to Frederick before we left. When the telegrams arrive, he'll call us, and we'll pick them up," Garth explained. "There it is. On the right." Garth pointed to the big blue bell with the letters AT&T printed on it.

I slid to a stop outside the telegraph office, peering past the empty sidewalk to the lighted building.

"I'll be right back," Garth called. He jumped from the car to the sidewalk to avoid the slush in the street.

I sat in the car and kept the engine running. The snow had stopped falling. However, the temperature seemed to have descended into the teens. My breath came out in clouds of steam. I threw my cigar butt out the window then reached into my jacket for another.

When I glanced out, I saw a Peerless Model 56 sitting next to me. I wiped the frost from the side window and stared at the auto. The driver had the canvas top up and the side window open. The large, hulking driver stared at me with rigid features. He had a thick black beard against a barrel chest and thick eyebrows under curly unkempt hair. I would have found his small derby perched on his head comical if he had not appeared so menacing. The dim street lamps parted the darkness, so I saw that he was alone. He said nothing; he merely glared at me. The look of hatred seemed to penetrate the auto.

His Peerless remained next to me for just a few moments. Then he nodded to me malignly as he moved off. He pulled onto the street and drove into the darkness.

"What are you staring at, Major?" Garth's sudden

voice, in the quiet of the night, startled me. I told him what had happened.

"How bizarre," Garth said. "However, it may have nothing to do with our case. Let's get on the road to Medina."

I put the Hudson into gear and headed south on 25th Street again. The road turned into Pearl Road as we left Cleveland. Farther on, the road name changed again to North Court Street. The memory of the bearded man tucked itself into the rear of my mind. I was surprised that Garth made nothing of the incident. All the same, I thought it best if I concentrated on my driving. The cold weather had frozen the dirt road to Medina. There was no messy mud to deal with, but the uneven tire ruts in the roadway were troublesome. The bounce of the auto and the cold air made for an uncomfortable ride.

The full moon peeked out from behind wisps of clouds that floated by. Occasionally, they brightened the night sky. Almost all of the drive was through farmland; February is not a month of growth or warmth. Whenever the sky allowed us to see, all was flat and barren. Mile after mile of wheat stubble covered by a thin layer of snow. Every few miles, a clump of leafless trees appeared. Their outstretched branches looked like scarecrows, warning us against going farther.

Garth, who held the map Margaret Spellman gave us, had me turn onto a narrow road. I noticed that the Spellmans had placed electrical poles along this stretch of road. I assumed we were close.

"There it is, Major," Garth called out. He slapped the back of his hand against my shoulder.

"Indeed, it is," I said as I examined the Edwardian

style home. It was a large, dark structure. Spires, sharply pointing to the heavens and silhouetted by the dim night sky, surrounded it on all four corners. The house stood four stories tall in the front, with only the first floor illuminated by electrical lights.

"It's good to see that the Spellmans have kept up with the times. Electricity and the telephone line are coming into their home," Garth remarked, with his gaze on the electric poles.

"I wonder if it's just the first floor that they've equipped with electricity."

"Good point. The upper floors are as dark as mud."

As we approached the front of the house, Margaret Spellman swung the double doors wide open; bright lights splashed from the mansion onto the drive. When we exited the automobile, she waved us up to the porch. "Why are we standing out in the cold?" she asked, as an introduction. "I cannot permit dawdling on the job." She stepped aside to allow us into the foyer.

"We were not dawdling, Mrs. Spellman," Garth said, removing his overcoat. "We were taking note of the house. All facts are important in an investigation."

"My name is certainly not Mrs. Spellman. I've never met a man who comes up to my standards to make me want to change my name. And, remember, you work for me."

"You may pay me my commission, but you won't interfere with the investigation." Garth stood toe-to-toe with the woman. "If you can't do that, I have a warm bed in Cleveland waiting for me."

Margaret's face turned red with rage. I sensed that no one had ever spoken to her as Garth had. She clenched her hands and glared into his eyes.

At that moment, Rachel Spellman walked into the foyer. "Oh, our guests have arrived," she exclaimed with a smile and a nod toward Garth.

"Miss Spellman," Garth said.

"It's good to see you again. We were about to speak of accommodations when you walked in."

"Yes, we have two rooms available for you." Margaret seemed to have a habit of interrupting her sister. I saw Rachel was about to continue the conversation but shied away when her elder sister spoke.

"However, since we are taking room and board from your commission," Margaret went on. "We have a large room for the two of you. It will cost you less."

I heard the implication in her voice. The woman peered down her nose at the policeman who, she thought, was desperate for money. "We'll take the two adjoining rooms if you don't mind," I said, as I ground my unlit cigar between my teeth.

"Now that that's settled," Rachel said. "Let me show you to the dining room. We've prepared dinner for you. I'm sure you can use a beverage after that arduous journey."

"Thank you, my dear. Coffee suits me well right now," Garth said.

After the sisters had left us in the spacious dining room, I pulled a new cigar from my vest pocket and lit it.

Garth thoughtfully considered the artwork that lined the walls and asked, "Well, Major, what do you think of our clients?" He laughed, knowing full well what I thought.

"The nastiest woman I've had the misfortune to meet. I can't see why you've taken her as a client. Especially after she had the gall to charge us room and board. I've never heard of such a thing." I was close to steaming at the thought.

"Margaret, yes. Poor little Rachel has quite a burden to carry," Garth said. A slight grin crossed his face. "You must remember, Major, she's a middle-aged woman who has, most likely, been eccentrically rude all of her life. She is not about to change to suit our fancy. It's the case that intrigues me. Margaret and Rachel are just pawns in the game."

"I'll tolerate her for your sake," I grumbled.

"Before we left Cleveland, you had a word with Fred. What was that about?"

"One of the swankier places in Cleveland is The Sparrow Club. A bartender there, Augie Holzer, is a friend of mine. I asked Fred to contact him and get the word out that we're in search of Henry Spellman. He has a crude grapevine that connects the clubs and restaurants in town," I explained, in hopes that Garth didn't think I'd gone over his head. "I told Fred to contact us here if he learns anything."

"My goodness, Major. You certainly have become resourceful," Garth said, leaning against the large oak dining room table.

Before I had time to respond, a heavy knock resonated on the closed doors to the hallway. Without our reply, the doors swung open and four uniformed policemen strode in. "Mr. Sherwood Garth?" the policeman with the sergeant stripes asked me.

"No, behind me." I stepped aside. Garth pushed himself from the table and walked forward.

"I'm Sherwood Garth," he said.

"You need to come with me, sir," the sergeant said.

"Lieutenant Brady, with Cleveland PD, told me we would find you here."

"What's happened, Sergeant?" I asked.

He eyeballed me and asked, "And, you are, sir?"

"Major James Mallory. Garth and I are partners in this case."

"Then, I'll need you both to follow Officer Parks and me," he said, as he started toward the front door. "I'm Sergeant Jack Markson with the Medina Police Department. Lieutenant Brady told me that you have a great deal of experience in cases such as this, Mr. Garth."

"Hold on now," Garth said, holding up his hand. "I'm not one to jump into the pot blindly. Where do you want to take us?"

The sergeant turned slowly and glanced at Garth, then me, then back to Garth. A fearful, lost expression crossed his young face. "I'm taking you to a murder scene. Henry Spellman has been murdered."

Chapter Six

A Dark Murder Scene

The tall, lean Sergeant Markson led us to a vehicle with the simple marking of 'Police' on the side. It was a plain Model-A Ford. There were no sirens, horns, or lights on the top.

"What about the Spellman sisters?" Garth asked, stopping at the door of the vehicle. "Shouldn't they be told?"

"That's why I left the other two officers behind," Markson answered, pulling his coat tightly around him. "The older man, Officer Beltran, has the experience and a gentleness about him. He can tell the sisters delicately. A younger officer, Jack Leonard, will tell the staff. Leonard also has a consoling nature."

The four of us jumped into the Ford and left. Garth

took the back seat next to Markson as I slid into the passenger seat with our driver, Officer Parks. Our windows were rolled up tightly but, even with the black canvas covering us, the frigid night air still penetrated. And the weak heater failed to warm us. Officer Parks and I shivered as we listened to the two men behind us.

"Where are you taking us?" I asked.

"To a deserted barn owned by the Spellmans," the sergeant said. "Their father, Edger, built it when he first moved to the area. I believe that it was in the 1840s."

"And, now it sits empty," Garth said. "Is Spellman's body the only one found?"

"Yes, Mr. Garth, he is sprawled out in the last stall. It seems someone stabbed him numerous times. I haven't done a thorough search yet. When I learned of the murder, I'd just gotten off the phone with Brady. I dropped off Officer Padua to secure the scene then came to you."

I turned in my seat to view the two men. However, the night was dark. All I saw were their shadows. "It does seem providential at that. Did Brady tell you we're here about the Spellman diamond case?"

"Yes, Brady said you were asked by the Spellman sisters to help find some diamonds. Mr. Garth, we know about your time as a detective in New York City. I've never conducted a murder investigation, so Lieutenant Brady suggested I consult you."

"I'd be glad to aid you, Markson. I assume no one has moved the body?" Garth said, his mind on the murder investigation.

"Besides the killer, no one has had the opportunity."

"Except maybe the person who found the body," Garth muttered, squinting at Markson through the dim light.

"No, that was Officer Padua, the man who is watching over the scene. He may be out of shape, physically, but he's a good copper," Markson defended his man. "He was on the outskirts of town dealing with a family fight."

"He drove by, witnessing a disturbance in the barn?" I asked.

"No, someone else drove by and saw a single lantern," the sergeant replied. "They called it in. Parks took the call. When Padua reported in, Parks gave him the assignment."

"What about the person who called, did you get a name?" Garth asked.

"No. It was a man, but the caller hung up immediately, without leaving his name." Markson said.

"Is that the barn in question?" Garth asked, pointing to a large rectangular shadow with a single lantern at the entrance.

"That's it," Markson said, then turned to our driver. "Drop us off next to the other squad car. I want you to drive into town, go to the hospital, let the coroner know what we've found. Have him come out with the ambulance to do his work. Then they can take Spellman to the morgue in the basement of the hospital." He added, "Tell him to bring his camera. We need some pictures taken."

"Will do, Sergeant. Anything else?" Parks asked. His breath frosted in the night air.

"Yes, go home and get a good night's sleep. Mr. Garth and Major Mallory may need my help. I want to depend on you to fill my shoes in the morning."

"That's considerate of you," Garth said. "However, I usually work alone. Now I have Mallory aiding me." He gave a lopsided grin as he left the vehicle.

I stepped out of the squad car and stood on the snow-covered ground. It had turned into an exceptionally dark night; clouds accumulated over us, blocking any light from the sky. The horizon held no buildings with lights on. I felt a cold blackness envelop me as I watched Parks drive off into the distance. His lights soon faded away.

"I certainly hope you have some flashlights," I said, not even sure someone was close enough to hear me.

"I've got one for each of us," Markson replied, placing one in my hand. "Padua should have a few lanterns inside the barn."

"Where did you get the lanterns?" Garth asked, flipping on his flashlight.

"I keep them in the trunk of the squad cars. We normally use them at accidents or road closures," Markson said, his teeth shining in the newfound light.

Garth pulled his brown coat snugly around himself and asked, "Where's this officer who's supposed to be securing the area?"

Sergeant Markson called out, "Padua! Where the hell are you?"

"Right here, Sarge," answered a big man, walking out of the shadows of the barn. As he approached, I realized he wasn't just large; he was obese. The policeman was bald with chubby cheeks that were as scarlet as strawberries. Padua rubbed his sizable hands together as he walked over to us.

"What were you doing in the barn, Padua? You didn't disturb the murder scene, did you?"

"Course not, Sarge," Padua replied, frowning. "I know my job."

"I suppose I won't get any footprints out here," Garth said, shining his light down on the snowy ground. "It looks like the entrance to Grand Central Station."

"Yeah, there were a lot of people stomping around out here," Padua said, meeting Garth's eyes. "But, you'll find two sets of tracks going out the paddock door, or what you might call the back door of the barn. Mine and the killer's. There's just enough snow to give you a shoe size and the tread of the boot."

"That'll be helpful, officer. It appears like you do know your job." Garth smiled at the big man who pulled himself up straight.

"Once I saw the prints, I backed off so I wouldn't disturb them," Padua added.

"You're a good man, Padua," the sergeant said. He then turned to Garth and me to ask, "Do you want to see the tracks or the body first?"

"We better examine poor old Henry first," I answered with a grin. "He may freeze solid anytime now."

Markson instructed Padua to stay at the entrance to the barn as he opened one of the rickety doors. I checked the rusty hinges as we entered. "These old doors are ready to fall off. How long has the barn been abandoned?"

"Nearly twenty years," Markson answered, holding the rotting door ajar.

"So, I can assume the barn doors weren't locked," I jested.

The sergeant laughed at the idea, then nodded toward the opening into the barn. Garth maneuvered in front of the sergeant and me to lead the way. "The body lies in the sixth stall on your left, Mr. Garth."

"Thank you, Sergeant. Forgive my rudeness, but I want to see what's ahead of us before we fall over it," Garth said. "I know what to look for in such cases."

"No need to apologize. We're right behind you," the sergeant answered.

We filed in and began walking cautiously. The barn had six stalls on the north side and four on the south side. There were no bales of hay nor tools of any sort along the walls. The wooden slats were separating, letting the cold air howl through. The numerous holes that covered the roof had allowed twenty years of rain and snow to fall on the floor. The damage appeared worst where the roof had collapsed onto the loft on the south side, crumpling onto the stalls below.

We continued our walk haltingly when Sergeant Markson announced, "The body is lying in the stall at the north end of the barn." Using his flashlight, he pointed it out. "There's the back door Padua told us about."

"I'm glad you have a photographer on the way," Garth said, still gazing at the stall floors.

"The coroner, Dr. George Polomsky, does that for us," Markson replied. "He's an amateur photographer and is good at it. He uses a Brownie camera to photograph what accidents we have in the area."

"When he gets here," Garth said, stopping in front of stall five, "tell him to photograph this stall thoroughly, the footprints out back, and the death scene."

"Why the fifth stall? The murder occurred in the sixth," the sergeant said, pursing his lips.

"Because the killer waited for Spellman in the fifth stall. It seems he waited a long time," Garth answered. His flashlight hovered over the dirt floor that the killer covered in cigarette butts and smudged boot prints.

I followed his gaze, nodding in agreement. "The killer paced back and forth in here, nervously waiting for

Spellman. That means Spellman had an appointment with someone he knew and wanted it where they wouldn't be disturbed."

"Good observation, Major. It seems they made the meeting for the sixth stall," Garth said. "The killer ambushed him from the fifth."

"Yes," Sergeant Markson added. "There doesn't appear to have been a struggle in the fifth stall, only in the sixth." He glanced around the old place. "I don't think we'll find any fingerprints on this rotting wood."

"I'll have to agree with you, Sergeant. However, we may get something from the cigarette butts," Garth said. "After the photographer finishes, I'll come back and collect them. Now, let's see the body."

I've had the misfortune of seeing dead soldiers on the battlefield. I no longer got queasy. I assumed Garth had seen his fair share of murder victims in New York. But, this was Markson's first murder, so I kept my eye on him.

Garth flashed his light around the sixth stall. There was evidence of a scuffle. However, it seemed to be over in short order. The next thing I noticed was that all of Spellman's pockets were turned out. His boots were yanked off and the cap he presumably wore, was turned inside out. "It appeared the killer was searching for something."

"Of course, Major. The same things we were hired to find," Garth said. "The diamonds. He searched Spellman while he was still alive."

"How do you know that, Mr. Garth?" Markson asked.

Garth's flashlight sent a beam along Spellman's outstretched arm to his hand. The light fell on two words and a letter. "He wrote, with his own blood, a clue. Lion's Head C."

I saw the words etched on the floor of the stall.

"I wonder what that means, Garth. And, what does the letter C stand for?" I asked, staring down at the last words Spellman would ever write.

"It, no doubt, is a clue to where the diamonds are," Garth replied. "It's disheartening he didn't last long enough to finish the word."

"I missed that earlier," Markson admitted. "I left in a hurry to find you."

"He's been dead a short time," Garth added, feeling the body. "Come here, Major. Feel the face, then put your hand under the overcoat."

I got down on one knee and did so. "I see what you mean. The skin exposed to the elements is dead cold. Spellman's body under the coat is still warm."

"Exactly. I would guess that he died maybe within the hour," Garth said to Markson, who was furiously taking notes. "An amateur committed the murder. Or at least someone who never killed with a knife before."

"How do you know that?" I asked, surprised by his quick assumption.

"See for yourself," he said, testing my reasoning skills.

I inspected the body from head to toe. There were knife wounds in Spellman's side and the wound in his throat. I remained silent for a moment, then my eye opened in recognition. "The cut on his neck! The killer originally tried to slit the poor fellow's throat, but he didn't have the stomach for it. The cut on Spellman's throat was only a scratch. He changed his mind and went to an area that was not as visible to him. It is easier to stick a knife in the victim's side than his throat. A man who has killed before would not be so squeamish about going to the throat."

"Excellent, Major. I'll make a detective out of you yet."

"Is there a chance Spellman may have overpowered the man when the fight first started?" Markson asked. "If so, we can search for a man with injuries."

"I doubt that theory; there's no evidence of a prolonged scuffle," Garth responded. "Look at Spellman's hands; there are only small cuts from the knife. It seems he had been overpowered quickly."

"You'd think the bastard would have finished the job cleanly. The killer must have known Spellman was still alive when he searched him," I commented.

"Yes, it takes a man longer to die from a stomach wound than a throat wound," Markson added. "That's what gave Spellman time to write his note."

"That's how I see it," Garth said. "Spellman was lying there, barely conscious. That gave the killer time to search Spellman's pockets. After the killer left, the victim retained just enough life to scrawl the note on the wooden planks at the bottom of the stall."

"I don't believe the killer is a woman, Garth," the sergeant said. "A woman wouldn't have the nerve to use a knife."

"In most cases, that's true, Markson. Women rarely use a knife to kill a man. Poison is the number one weapon used by women, followed by guns," Garth explained. "However, if we're dealing with a psychopathic woman, anything might be true."

Garth bent over the body, peering closely at the wounds. "When one compares the tear in his coat to where the body wounds are, it appears as if the knife went in at an upward angle."

Garth again waved me toward the corpse, "See here,

Major. When you pull the coat down, the tears in it are below the wounds. I believe we are searching for a short man with no military experience and no record of violence," he went on dryly as we listened. "It appears that the knife was double-edged and penetrated the kidney," Garth said, closely examining the wound. "However, I'm not a doctor; we'll wait to see what the coroner has to say."

"Speaking of the coroner, I hear a truck engine," I said, turning my flashlight to the front of the barn.

"That would be our makeshift ambulance. It's a truck we use to carry bodies to the hospital where our morgue is located."

"I'm finished here," Garth said, calmly. "Markson, you and your men can remove the body once your multi-talented doctor finishes the photographs."

Chapter Seven

Following the Prints

"Our night's work is not done, Major. We need to examine the footprints out back."

The rear door of the barn stood a few feet away from the sixth stall. I trained my flashlight on the door, examining it closely. I doubted there were fingerprints to find there. The door was nothing more than three rotting boards hanging from a crossbar at the top. The doorknob was gone, and no metal hardware remained that would yield any prints.

We pushed through, and I immediately saw the large boot marks made by Padua. A few feet away, on the right of the trail, I noticed the smaller footprints of our suspect. Garth pulled out a measuring tape and gingerly reached over to the footprints. Without disturbing the snow around them, he measured two of the prints.

"Well, Major. Our quarry is a man who is possibly five feet nine inches tall and maybe one hundred and thirty pounds," he explained. "Before you ask, I can surmise this by the size of his shoe and the depth of its indentation. Padua's print is a great deal larger, compared to our suspect's. I would say the killer wears a size nine."

"He also smokes a lot and needs money," I added. "That leaves out the man who spied on us in Cleveland. He'd wear a shoe size much larger than these."

"You mean the man who gave me that killer glare in front of the telegraph office? You undoubtedly took his parking spot," Garth quipped, a big smile pasted across his face.

"Shouldn't we follow the footprints and see where they lead?" I asked, pulling my overcoat snugly around me.

"If you're willing to freeze your ass off, I'm ready," Garth groaned.

"After all, you said the murder occurred only a little over an hour ago. We may catch the man out there in the fields," I said, swirling my flashlight beam around in the snow.

"Good point, I'll lead the way." Garth moved ahead of me. "Try to stay away from the prints; follow them from a distance."

The snow coverage was only an inch or two. We followed the tracks with ease. In some areas, the wind had blown the prints away entirely. We regretted each step because of the cold but kept moving slowly along. The killer's footprints were the only man-made ones in the wheat field. Only the prints of wildlife crossed them. If not for the flashlights, we would have been traveling blind, but I knew that the batteries in our lights were only good for a half-hour.

"Our quarry is making this very easy," he said. "He's traveling a straight path, as if he knows where he's going."

"That would be another clue that the man hadn't killed before," I guessed. "He's making it too easy to follow him."

The footprints made an abrupt turn to the left. "I have an idea where the killer's going," Garth said.

"Tell me then."

"The road that runs south to downtown Medina. The other direction leads north through the farmlands." Garth used his flashlight to point both ways. "That's where the Spellman place sits," Garth said softly, almost to himself. "Along the road to the north."

Sure enough, the footprints ended at a right angle to the road we'd taken earlier. We searched across the roadway, looking up and down its shoulders. There were no more tracks.

"It's as if he vanished into thin air," I grumbled, disappointed we didn't catch the guy.

"No, Major. People don't vanish without cause. Like I said earlier, he had a confederate pick him up here. Or, he may have been given a lift by an unwary resident of the area. If he went the opposite direction, he might have gone to the Spellman mansion."

"Or any of the farms in the area," I pointed out. "Or the Good Samaritan, who picked him up, took him all the way to Cleveland."

"Since we don't know which direction he traveled in, I'm all for getting out of the snow and cold." Garth rubbed his hands on his overcoat. "The Spellman house is but a mile or so from here."

"All right, we'll begin the search again in the morning," I said as I led the way. My longer strides were outpacing Garth's. He had to double-time to keep from being left behind. Gazing to my rear, I saw him scowling with displeasure. "What's the matter, Garth? Can't keep up?"

"No, I'm doing fine. I'm purposely moving at a slower pace so as not to miss anything. Just don't slow down, I might trample you." We both laughed and made our way to the Spellman's home.

* * *

"Welcome back, gentlemen. I hope the trip wasn't too strenuous for you," Rachel Spellman said as she brushed back loose hairs from her forehead. "I kept your dinners warm if you're still hungry."

Garth and I tried to conceal our amazement. The woman recently became aware of her brother's murder, and she was showing no emotion. "Is your sister at home, Rachel?" Garth asked.

"Oh, no. Margaret left about half an hour ago to drive our maid home. Oda had no transportation, so Margaret volunteered; she'll be gone for an hour. She was a little put off by Henry's death and needed to get out into the fresh air."

"That's just as well," Garth said. "I needed to speak to you alone. You didn't have much to say at our last meeting."

We followed Rachel into the dining room for a late dinner. "Margaret has always been the dominant member of the family. What she told you was all there was to say." She shrugged and proceeded to spoon out two bowls of chicken soup for us.

"Not quite, Miss Spellman," said Garth. "It is obvious Margaret has little compassion for your brother. What are your feelings for him?"

She smiled, gazing thoughtfully toward the chandelier hanging from the center of the high ceiling. "My brother …" she paused for a moment. "Henry had been spoiled all his life. Our mother died in childbirth, giving me life. Father passed away a few years later. He left a will that gave eighteen-year-old Margaret not only all his possessions and money but also the task of raising Henry and me." Rachel set the bowls in front of us and sat down across from Garth, folding her hands in front of her. It seemed to me that she spoke with more control and authority without her sister in the room.

"Without any experience with children, she made the mistake of giving our brother whatever he wanted. She, of course, would not admit guilt in his poor upbringing. Instead, she blamed heredity. If Henry needed money for anything, he knew where to get it."

Garth glared sternly across the table at her. "That doesn't answer the question; what do you think of him? Not to be unkind, but do I hear a hint of jealousy in your tone?" he asked, beginning to drink his soup.

"Not at all," Rachel snapped back. "I am quite comfortable here and wish for very little. Henry was continuously off to some remote corner of the world to find his fortune. I prefer to remain where I am. I am quite content with the comfort of my home and my life." She tucked strands of her sandy-colored hair into her bun and continued. "I hadn't envied him, nor had I condemned him for his lifestyle. To be honest, at times he seemed like a stranger to me. I have no feeling for him, good or bad."

She leaned forward, her fingers knitted together.

I sipped the soup before me, realizing how cold and hungry I was. Then Garth asked, "Did he ever borrow money from you instead of your sister?"

"No, Major, he didn't. You see, I have very little money of my own. As I told you, Father left everything to Margaret. He blamed me for our mother's death, so he left only a small allowance, distributed monthly. At the time of Father's death, it seemed substantial. With inflation the way it is, the money is now but a pittance. Margaret, on her own accord, increased it for me. However, it is still a small amount, and I have to live frugally."

Garth and I glanced at each other silently. I understood the reasons for her coolness toward her brother. However, it still inwardly stunned me.

"Where did your brother spend the money that Margaret lent him?" Garth asked.

"Mostly in Cleveland at the clubs," Rachel replied, a sly grin on her face. "He has a female companion, Karen Bender. She's a very shrewd woman, Mr. Garth. Beautiful and shrewd, with no scruples, make for a dangerous adversary."

"Yes, you had mentioned her earlier. How often did he go into the city?" I asked.

"Maybe once a week," she replied, still watching Garth. "I've been told that she comes to Medina to visit him at times."

"Where did you get that information?" Garth asked.

Rachel stayed quiet for some time. I felt an awkward cloak fall over us in the silence of the room. She was hiding something. She then responded, "I have my sources."

"Maybe you can tell us something about the servants,"

Garth requested, finishing his soup. "Did they get along with Henry?"

"The servants? I don't know how well they got along with Henry." She leaned back, seeming to be in deep thought for a moment. "Well, there's Cynthia Browning," Rachel said, coloring faintly.

Margaret had told us Cynthia was her lady-in-waiting.

"Cynthia is paid better than the rest of the staff because she agrees with everything Margaret says and does. My sister enjoys ass-kissing servitude."

I felt a moment's shock at demure Rachel's crude language. I looked over at Garth and saw his mouth agape, but she continued speaking. "Cynthia seemed to charm your policeman, Jack Leonard. When he informed the staff of Henry's death, he seemed to pay special attention to Cynthia."

Garth nodded. "What about the rest of the staff?"

"The scullery maid, Katy Sparks, is a dear little girl," Rachel said, smiling. "I haven't seen her with Henry or heard her speak about him. Oda Rogers, our maid, lives in Medina. She leaves soon after dark each night. She drops the gardener off at his home, along the road a bit, and heads home. Her husband, Craig, is a double amputee. He lost both legs in France last year. Poor Oda must work and care for her husband. Her mother-in-law also lives with them. From what I hear, they don't get along very well. So you see, she has too much on her mind to worry about Henry or any of our family matters."

"Your sister is taking her home now?" I asked, thinking about the late hour.

"They left soon after we were informed of Henry's death. It is a bit odd that she stayed so long. Oda was waiting for Joseph to return with her auto. Fell asleep in the parlor and only woke when the police came."

"You mentioned that Henry went to local bars and restaurants to spend his evenings," Garth asked. "Do you know the names of these establishments?"

"Oh, that's easy." Rachel gave her flirtatious smile again. "There are only three nightspots in the area. The best of the three is a restaurant on Chippewa Lake called The Lajon Bostad. Then there's The Medina Lounge, which is a real frolic pad."

"A frolic pad?" I questioned. "What the hell is a frolic pad?"

"You know, a clip joint, a dance hall, a place where the young go to kick up their heels." Garth gave a wink.

"Why didn't she just say so?" I scolded.

"I'm sorry, Major. I sometimes use the new slang terms." Rachel placed her hand on my arm. "The third place is Billy's Place. It's a real gin mill. I've never been there myself, but Henry told me about his visit there just last week."

"He certainly got around, didn't he?" I massaged the back of my neck to ease my tense muscles.

"He certainly did," she giggled.

"What about Joseph Polletti?" Garth asked.

"Oh, Joseph. I don't know much about him. He came over from Italy four years ago. I don't spend much time in the garden, and he doesn't talk much when he drives us anywhere. All I can tell you is that he's a handsome young man in his thirties. He comes into the kitchen in the evening to wait for Oda to drive him home. But, I've never really talked to him."

"We'll need to speak to the four of them," Garth said.

He walked to her chair and bent down, taking her hand. "You've been a wealth of information, my dear."

"Oh, where are my manners," Rachel said as she jumped up. "All I've served you is the chicken soup. Allow me to bring you a more substantial meal. I'll go to the kitchen and find the fried chicken Margaret prepared for tonight."

After she left, I asked Garth, "What have you gathered from Rachel Spellman thus far?"

Garth shrugged. "She revealed a lot about her sister and her deceased brother. Rachel doesn't seem to care that he's dead. Why should she? He was a virtual stranger to her, one with a weak, selfish character. I would suppose there is no love lost in this household. She didn't actually reveal much about Henry's relationships with any of the help—maybe she doesn't know whether they got along."

"So, Margaret's hatred for Rachel, and maybe Henry's hatred as well, stems from something out of Rachel's control," I ventured to guess.

"That's part of it. However, when she passed by us in the hallway earlier, I smelled the distinct odor of cigarette smoke and whiskey. Considering Margaret's puritanical attitude, there may be more to their animosity than the mother's death. But, let's keep that to ourselves. I think we'd be better off finding the diamond hunters from Africa. That may be where the answer lies."

"That would be Holdsworth, Jackson, and Allen Douglas?"

"You forgot, Major, Holdsworth is no longer with us. Judging by the length of time Spellman has been home, the other two may already be in the area. If so, they are our most likely suspects." Garth leaned across the table with a glisten in his blue eyes. "It takes a week to cross the pond from Great Britain. If they set off from Cape Town to London, then caught a ship to New York, they would have arrived here a few days before Spellman disappeared."

Chapter Eight

Word From Augie

The next morning, Sunday the tenth of February—because of the long night at the barn, Garth and I left our beds past our normal time. I dressed casually in my tweed jacket and brown trousers. Garth seemed to favor his tastefully styled black and gray striped suit, topped off with a black homburg. I wasn't sure if it was to impress others or himself.

We weren't the only ones up. We came down the stairs to the sound of the telephone ringing directly below our feet. The Spellman family had the instrument installed in the customary alcove beneath the staircase.

I heard Margaret answer it in her usual grumpy tone, "Yes, I'll get him. I don't know why you need to call at such an ungodly hour."

"That must be for me," Garth said, stepping around to meet Margaret. "I'm expecting a telephone call this morning."

"Yes. Mallory's man Frederick wants to speak to you."

Garth took out his notebook. He began jotting down page after page of information Fred relayed to him. When Garth responded, he spoke in low tones. "Excellent, Fred. Now, for the second half of your assignment." After giving Fred additional instruction, Garth hung the earpiece back onto its cradle and stepped away.

"Well, when are you going to begin searching for the stones, Mr. Garth? I hope you won't waste any time," Margaret demanded as we walked toward the dining room for breakfast.

Before anyone responded to her question, the telephone rang once more. Margaret gave Garth a displeased sneer and asked, "Are you expecting another call?"

Garth shrugged, "It's not for me."

Margaret answered the telephone and quickly slammed down the receiver, almost dislodging it from the wall. She stepped from under the staircase. "It's that blasted caller again. The man after the diamonds. I'm fed up with him," she bellowed.

Rachel had just stepped out of the dining room. Her face turned pale; her eyes grew large as she covered her mouth, ran to the staircase, and disappeared upstairs. We all followed her with our eyes, speechless.

"Is she all right?" I asked.

"Don't worry yourself about her, Major," Margaret responded unsympathetically. "Rachel normally handles stress better than that. She may be putting on an act for you. She enjoys being pitied. But you must admit, the situation is quite distressing. I better check on her, or I'll get no rest."

Garth and I watched as Margaret, with great difficulty, climbed the steps. Once she was out of sight, we entered the dining room and filled our plates with fried eggs and potatoes. We each grabbed a cup of coffee and sat at the table.

Garth glanced at the door to be sure we were alone. "Fred learned a great deal from Augie, the bartender at The Sparrow Club. Henry Spellman was a frequent visitor when he was in Cleveland. He chummed around with whoever frequented the bar.

"I received the address of Karen Bender, that young woman Spellman was close to. There is also a man who has been searching for Spellman. He's a big bear-like fellow with a beard to his chest. He wears a checkered suit and derby. Does he sound familiar?"

"Indeed he does. The man in front of the AT&T office."

"There's more," Garth said, as I finished my eggs. "Augie put the word out to other bars and restaurants in the area."

"Did he receive an answer through his grapevine?" I asked, picking up my coffee.

"Yes, a waiter at the Trivoli Garden Italian Restaurant, Eddie Bennett, overheard the bartender talking to Augie early this morning. When he heard the name Henry Spellman, he interrupted the bartender and took the phone. He had customers earlier that morning who were asking about Spellman. That was before two a.m."

"Is Bennett willing to talk to us?"

"Yes, but he doesn't start his shift until three this

afternoon. He'll meet us at two at the restaurant," Garth answered, wiping his mouth with his napkin. "I love Italian food. Maybe we'll have time for a bite to eat."

"You just finished breakfast, and you're thinking of food again. How do you stay so thin?"

"A lot of running around with you," he said, smiling. "Seriously, I just burn more energy than most." He took a quick view of the entrance; no one was in sight. He leaned forward, staring at me. "What did you make of the sisters' reactions to the second phone call?"

"Margaret's scene of anger was expected," I said, pushing my empty plate away. "She seems to respond to every situation in that way." I fiddled with my goatee as I thought of Rachel. "I was somewhat surprised by Rachel's faintheartedness."

"I fully agree. That was Fred on the second call. We pre-arranged the call so that I could witness their reactions. I wonder why Rachel was so fearful of the call?"

"She possibly thought the caller was her brother's killer and is afraid he will come after the sisters next," I responded.

"Quite feasible. Before Spellman's murder, they received daily calls from someone demanding to talk to Henry. I'll have to think about this once we learn more."

"We have a full day ahead of us, Garth," I said, pushing away from the table. "Talking to Karen Bender would be a good start."

"No, Major. We'll be better off going to The Sparrow Club after dark to find her. After a few drinks, her lips may be loosened for us. We need to know the best time to meet her."

Once Garth finished his second cup of coffee, he rose

to head out on the hunt. However, another obstacle held us back. Rachel rushed downstairs, stopping in the doorway.

"I must apologize for my rude conduct earlier," she said. "Please do forgive me for acting as I did."

"There's nothing to forgive. You were acting under stress."

"Yes, my dear. I agree," Garth said, winking. A blush appeared on the girl's face when he spoke to her.

"To make up for it, let me give you a tour of the house," she offered. "With all that's been going on, we haven't been able to show you around."

We accepted the invitation eagerly. The more we learned about the Spellmans, the easier our job might be. The tour started in the parlor, the first room past the hall entrance. We continued to the library, her father's seldom-used den, and a music room.

The music room held a grand piano. Garth ran his hand across the smooth yellow birch wood on the keyboard caps. "Who plays this lovely instrument?"

"Oh, I do, Mr. Garth," she replied, running the back of her fingers over the keys, close to his fingers. "Music is one of my passions. Margaret tells me I need to work, but the staff enjoys listening to me play. Would you like to hear me play something? I love Antonio Vivaldi."

"I would love to," Garth answered, "Vivaldi is one of my favorites as well. As is Chopin and Joplin, but we have to deal with this ugly business. Some other time."

She seemed dreadfully disappointed, so I said, "I hope that invitation was for me as well. I'd love to hear you play."

"Oh, of course, Major. Whenever you two have the time." She turned back to Garth and winked. "Yes, I do play Joplin as well. I keep up with the latest music."

The family had richly decorated all the rooms with antiques and fine artwork. Rachel and I spoke openly about the regal *objets d'art* that filled the house. However, Garth remained silent once we left the music room. He gazed over everything in the rooms as we walked through. I remembered him telling me he had a photographic memory. I imagined the camera in his head was photographing the entire house.

We reached a large room in the rear that had French doors leading to the garden. It was the trophy room. "I see your father did a great deal of hunting, Miss Spellman," Garth noted, pointing at a stuffed brown bear's head fixed to the wall next to a gun rack.

"Oh, no. Father did little traveling; all of these mementos were Henry's. He was fascinated by taxidermy. He brought the bear back from Alaska, the caribou and the moose from Northern Canada, the tiger came from India, and the lion and gazelle from Africa. As you may expect, Henry was very proud of this room," she said, scanning the animal trophies. "In fact, he spent most of the past three weeks in this room. I don't know what we'll do with all this now that he's gone."

"This would make a good tea room for you ladies when you have callers," I suggested.

"We rarely have callers, Major," she said somberly. "But that may change shortly. And, you're right. Minus the animal heads, it would be perfect for a tea on a spring day when the garden outside is in bloom."

Garth spent a few moments mulling over everything in the room. I watched his eyes scan each object. I then noticed Rachel studying Garth as if he was to be her own trophy, and I saw her in a totally different light. Liz had described her as a delicate porcelain doll. However, when Margaret was not in the room, Rachel came across as a self-willed woman. She was still an enigma; someone who seemed to be different at each encounter.

Returning to the dining room, we found that Margaret had come downstairs, dressed from head to toe in Victorian-style black. Garth and I knew it was for show, unless Margaret, indeed, had feelings for her brother and covered them by her self-imposed aloofness.

"I hope Rachel has been hospitable in my absence," she said.

I felt an air of tension rising in the room as Rachel fell into her unassuming pose. It was like a reverse metamorphosis. The butterfly reverting into the unattractive caterpillar. It was hard to distinguish if she subconsciously made the changes, or they were part of an act for Margaret's benefit.

Trying to exonerate Rachel of a social faux pas, Garth gave an exaggerated report of her laudable conduct. It satisfied Margaret and cheered Rachel. "We have much on our agenda, Miss Spellman," Garth announced, with a curt bow to Margaret, then turned to Rachel. "Thank you for the tour, Miss Rachel." With a second bow to the younger sister, Garth walked toward the kitchen and the cloakroom.

I gave my salutations as well, returning to my room to clean up before leaving. I went to the sink in our adjoining bathroom, looked around to be sure Garth wasn't watching, then removed the patch from my left eye. Splashing water on my face, I quickly dried off without bothering to shave. After positioning the patch over my eye socket, I headed down the hall to join Garth and make our way to Cleveland.

Garth stood at the rear door, waiting for me. He held an anxious frown as I walked toward him. "Are you in a hurry?" I asked.

"Yes," he answered, waving a note in the air. "Much has happened. We've got an appointment at Markson's office. New evidence has been found. We'll have to postpone our drive to Cleveland for now." His eyes were gleaming with anticipation.

Throwing on my jacket, I joined him. Oda was waiting at the door with my overcoat and cap in hand and ushered us out into the cold morning air. The two of us left in my Hudson, headed for the Medina City Hall.

Chapter Nine

A Suspect at Medina City Hall

As we expected, Sergeant Markson's team found no fingerprints in the old barn. The county coroner, Dr. George Polomsky, spent the night on the autopsy but hadn't yet developed the photographs of the scene. His work added no clues that Garth and I hadn't already known about. However, he did confirm that there were six stab wounds to the torso. They came from a low angle and were thrust upwards, as Garth supposed. The doctor also confirmed the slight bruises and cuts on the neck.

Dr. Polomsky left two small paper bags containing the cigarette butts that were found in and around stall number five. The first bag held eight cigarette butts, each with a distinctive cut along the end of the cigarette. The other bag held only two, but they had a hint of lip rouge on the tip.

Markson took us to his office for a private consultation. "There's a pot of coffee on the side table there, under the window. Help yourselves." The sergeant waved his hand in the direction of the ill-kept table. "I have someone of interest in the interrogation room. I believe you may want to speak to him," Markson continued, sitting down behind his small desk. "He had reason to want to see Spellman dead."

"Indeed," Garth said, sliding onto a wooden bench against the wall. "Tell us about him, Sergeant."

"Herbert Longfellow. He's a crotchety old man with a nasty disposition but with a good cause not to like Spellman. Last year, Longfellow's son, Herbert Junior, went on a hunting trip with Spellman and two other men to Alaska."

"Would these two other men be Allen Douglas and Steven Jackson?" I asked, as I sought out and found a box of pastries.

"Yes, the same men who accompanied Spellman to Africa. To make a long story short, young Longfellow was killed in a shooting accident. Mr. Jackson fired the bullet that killed the boy, but Spellman was witness to the shooting and testified that it was an accident."

"Longfellow believes his boy was murdered, doesn't he?" I asked. "He wouldn't be seeking revenge if he thought otherwise."

"Excellent, Major. Just what I was thinking," Garth said. "Is there anything that connects him to the murder, Sergeant?"

"We found him in the barn this morning," Markson answered. "Mr. Longfellow was walking toward the murder scene when Officer Padua stopped him. He brought Longfellow in for questioning."

"Your man, Padua, is a good officer." Garth removed his homburg and brushed his hair back.

"One more thing," Markson said, standing up. "While the foursome were in Alaska, they did some panning for gold."

"Don't tell me," I said. "The men struck it rich, but Spellman held onto the gold, and the others never received their share."

"Not entirely correct, Major. Spellman shared it with Douglas and Jackson but decided that Longfellow forfeited his share when his son died."

"What a cad, this Spellman was." My lips pressed tightly as I thought of his cruel ways.

"The most damning evidence just came in this morning," the sergeant said, dropping a thin envelope on his desk.

Garth finished his coffee and picked up the envelope. "What have we here?" Garth opened the expensive envelope, slid out a single sheet of paper, unfolded it, dropped the envelope, and read it aloud to the three of us.

Mr. Henry Spellman:

I've told Herbert numerous times to stay clear of trash like you, but he wouldn't listen. He allowed himself to be coerced into the hunting expedition in Alaska, and now, he is dead. It is all on your head. You didn't pull the trigger, but you may as well have. My son is no longer with me because of you.

You know this truth all too well. What you don't know is that you'll never come back to Medina. If you ever show your face anywhere around the city again, you're as good as dead.

Longfellow

"Have you compared the handwriting to Longfellow's?" Garth asked.

"Yes, it matches. Longfellow admits writing the letter. But, the old man said that he never planned on carrying through on the threat."

Garth picked up the envelope and read the address on its face. "The letter was sent to a South African address last month." Garth turned the envelope over; he saw that there was no return address. "Where did you find this, Markson?"

The sergeant leaned back in his chair. "Tucked away in Spellman's luggage. I didn't notice it the first time I went through his steamer trunk, which was sent directly from South Africa to Cleveland before his leaving for London."

"It was stuffed in a side pocket," Markson said. "Oh, I almost forgot, there was a second bag delivered to the Spellman's place. The New York Central lost it when Spellman arrived from Europe."

"Was anything of interest found in it, Markson?" Garth asked.

"Not that I know of. Margaret had thrown it in Spellman's wardrobe after removing his dirty clothes. She only called me moments ago to tell me about it."

"Good, I'll comb through it when I get back," Garth responded. He gave Markson the once-over, asking, "As to Longfellow, do you think there's enough evidence for an arrest, let alone a conviction? A good lawyer will rip this letter to shreds in a courtroom."

"We have a witness to an argument between Spellman and Longfellow, at Longfellow's real estate office," Markson said, pouring himself a cup of coffee.

"The day before Spellman's death, he went to see

Longfellow. It was about noon. Longfellow's young clerk, Raymond Perkins, was on his way out to lunch when Spellman passed him at the door. Perkins recognized him and waited at the door to listen to the conversation."

"Does he always eavesdrop on his employer?" Garth asked.

"No, but in this case, he felt there could be trouble. He knew of the old man's hatred for Spellman. In any case, he did stay and he overheard the conversation. Spellman wanted to repurchase the barn. He told Longfellow he wanted to preserve the family legacy. Longfellow would have nothing to do with him. I don't believe his refusal to sell had anything to do with the value of the barn or the ten acres it sits on. He simply wanted to annoy Spellman. They exchanged a few insulting remarks, then Longfellow made yet another threat to Spellman's life."

"It sounds like Longfellow still has a vendetta against Spellman. Let's go talk to the elderly gentleman." Garth rose from the bench. "Show us the way, Markson."

* * *

"Mr. Herbert Longfellow, I presume," I said as I bit off the tip of my first cigar for the day.

"Yes, and you are Major Mallory. And, that's Sherwood Garth. The sergeant told me he had a Pinkerton man who wanted to see me." He glared at Garth with disdain. "What is it you want from me?"

Longfellow sat at one end of an old table that was scratched and tarnished by years of use and neglect. Garth sat down across from him. I stood back, toward the closed door, leaning against the wall. I lit my cigar and listened.

The eighty-something-year-old Longfellow was a short, thin man with a misshapen hump on his back. His fierce eyes glared at Garth from under thick, white eyebrows and hair that hung untidily over his ears.

"First of all, Mr. Longfellow, what were you doing at the barn this morning?" Garth asked.

"I have a right to be on my own property, Mr. Detective. I own that barn."

Garth remained quiet for a moment then said to Longfellow. "I was under the assumption that the barn was on Spellman property." I saw Garth's game. He was testing the old man's anger.

"Then you'd better do some homework," Longfellow chided. "I bought the barn and the ten acres it sits on. Margaret Spellman sold it to me last month. She insisted the purchase remain a secret. The old battle-ax didn't want anyone to know they needed cash."

"It still doesn't explain why you were there, Mr. Longfellow."

"I heard about the murder and wanted to evaluate any damage done to the barn," he responded. Longfellow then pointed a long bent finger at Garth. "It's my barn. I have a right to visit it whenever I want to."

"Indeed you do, sir, if it weren't the scene of a murder," said Garth, unmoved by Longfellow's indignation. "However, from what I've seen of the barn, it was ready for the garbage heap already. But, as you say, it's your barn. How well did you know Henry Spellman?"

"Hardly at all," he snapped. "He was an acquaintance of my son. Since Herbert's death, I haven't seen the man at all."

"Did you approve of their friendship?"

"It was none of my business who my son took up with," he snarled. "Herbert was a full-grown man and able to choose his friends at will."

"What about Allen Douglas?" Garth asked. "What do you know about him?"

"A family friend," Longfellow answered. "He and young Herbert went to school together. I became fond of the man. I'm sure you know Allen spent the night at my home the night of the murder. He's my alibi. Talk to him, Mr. Pinkerton man."

"You knew Henry testified in a court of law that your son's death was an accident," Garth continued, undeterred. "What did you think of that?"

Longfellow bent his head forward, glancing side to side, a deep frown crossing his brow. "I think nothing of it. It's the past. If you're trying to implicate me in the murder of that young scallywag, you're wasting your time. I have no remorse that he's dead, but it wasn't me. I was at home all night and have a friend to prove it."

"Yes, a friend who has equal reason to see Spellman dead. One last question before you leave, sir. What brand of cigarettes do you smoke?"

"I don't smoke, Mr. Garth. Never have. I can't stand the smell of tobacco, such as that vile cigar the Major is puffing on."

"I'm sorry, sir. I didn't realize it offended you."

"Yes, it offends me—*you* offend me," he said, swinging his thin arm at us. "You *both* offend me." He glared at us, then stood, grabbed his walking stick, and hobbled toward the door. Longfellow stopped and turned around. "If you want to find someone with a reason to hate Spellman, consider the maid's husband. He's a crippled man who can't care for his woman."

"Why do you suspect him?" I asked.

"He's an extremely jealous man, with good cause. He thinks Spellman was having an affair with his wife, Oda. And, while you're at it, ask Karen Bender a few questions. I'll bet she's all tied up in this." Longfellow didn't wait for a response. He merely stomped out of the room.

"We'll have to look into that," Garth said, remaining in his seat.

I gazed at Garth as I continued to puff on my cigar. "The old man has a horrible disposition. Why didn't you ask him about the letter?" I asked. I was dumbfounded by the missed opportunity to seal the case against Longfellow.

"Because he would lie about it," Garth answered. "He lied about most everything else; why waste my time?"

"I wonder where he got the information about Oda's husband," I pondered, tapping the ash from my cigar and wondering how Garth was so adept at spotting lies.

"That's a good question. We'll check into Oda's husband ourselves. Nonetheless, we'll have Jack Markson check his alibi," Garth sighed.

After a moment of thought, I said, "The name Karen Bender keeps coming up." I fiddled with my goatee and added, "That name sounds familiar, somehow. It's bothered me ever since I first heard it. I suppose it will come to me in time."

Markson walked into the room, finding Garth ready to leave. "You know, Spellman owed Longfellow a share of the gold they found in Alaska," the sergeant said. "What if the two men planned on meeting at the barn to settle up?"

"That's a longshot, Markson, don't be too hasty. I don't think Spellman would settle up with anyone, Longfellow would have known that. Spellman was a thief and a cheat and maybe worse. Judging by Longfellow's condition, unless he had help, he couldn't harm a fly. No, Sergeant, we'll keep our eyes on the old codger, but we must hunt elsewhere."

"Why would he go out of his way to meet in the cold barn?" I asked. "He had a cozy, warm office to conduct business in."

"In any case, I'm going to follow up on him and his alibi," Markson said.

Garth turned to me. "Come, Major. Let's be off."

Chapter Ten

Detour

"Where are we going now?" I asked my companion as we walked out of city hall. We stopped in the foyer before going out into the cold. "Garth, where—"

A tall, willowy woman stepped away from the counter a few feet away from me. I heard her cheery voice as she said goodbye to the clerk. She turned and strutted out of the building. The fur collar of her green coat was turned up so that it covered her face, but—

"Major, are you with me?" I heard Garth say, fiercely. "Let's keep our minds on the case." He glanced at the woman himself, then shook his head.

"Go on, Garth. Where are we going?"

"A little detour before going to Cleveland. I want to talk to Rogers." Garth led us out of the building and to my Hudson. He reached into his breast pocket, producing the pad of paper he had been taking notes on. He flipped through the pages. "Ah, here it is. Can you get us to 2711 E. Friendship Street?"

"Not a problem, Garth. That's not too far from here. But, Oda is at the Spellman place, working. We can talk to her there."

"It's Craig Rogers, her husband, I want to speak to."

* * *

The Rogers family resided in a small bungalow at the end of Friendship Street. It struck me as a home not well cared for. As we walked on the path to the house, we passed by a woman who was hastily leaving. Although I didn't see her face clearly, I noticed red locks protruding beneath her cloche. Garth shook his head at me as I watched her walk down to the street and get into a car. "Something appears familiar about her."

"She's the woman you stared at when we were at city hall."

"You may be right." I glanced away and walked up to the front door. I took note that the paint on the door was peeling, and the entire house needed repairs. Because of Longfellow's crude comment about Rogers' condition, I wondered if Rogers would answer the door himself. However, it was answered, not by Craig, but by an elderly lady. "What is it you want?" she asked through the open door.

Garth introduced us, asking, "Can we have a word with your son?"

"How do you know I'm his mother?"

Garth smiled appealingly at the elderly lady. "You certainly wouldn't be a servant; you're too well dressed. Your countenance is unlike Oda's, so I assumed you were Craig's mother, here to help care for him while Oda is working. May we speak to Craig?"

"Well, you assumed correctly; Craig is the oldest of my three children." She softened her response as she opened the door wider. "Craig's in the kitchen. I'll go see if he wants to speak to you. You can wait in the front room."

The wait wasn't long. The woman came into the small, sparsely appointed living room, pushing her son in his wheelchair. He was a young man with strong features and a shroud of sadness.

"Good morning, sir," I said. "I'm Major James Mallory and this is Mr. Sherwood Garth," I introduced as I discreetly glanced at him.

"Craig Rogers. Oda tells me you are investigating Henry Spellman's death. I'm sure you're not here to accuse me of that crime." He nodded down to the stumps of his legs.

I'd seen the condition before when soldiers returned from the front lines in the Philippines. Artillery shelling did a great deal of damage to our young men. I saw pity in Garth's eyes at the sight of the man. I hoped Rogers didn't see it. But I think he did.

"No need to feel sorry for me, Mr. Garth. I was at the Battle of the Somme. A captain in the Canadian Army. In August 1916, I transferred to the village of Courcelette, which the Germans bombarded heavily. I got in the way of one of their shells." He swiped his hands across his lap. "This is the result."

"I'm sorry," Garth said. "I didn't mean to stare. I was told that you had a reason to kill Spellman. However, physically that would be quite impossible."

"Who told you that? Old lady Margaret?" Craig's mother asked. "She's got a dislike for my boy."

"She's got a dislike for everyone," I said. "But, we can't reveal who gave us that information."

"How do you feel about Oda working at that house?" Garth asked, with what I took to be a warning in his eyes, telling me to let him guide the conversation. I sat back and listened.

"I don't like it at all." Rogers stiffened, pursing his thin lips. "The Spellmans work her hard, paying just enough to keep us alive. I've always been a man who took care of my wife. I was a well-respected officer, a man of action, and now this. You understand, don't you, Major."

I did, but Garth answered for me. "Yes, Captain, we both do. Has Oda told you anything about the household that would be pertinent to my investigation?"

"Hell, the whole family is batty. Margaret thinks she still lives in the Gilded Age. Rachel acts like a nun, and Henry was a parasite. I suppose that's why your informant thinks I have a reason to kill the guy. Oda loves me, Mr. Garth. She wouldn't be running around."

The entire time Garth was speaking to Craig, his mother circled the room. To all appearances, she was merely straightening the knick-knacks on the shelves. However, I saw that she was listening carefully to the conversation.

"What about the late nights …"

"Don't try to imply anything, Garth." Rogers' jaw tightened. "She loves me. She wouldn't go through the indignity of working for those people if she didn't have to."

Garth persisted, undaunted by Rogers' indignation. "I don't mean to imply anything, Captain. What about the other servants? Does she talk about them?"

Rogers outwardly appeared to relax a bit. "Katy, the kitchen maid is just a kid. Oda likes her. The others, I don't know about. Believe me, Mr. Garth, Oda loves me. She wouldn't do anything to hurt me. Mother, please show these men to the door. I think I've said enough."

"Before we go, I'm embarrassed to ask, but may I use your bathroom." Garth sheepishly bowed his head.

Craig Rogers, still upset with us, nodded, "It's down the hall, go through the bedroom."

The conversation ended as abruptly as it had started. I didn't think we'd learned much except that the poor man felt emasculated by his war injury. No man wants to use a wheelchair and see his wife work to support him. The wait in the hallway for Garth was slightly uncomfortable. Rogers' mother stood quietly by as we waited.

Once he finished, Garth rejoined me. Mrs. Rogers followed as we went to the front door. Craig wheeled himself into another room.

The front door closed behind us, but Mrs. Rogers had followed us out. We turned to see her bent, thin frame wrapped in a shawl. "Gentlemen, please wait."

"What is it?" Garth asked. He seemed surprised to see her still standing on the stoop.

"You need to know. Oda has been playing my son. Sure, she's working there and working hard, but she's also staying late without cause."

"How do you know that she has no cause?"

"Margaret has a schedule the staff keeps. Margaret told me that the staff is off at eight every night, no exceptions. When Oda comes home at eleven, she tells Craig she's worked late."

"And you don't believe it?"

"No. She's been working late ever since Henry came home from Africa," Mrs. Rogers whispered, glancing into the house. "Craig believes her, or so he lets on. I hate to say this about my poor boy but, as you may have guessed, he can't perform like other men. Oda is still young and has needs. I think she satisfied those needs with that cad Henry."

"You realize what you're saying points the finger at Craig. It gives him a reason to kill." Garth wondered about the old woman. He was trying to discover the truth and her motive for talking to us.

"Of course not, young man. Craig isn't physically capable of doing such a thing. The night of the murder, he was home with me, not with Oda. She, again, came home late, well after eleven. Margaret Spellman brought her home. Oda's an attractive woman. She'd love to get hold of those gems and run off. Henry may have done her wrong, who knows?" she asked with a shrug. "My poor boy can be better cared for at my place in Canada, than here. He has family up there. He came down here because Oda insisted. I never understood that woman."

"I see," Garth said. "Thank you for your honesty. We'll weigh it all with the rest of our evidence."

She turned and scurried into the house as he joined me by the Hudson.

"What was all that about using their bathroom? That was quite odd."

He pulled his hand from his overcoat pocket, holding up a couple of hankies with lip rouge on them. "It's not odd if you're able to retrieve evidence."

We sat quietly without starting the engine. Garth saw me run my fingers through my shaggy hair then pull my cap tightly over my head. "What do you think of all that, Major? Any conclusions?"

"It's obvious Craig's mother doesn't like her daughter-in-law and wants us to think she is in on the murder. The mother might think that Oda is after the diamonds so she can leave Craig."

"Indeed," Garth responded. "I also noticed Craig seems to overstate his wife's affection for him. Is he trying to convince himself or us?"

I sat and thought for a moment. "We'd best move on to Cleveland. Brady is waiting for us." I jumped from the motorcar, gave the crank a turn, and we were off.

Chapter Eleven

On to the Cleveland PD

Garth remained silent as we proceeded out of town, north to Cleveland. He buttoned his brown overcoat and tugged his homburg over his eyes. There was no snow coming down, nor icy winds to hamper us, but cold air still circulated through the passenger compartment of my Hudson.

Garth broke the silence by bringing up a subject we hadn't discussed before. "I don't understand Allen Douglas' motives for involving himself with Spellman. Douglas has a good reputation with the press. He has been in the papers on occasion, but only in dealing with the U.S. government and foreign policy. He's been a close advisor to Senator Franklyn Ward. You'd think a man in that position wouldn't have time for a long stay in South Africa."

"Or Alaska, now that you mention it. Perhaps he's just as greedy as the rest of them and sought an easy fortune." My attention reverted to the icy road. "Gold from Alaska—diamonds from Africa; maybe he thought he saw instant millions for the taking?"

"In that case, there is a lot of money for the taking in Washington," Garth said, shaking his head. "There's a piece of the puzzle missing on Mr. Douglas."

"What about the other man, Steven Jackson?" I asked.

"I know as much as you do, old man. Just that he is from California."

"The final partner? Sir Chadwick?"

"We'll learn more about what happened to him once my telegrams come in," Garth said. "I am also waiting for an answer from a colleague of mine from my Secret Service days in San Francisco. I hope to learn more about Jackson from him."

We arrived at 26 Sumner Street just before noon. Liz served lunch and prodded us about what had happened. But Garth saw the two telegrams on the tray and sidestepped her questions.

"Ah," he said enthusiastically. "Here are a few pieces of the puzzle we need." He stuffed one telegram in his pocket and tore open the one from England. For a telegram, it was quite long.

Garth read it, then laid the paper down and sighed. "This adds another dimension to the story."

"What does it say?"

"As we knew, Sir Chadwick Holdsworth is dead," Garth said. "My source tells me that he came back to England three weeks ago. He was accompanied by a young American man, whom Holdsworth had dealings with while in South Africa."

"That sounds like Spellman."

"Indeed, it does," he agreed. "They spent a few days in London, visited the British Museum of Antiquities, then the two of them went to Holdsworth's estate in Leeds. Five days later, after a long search of the property, his servants found Holdsworth's body stuffed under his gazebo. He had been dead those five days, and there has been no sign of the American."

"It all implies that the two plotted to keep the ill-gotten gains to themselves," I said. "The proverb seems to be true; there is no honor among thieves."

"And now he's dead," Liz chimed in. "What a terrible mess."

"The Major and Mr. Garth will figure it out," Fred said. He had been leaning against the doorframe to the dining room listening as well. "Who sent the telegram, Mr. Garth?"

"A former consulting detective in London."

"If you need any more help with the investigation, let us know," Fred offered.

"I certainly will, Frederick. For now, the Major and I are on our way to see Brady."

In a mere ten minutes, we drove down 14th Street to the central police station. Leaving the Hudson parked on the street, we went to the second floor, finding Lieutenant Brady's small office. The room wasn't large enough for anything more than his desk, a few wooden chairs, and a filing cabinet. The drab olive green walls were bare except for the three commendations hanging on the wall behind our friend's desk. His bald head was bent over a stack of papers, which he was signing, one after another, as we walked in. He heard our steps and asked for our patience as he completed his work.

"I have some news that should be useful to you." He threw down his pen and jumped to his feet. "My men found one of the partners, Steven Jackson."

"Excellent," Garth exclaimed, grinning. "Tell us more."

"Surprisingly, he's been here in Cleveland for over a week. He's staying at the Hollenden Hotel on Superior and Sixth Street."

"I know the hotel," I said. "It's an outstanding place to stay."

"It costs a sawbuck a night," Garth added. "It should be a tiptop place."

"Be careful, if you want to talk to him," Brady warned. "He has a long record of assaults going back to his teen years. He's a mean character."

"What about Allen Douglas?" I asked.

"Well, that's an interesting case. Douglas arrived from New York City just two nights before the murder. That would be Thursday, the seventh."

"We know that Douglas was with Longfellow's son when he died in Alaska. However, Longfellow Senior opened his home to Douglas," Garth said. "Something doesn't sound right about this."

"Don't be so sure," Brady corrected, sitting back down in his chair. "Allen Douglas and Herbert Longfellow, Jr. were classmates and close friends in college. Douglas became a family friend as well; the old man didn't hold him responsible for what went on in Alaska."

"We just came from Markson's office in Medina. Longfellow didn't say anything about Douglas staying with him." Garth studied Brady's face for a reaction.

"Maybe I ought to talk to Markson. We need to

compare notes to see what comes up." Brady leaned back in his chair. "Why were you talking to Longfellow at the police station?"

"Markson seems to think Longfellow is the killer. The Major and I have our doubts. You can make your own assumptions. So who told you that Douglas spent the night of the seventh at Longfellow's? Where did he go from there?"

Brady reached for some papers on his desk and flipped through them. "Our source is an employee at the train station. He spoke to us anonymously. Supposedly, Douglas arrived in Cleveland on the morning of the seventh. There's another reason I need to speak to Markson. We know Douglas was seen the afternoon of the ninth at the train depot. He met with two nasty characters getting off the train from New York City. You may know them, Mr. Garth. Stefano Rizzo and Angelo De Luca."

"Good Lord, yes, I do know them. Two of the meanest members of the Black Hand."

"The Black Hand?" I asked. "What in the world is that?"

"You need to read the papers more often," Garth said. "The Black Hand is a criminal syndicate, the members of which would scare the demons back to hell."

"Well, it seems like you may need my muscle after all," I said, weakly grinning at him.

"There's nothing to grin about when it comes to the Black Hand, Major." Brady stood and walked around his desk. "I would suggest you wait a few days before going after Allen Douglas. We have men searching for him and his friends. I'll let you know what I learn from Markson and if we find the three men in question." Brady stretched his long arms over his head and changed the subject. "How are you two getting along at the Spellman house?"

"We aren't spending a lot of time there," Garth replied. "They put Mallory in a room next to mine; his snoring keeps me up half the night."

I gave a snort and replied. "Sorry, but your infernal pacing does the same to me the other half of the night. But, all in all, Garth isn't hard to get along with. I've shared tents in the field with men who annoy me a lot more."

"Well, thank you. We'll have to spend a week camping when the case is over," he offered as he flipped his homburg rakishly onto his head.

"Oh, before I forget, Brady." Garth rummaged through his jacket pockets. "I received news from London this morning." He finally found the telegrams, handing them to Brady.

The Lieutenant picked up his bulldog pipe and chewed on the stem as he read them. "This case is protracting more each day. May I keep these telegrams, Mr. Garth?"

"Go right ahead, Lieutenant. I have them memorized. We've got people to see. Have a good afternoon," Garth threw his coat back over his shoulders, giving me a tight-lipped grin. "It may be best to confront Steven Jackson today. I hate putting you in danger, Major …"

"I volunteered for this, Garth. I'll follow through. Don't worry about me. I've faced tougher obstacles than that bear of a man and a couple of New York hoods."

"That's a good man. Now, show me to the Hollenden Hotel."

"You might want to go see the informant at the Trivoli Restaurant," Brady suggested. "Once he starts his shift, he may not be able to get away from his duties and speak to you."

"How did you know about Eddie Bennett?" Garth

asked, suspicion glaring in his eyes.

"Fred keeps me informed too," Brady answered.

"I didn't know about him," I said. "No one tells me anything."

"I'll fill you in Major," Garth promised. "Come along now."

Chapter Twelve

Dining Out

"We're here, Major. Pull into this parking lot."

We walked up to the Trivoli Garden Italian Restaurant just before two in the afternoon and knocked on the front door. It took a few minutes to get someone's attention. When it opened, we were met by a well-dressed man with a pencil mustache and long sideburns. He held the door open and said, "The restaurant doesn't open until two p.m., gentlemen. Come back then, please."

"We understand that," Garth responded. "We wish to speak to Eddie Bennett. I believe he is working right now."

"Yes, but I don't allow personal visits when my employees are on duty."

"Ah, so you're the manager," Garth said, a glint in his eyes. "Then you must know about the message from Augie at The Sparrow Club."

"And, you're Mr. Garth." The man nodded in approval. "Augie said you were coming down. Make it quick; Eddie has work to do." The manager's voice quickened as he glared down his pointed nose at us. He looked in the direction of a young man taking chairs off the tables.

"We'll only be a minute." I said, as we passed into the dining room.

Eddie Bennett was only in his teen years. He stood tall and lanky in a tuxedo that hung loosely off his shoulders. "Mr. Bennett, may we have a word with you? I'm Sherwood Garth, this is my partner, Major James Mallory."

"Um, just a quick word. I don't want to lose my job over this," Eddie replied with a taut voice.

"Sit down, we can talk here." I pulled out a chair.

"I know what you're here about," Eddie said, sitting across from me. "The manager was speaking to Augie the other night; I happened to overhear their conversation."

"You heard the name of Spellman …"

"Yes, just before that, I had a customer who asked about him," Eddie interrupted. "There were three of them sitting at the table in the corner over there." He pointed to a corner table. "The guy who spoke seemed like a real gentleman. He was well-dressed in a business suit and wore a handlebar mustache. I even noticed that he had his fingernails manicured. A real dandy, he was. The other two were a couple of thugs. I recognized the type. Both had broken noses that didn't set right, cauliflower ears, and a few deep scars."

"What did they ask you?" I questioned.

"The gent asked if I knew Henry Spellman," the kid said. "Course, I didn't. I told him Cleveland's a big town; I can't know everybody."

"Did he act upset over that answer?" Garth asked, knitting his fingers together.

"Naw, he was okay. But, the two mugs with him gave me a scowl that sent shivers down my back. So, I figured I better watch my words," Eddie whispered, smiling nervously. "Anyway, the gentleman didn't act like the other two. In fact, he gave me a good tip."

"Did he say why he was asking about Spellman?" Garth asked.

"No. Not to me. I kept my ears open while I served them. The gent spoke in a level tone. He didn't yell or nothin'. But, when I was setting their plates in front of them, one of the thugs said something like, 'If you can't get the rocks, we'll get them ourselves and leave you hanging.'"

"I hope they didn't know you were listening," I said. "Those men are with the Black Hand."

The color drained from Eddie's face, and his jaw dropped. "Geez, I didn't know that. Those guys are killers."

"Don't worry," Garth said, grinning to ease Eddie's fears. "If they thought you heard them, they wouldn't have spoken of anything incriminating. Did you hear anything else?"

Eddie's face scrunched up, deep in thought. "The one thug said to the other that he knows how to find the place. That's all I remember."

"What time did this all transpire?" I asked Eddie.

"Pretty late. I remember because I had a date after work, so I kept an eye on the clock. It was about a quarter past ten."

"On Saturday night?"

"No," he corrected, waving his hand. "The night

before, Friday, the eighth."

"You've been very helpful, Eddie." Garth dropped a five-dollar gold piece on the table. "If these guys come back tonight, give Augie a call and let him know. He'll get word to us." Garth pushed back his chair and stood.

"You'd better get to work," I suggested, scanning the bar, seeing the manager frown at us. "I don't want you to get in trouble."

Eddie scurried off to his duties while I shifted in my chair to face Garth. "Did you hear what he said?"

"Every word of it."

"The discrepancy of dates, Garth. Brady believes that the Black Hand arrived on the ninth, the day of the murder. Eddie said the three of them were in the restaurant on the eighth."

"Yes. I don't believe the young man would make a mistake like that with a young lady waiting for him. I'll need to double-check on that. If you like Italian food, Major, we can stay and have an early dinner."

"Indeed I do," I answered, a little taken aback by the change of topic. "Trivoli has a reputation for excellent cuisine. I recommend their Carbonara. It's one of my favorites."

"So, we'll eat here before moving on."

* * *

After an enjoyable dinner at Trivoli's, we headed toward the Hollenden Hotel. I was a little confused as to why we were going to see Jackson. I assumed our next stop would be The Sparrow Club. After all, Karen Bender would be a fountain of information about Spellman. She knew what

Spellman's plans had been before his death. She should be able to answer so many other questions.

"It was a good idea, Major," he said, as if reading my mind. "I was planning on seeing Miss Bender tonight but changed my plan."

"Why is that?"

"Because it's Sunday, and The Sparrow Club is closed." He took off his homburg, tossing it into the back seat. "When I spoke with Fred this morning, he mentioned that Miss Bender rarely goes to The Sparrow Club on Mondays. However, she's always there on the weekends."

"Ah, you didn't mention that to me," I grumbled, glaring over at him. It was already becoming dark as I drove down Superior Avenue. "You have to be more open with me, Garth. How am I supposed to help you if you're keeping information like that from me?"

"You're right. I apologize. I'm not accustomed to having a partner, someone I can trust."

I smiled as I heard the man who trusts no one, tell me that I have his confidence. "Now, what have you got planned for the rest of the evening?"

"It's getting late. We have just one more stop to make."

"You mean Steven Jackson?"

"Indeed. He should be back at his hotel shortly. I want to get this visit out of the way as soon as possible," Garth said, glancing toward me. "Then we need to head back to Medina. However, I have something special planned for tomorrow evening. Something you'll enjoy a great deal."

"What is that?" I blew out smoke after lighting a cigar.

"We're going out clubbing, old man."

"Clubbing? What on earth for?"

"I want to dig around the local bars and see how much

I can learn about Henry. Rachel told me that he spent most evenings on the prowl. There are only three local bars in Medina." Garth pulled out his notebook and flipped past a few pages. "We are going to two of them tomorrow evening. The Medina Lounge and Billy's Place. Remember, Rachel said they are vastly different in their clientele. The lounge is a bit upper-crust, and Billy's is more of the working man's bar."

"What about the third place?" I asked.

I glanced over at him, catching a smile on his face. "The third I want to give a little more time to. It's called The Lajon Bostad Inn."

"Good Lord, Garth," I exclaimed. "What's a French restaurant doing out in farm country?"

"I found that intriguing, as well. We'll discover that when we go there. In the first two, I want to ask about Spellman's friends. I expect our visit to The Lajon Bostad Inn to be quite lengthy. Supposedly, when Karen came to visit Henry in Medina, The Lajon Bostad Inn was where they'd meet. Spellman seemed more apt to visit a European lounge. That's why I wish to devote more time there."

"I see what you mean. Learn more about the man and his relationship with Miss Bender."

"Precisely. For tonight, we go to see Mr. Jackson, tomorrow we go to the first two bars, the following night, The Lajon Bostad."

Chapter Thirteen

The Bear

We walked through the revolving doors of the elegant Hollenden Hotel and approached the front desk.

"Jackson must be well-off to be able to afford a room here," I said, walking under a gigantic chandelier in the center of the lobby.

Ignoring my comment, Garth went directly to the desk and addressed the clerk. "Good afternoon. We are searching for a man we presume registered here. Mr. Steven Jackson. Would you be kind enough to tell us his room number?"

"Are you two policemen?"

Garth opened the lapel on his jacket, flashing his badge. "No, I'm a Pinkerton agent." The immaculately dressed little man answered without consulting his register. "Mr.

Jackson is in room 347, sir. However, you won't find him there; he stepped out a few moments ago. He always goes to dinner at five. Would you care to leave a message?"

"No, thank you. We'll come back later." Garth began to leave but turned and leaned on the front desk. "Tell me, how is it that you immediately knew the man's room number?"

The clerk nervously smiled. "Mr. Jackson is not easy to forget. A bear of a man in his appearance and demeanor. He's a very intimidating character. The manager asked Clyde and me to watch him. The boss thinks Jackson may be trouble."

"Does Mr. Jackson go out of town much?"

"It's funny you would ask that," the clerk said, leaning forward on his desk with his hand out. Garth understood the gesture and dropped a couple of coins in the man's palm. "No. He arrived a week ago, on the twenty-eighth of January. Just about every night, he goes out to the local bars and returns to his room by eleven. Then Saturday morning, he was speaking to the doorman, Clyde, who pointed out the Spellman sisters for him. Jackson had been asking about them. There they were, driving down the street. Jackson jumped into his rented car and followed them. It was the last we saw of him until half past eleven that night when he returned. If you want to see him, come back in an hour. Remember, he's a tough character."

"We'll keep that in mind." I stepped back into the openness of the lobby and was on my way to the entrance of the hotel when I felt a tug on my sleeve. I turned around and saw what Garth had seen. The desk clerk walked off into a back room. We made an abrupt change and headed for the staircase.

"Where on earth are we going, Garth?"

"Room 347, where we intended to go," he said, leaping up the stairs, two at a time. "We have a chance to search his room before we are interrupted."

We reached the third floor and found room 347. Garth rapped on the door loudly as he searched the hallway. He then slipped his hand into the pocket of his overcoat, bringing forth two metal prongs. He bent forward and went to work on the keyhole.

"You do realize what will happen if we are caught breaking into this room?" I reminded him.

"Of course I know, Major. Remember, I was a police officer some time ago. However, I don't plan on being caught. Now, be quiet and watch for Jackson." He quickly had the door open. We passed into the room.

"Keep the door open a crack and watch for the big man, so I can explore." He headed straight for the desk, which was cluttered with clothing and newspapers. He went through the mess, then began to rifle through the drawers and pulled out a bundle of letters. After reading the top of one, he stuffed the rest into the pocket of his overcoat.

From the next drawer down, he removed a large hunting knife in a leather sheath. Holding it between his fingers, he held it up for me to see. "What do you make of this?"

I grinned at his ploy to catch me in the wrong answer, "Absolutely nothing, *young* man," I responded. "That weapon is far too big and thick to be the murder weapon. The killer used a stiletto, as you recall, a two-sided blade if I remember correctly."

Garth smiled back. "Very good, Major. Just trying to

keep you on your toes." He slipped it back into its sheath and put it in the drawer.

He allowed his gaze to circle the room and was ready to go when I noticed something. "Over there, Garth." I pointed to a small end table next to the bed. "Even from here, that piece of paper appears to be a train ticket."

Without uttering a word, he ran to the nightstand. "Indeed, you're right. It shows that Jackson arrived in Cleveland on Monday, January twenty-eighth, just as the clerk said." Garth rummaged through the table's small drawer.

"That's almost a full week before Spellman's murder," I pointed out. "What was that you found on the table?"

"A letter from a college in California. It's to congratulate him on earning a degree in mining. Another reason Spellman brought him along to Africa."

Garth stuffed the ticket into his pocket. "Let's get out of here, Major, before Jackson comes back." I peered out into the hallway and signaled an all-clear. Garth followed me, closing the door behind him and relocking it with his tools.

We headed toward the staircase when, from around the corner, stepped a giant of a man. I recognized him immediately. His full, black beard came down to the center of his huge chest. His equally dark hair hung limply on his shoulders. He still wore the pinstriped suit and bowler he had on the other night. As he approached us, Garth called out his name.

"How do you know me?" he asked, stopping to glare at my friend.

"You fit your description admirably," Garth said. "May we have a moment of your time? I am Sherwood Garth, and this is my friend, James Mallory."

"I suppose you can," Jackson said, then thought again. "You ain't coppers, are yah?"

"No," I answered. "We're private investigators. We have no police authorization, so you have nothing to fear by talking to us."

Without answering, he turned, leading us to the room we had just left. He had to duck his head or risk damage to the woodwork. He flung his jacket on the desk and sat down on his unmade bed.

Garth started the interrogation abruptly. "Are you aware that Henry Spellman is dead?"

Jackson's eyebrows became knitted together, "What's that to me? I don't know the man."

"Oh, I believe you do know him. We know about the mishap in Alaska, the fact you worked with Spellman in South Africa, and that Spellman walked off with everyone's share of the diamonds. You're here in Cleveland to confront him. Now if you'll be so kind as to explain where you were Saturday night. It will settle matters for you."

"I was out having a few drinks. As I said, I don't have anything to do with your Henry Spellman," he said, with fire in his eyes. "I don't give a crap if the man is dead."

Garth heaved a heavy sigh and shook his head. "It would be best if you were honest with us, Mr. Jackson."

Jackson rose from the side of his bed, glaring at both Garth and me. It appeared he didn't like us catching him in a lie. "Okay, so you're smarter than you look, but if you're here to accuse me of killin' that piece of dung, you're wrong. You can get outta here, right now."

"No one's accusing you of murder, Mr. Jackson. After all, you have Major Mallory as an alibi. Remember, he saw you at half past ten on the night of the murder. We just want to know what you're doing in Cleveland," Garth pressed. "Is it to collect your share of the stones? Or is it about what happened in Alaska?"

"I told you, Alaska ain't none of yer business," Jackson growled, pointing his finger into Garth's face.

"Come, come, Mr. Jackson. I know Spellman was the only witness in the trial that proved Longfellow's death was an accident. Did Spellman hold anything back at the trial?"

"I told you to stay the hell out of it!" Jackson bellowed as he came at Garth. His face turned scarlet with rage; his claw-like hands stretched out to grip the lapels on Garth's coat. With his brute strength, he lifted Garth off his feet, pinning him against the wall. Garth's feet kicked in midair, not hitting their target, and he pulled at Jackson's arms, to no avail.

I grabbed the first thing in reach, a small wooden chair. Raising it above my head, I sent it crashing across Jackson's back. It stunned him enough to make him drop Garth in a heap on the floor, but it didn't stop him. He turned on me and charged like a bull. His huge left fist landed squarely on my jaw. The punch staggered me, but I remained on my feet.

I was done playing with the brute. He rushed me again and took another swing. I flung my arm up and blocked it. I stood directly in front of him and threw a string of punches into his massive chest and face. I aimed my punches to the back of his head through his face. I gritted my teeth and cupped my hands, smashing against both of his ears. He staggered backward with each blow, his nose bleeding and a welt already rising on his cheek. He held both arms in front of his face, leaving just the opening

I needed. With all the strength I could muster, I sent my fist into his midsection, straight to the solar plexus. At the same moment, Garth threw a tackle across Jackson's knees that sent him sprawling to the floor, with me still on top of him. Jackson curled up in the fetal position, gasping for air. The bluster was gone—for now.

Garth and I simultaneously jumped to our feet, ran out of the room, out of the hotel, and into my Hudson. We cranked the car to life and roared into the traffic.

"I'm indebted to you, Major. I was helpless in that man's grasp," Garth wheezed.

"I suppose I should expect a bruise now and then if I continue working with you," I said, lightly touching my jaw. The slight touch sent streaks of pain to my head. I eased my motor car into the traffic on Superior. "What was all that about Longfellow and Jackson? You seemed to know more than I do."

"Sorry, I failed to show you the telegram from San Francisco and the newspaper clippings I found in Henry Spellman's bedroom at home." He quickly recapped the hunting accident and death of young Longfellow.

"That's all that the newspapers wrote?" I asked. "There are a lot of holes in that story."

"That's what I thought," Garth said, rubbing his chin. "My guess is that Spellman was blackmailing Jackson, which explains his presence here."

"Along with trying to get his share of the hot rocks," I added. "Jackson doesn't seem to be an astute man." I grinned as I glanced over at Garth, noticing a smirk on his face, as well.

"He did have the degree in mining," Garth reminded me. "I suppose that's how he made his living."

"That's about all he can do efficiently," I responded. "If he was allowing Spellman to blackmail him over the incident in Alaska, he should have known he was wasting his money. They can't try him for the same crime once he's acquitted."

Garth sighed and shook his head disgustedly. "Another theory that's too obvious. Why wait until he came home from South Africa to kill him? It would have been easier to do the deed in Africa and leave Spellman's body to the lions and hyenas."

"Don't forget the elder Longfellow. This latest information about Alaska shines more light on him. He may have blamed Spellman for allowing the killer of his son to go unpunished."

"That's true. Mr. Longfellow may not have known Jackson was in town, but he did know Spellman was," Garth said, as we cut over to Fourteenth Street.

"There are many reasons people wanted Spellman dead," I said, chewing on the unlit cigar. "And, there are many suspects. Longfellow is one of them."

"As is Jackson. Nonetheless, it is altogether too early to pin the murder on anyone," Garth responded. "Let's get back to Medina."

Chapter Fourteen

A Chat With Katy

The bed that the Spellman sisters provided for me was one of the most comfortable I've ever slept on. The double sized mattress held me in its clutches until well past my usual wake-up call. I rolled over, glaring at the clock on the end table, and sighed at my laziness. "Eight-fifteen," I said to the walls. I threw off the thick quilt, feeling the chilly morning air engulf me. "Damn, I've wasted hours sleeping in."

I reached over to the chair by the bed. Instead of grabbing my dressing gown, I felt a sheet of paper. I sat up and focused my eye on it.

Garth had risen early and left for Cleveland to meet with Lieutenant Brady and check with one of Brady's connections at Union Station. The note said he would fill me in when he returned around noon. However, Garth had left a task for me to handle. We had neglected to speak to the staff at the Spellman mansion, so he assigned me to that job. 'Your opportunity to prove yourself' is how he put it. We'd planned on questioning the staff but decided to consider the partners first. Now it was time.

I sat on the edge of the bed, sliding my feet into my slippers. It occurred to me that both Margaret and Rachel were probably still in bed, fast asleep. Both had the uncanny ability to sleep for hours. I had taken part in interviews alongside Garth, so I shouldn't have much trouble if I followed his methods. I washed and dressed in a casual gray wool suit and headed for the kitchen.

Following the smell of freshly brewed coffee, I found the kitchen maid, Katy Sparks, hard at work. She stood at the cutting table, dicing onions and potatoes, mixing them with the beaten eggs. "Good morning, young lady. May I have a cup of coffee?" The young cook-in-training wore an ankle-length gray dress with a full white apron covering it. Her auburn hair was tucked up into her bonnet. "May I call you Katy?"

"Why, of course, Major. Help yourself to the coffee," she offered. "My hands are a bit occupied." She turned from her work to give me a sweet smile. She had not yet turned seventeen, but she had the beauty of a woman about her. She had dark blue eyes and very prominent dimples when she smiled.

"Why don't you take a break?" I suggested. "If you don't mind, I'd like to ask you a few questions."

"About the murder?" she asked, her smile fading. "I don't know anything about that."

"I'm sure you don't, Katy. I just want to ask you about

the people who work and live here," I said, pouring my coffee. "You seem to be a smart girl. You see what goes on around here."

"It's true, I keep my ears open and my mouth shut," she said, the smile creeping back. "But I don't want to be a gossip. Miss Spellman said I shouldn't gossip about people here."

"I understand, but I'm investigating a murder, my dear." I set my cup down. "The only person who'll get into trouble is the killer."

"Do you think Mr. Spellman's killer is in this house?"

"I honestly have no idea. That's why I need to talk to you," I said, shrugging to disarm Katy's fears with a casual attitude.

She sat down at the kitchen table after drying her hands on her apron. "Okay, what do you want to know?"

"Good girl. Let's start with Mr. Spellman. How close were you to him?"

"Oh, not close at all," she responded. "I was hired last year while Mr. Spellman was in Alaska. When he came home, he kept to himself, then off he went to Africa. I must admit, I didn't miss him that much. He only talked to me when he wanted something. The other servants felt the same way about him. We sensed that he didn't want us around."

"Did they tell you that?" I asked.

"Who?"

"The other servants."

"Oh yeah, we talked about him here in the kitchen when the ladies weren't close by," she admitted. "I know, that's gossiping, but we have time on our hands so…"

I remembered about the nightspots in Medina and

softly asked Katy, "Do you know about Henry Spellman's nights out?"

"Cynthia told us about that too. He went to Cleveland some but went to the local clubs more often."

"Did she ever mention a French restaurant named The Lajon Bostad Inn?"

"Oh, sure," Katy smiled and waved her hand. "He would meet someone there at least once a week before he left. And it isn't a French place."

"Really," I exclaimed. "It certainly sounds French."

"I thought so too. But it's owned by an old man from Sweden. It's run by his three daughters." Katy picked up a dishcloth and absently cleaned the table. "They serve Swedish food along with domestic beer."

"You sound like an expert. Have you been there?"

"Of course not, Major. I'm too young. But I met the twin sisters, Gerda and Greta. I was shopping and had a friendly conversation with them."

"Tell me about Oda. How does she get along with everyone?"

"Oda's such a sad person," Katy murmured. "Her husband got blown up, or something, in the war. They had to cut off his legs. Oda needs to work to support him, and he's a flat-out grump about it. She tries to act cheerful, but we can tell she's sad. I feel sad for her," Katy said. "But Joseph seems to be able to cheer her up."

"That's the gardener and driver here?"

"Yeah, he doesn't have a car of his own, but he's Miss Margaret's driver." Katy's head tilted to the left.

"Does Joseph live here?"

"No, he rents a little bungalow down the road. It's on the way to Cleveland, so Oda has to double back to Medina after she drops him off."

"So, Oda drives him home after work?"

"Every day," Katy answered with a wink. "They seemed to like each other."

"How can you tell that?" I asked, leaning casually back in my seat, listening.

"He makes her laugh," she answered with a shrug. "That's what she needs. Someone to make her laugh. I just hope he doesn't hurt her."

"I hope not, either," I said, to keep Katy from closing. "How would he hurt her?"

"Well, Joseph likes Cynthia too. But differently. When Cynthia finishes with Margaret's hair, she waves Joseph inside and they go up to her room." Katy said, her nose crinkling. "I'm no dumb kid; I know what they're doing."

"Seems like he's not treating Oda fairly."

"I know, especially since she drives him home. That reminds me," she glanced out the window.

"What's that?"

"On the night of Mr. Spellman's murder, Oda didn't drive him home."

"You mean she left without him?"

"No, I looked out the back door to where she usually parks her car, and it wasn't there," Katy answered. "I asked her about it; she said that Joseph had to borrow it to do something important and he would pick her up in the morning."

"That's why Margaret had to drive Oda home that night."

"Miss Margaret was none too happy about it."

"What time did he take the car?" I asked.

"I'm not sure," Katy answered. "But he worked his

full shift, which ends at eight. When I looked out of my window, it was after nine and the car was gone. And, I'd just seen Oda in the kitchen moments before."

"What about Cynthia? What do you think of her?"

"She's the cat's pajamas. Absolutely beautiful," she chimed, showing her dimples again. "But, she's a bigger gossip than anyone else in the household."

"What does she talk about?"

"Well, while she's helping Miss Margaret with her hair and dressing, she listens to every word her mistress says. I'm sure Miss Margaret doesn't want everything she says spread around to everyone. But Cynthia loves to tell us everything she hears. When Miss Margaret goes out, Cynthia comes to the kitchen, blabbing it all."

"She would lose her job for that," I reminded Katy.

"If anyone told Miss Margaret she would, but no one has the nerve."

"Did Miss Margaret ever tell her about the diamonds?" I asked, hoping for a revelation.

"Cynthia told us that she talks about them all the time. Oda asked her what the old bag told her." She stopped, looking embarrassed. "That's her words, 'the old bag.' I would never say that. Well, then Cynthia said, 'that's a topic I only share with Joe.' She meant Joseph, but I suppose when they're upstairs, she calls him Joe."

"That's telling," I said, stroking my goatee as I thought about what she'd told me. "Where is Mr. Polletti now?"

"Out in the garage. Miss Margaret wants him to drive her into town for some shopping. Joseph is warming up the engine in the car. She'll be down a little later. I have to get a wiggle on it and get back to work, Major Mallory. Have I helped any?"

"You have been exceedingly helpful, my dear. If anyone should ask, don't tell them we spoke. I won't tell anyone either. It will keep us both out of trouble."

Katy laughed. "Okay. Mum's the word."

I decided to find Polletti in the garage before he left. "It seems cold out there," I said to Katy, peering through the glass window in the back door. "I'd better get my scarf." I started for the foyer to the main staircase when Katy stopped me.

"You can use the servant's staircase." She nodded to a door to her right. "It's narrow, but even a big guy like you can fit," she quipped, with another dimpled smile.

I grinned back and started climbing the uncarpeted steps. They creaked with every step I made. Halfway up, after a sharp turn in the stairway, I abruptly stopped as I faced an attractive young woman coming down. She wore an orange and white silk kimono loosely held together by a red sash. She took a few steps before seeing me, with each step down causing a jiggle in her feminine attributes. I presumed this was Cynthia Browning standing before me.

"Oh, my," she exclaimed, pulling the sash tighter. "I didn't expect to see anyone except Katy on these stairs at this hour."

"I'm sorry to startle you, I'm …"

"You're Major James Mallory. I know. I've seen you and that other man."

"Well, we haven't been formally introduced, and we are in an awkward position," I hinted, nodding to her kimono, slightly open above her knees.

She batted her eyes, blushing red as she closed the kimono. "I'm Cynthia Browning, Miss Margaret's personal assistant. She calls me her lady-in-waiting."

"Good, I've meant to talk to you. Can we do that now?"

"Now?"

"Not exactly now," I said, blushing as much as she was. "You can dress, and I'll meet you in the …"

"There's a sitting room upstairs, Major. The third door down the hall, close to your room. I'll meet you there. I need to get my coffee and dress. That'll take me about an hour."

I thought a minute and realized I had other plans. "Can we make that at seven this evening? If that would suit you?"

"That's fine, Major. Now, may I pass?"

I turned sideways to allow her to walk down the steps to the kitchen. She gazed up at me with a pair of alluring green eyes. She softly brushed against me as she descended. I wondered if that was done purposely.

My eye was glued to Cynthia as she descended the narrow staircase and disappeared into the kitchen. *She's a suspect, James. Maybe a murderer. Keep yourself under control.*

When I reached my room to get my scarf, I was met by Oda in the hallway. "Well, there you are, Major," she mused. "You're a hard man to catch up with."

"You found me, what can I do for you?"

"Nothing for me," she replied, her voice sharp. "You're wanted on the telephone, downstairs. Follow me."

The little woman turned toward the main stairs, leading me below to the telephone under the staircase. "Thank you, Oda."

She shrugged and walked to the kitchen. "I've got work to do. I don't need any more interruptions."

I picked up the candlestick phone and spoke loudly into it. "Hello? Who's calling?"

"It's me—Garth. I'm in Cleveland, as you well know,

but I can't come back to Medina until tomorrow."

"Why?"

"The Pinkerton office is holding me up."

"Are you in any trouble?" I asked, smiling to myself.

"Wipe that smile off your face. I can hear it in your voice. No, I'm not in trouble. But, they were concerned about getting their part of my income. Remember, I'm under contract with them. Any income I make while in their employment is to be divided. They get thirty percent. That's why I needed to be aggressive with Margaret on our fee."

"Understood. Well, then, I'll find something to keep me occupied. I spoke with Katy a few minutes ago," I said, leaning against the wall.

"Good for you. But, I want to be there when we speak to the others in the household." His voice began to fade. "Our telephone line's not doing well, Major. We'll have to talk later."

At that point, we were cut off before I had a chance to argue about my interviewing the others without him staring over my shoulder. I supposed he had a reason, but there went my planned interview with Joseph. Being a good soldier, I obeyed his orders.

Nonetheless, I wasn't happy being ordered about. I'm usually the one giving orders. I grumbled to myself, then punched the wall under the staircase and walked away.

Chapter Fifteen

A Visit to The Lajon Bostad

After my conversation with Garth, I walked back into the kitchen and found Katy washing dishes. An idea came to mind. "Uh, Katy. Do you know the way to The Lajon Bostad?"

She turned around, smiling graciously. "Why, of course, Major." Katy opened a drawer and found a pad of paper and a pencil. She jotted down the directions to The Lajon Bostad with a simple map showing Chippewa Road, which led southwest and ended at a rather large lake. "It's gorgeous out there. Especially at Christmas time. The pine trees and the building resemble a winter wonderland. But, Major, Mr. Garth took your motorcar."

"Oh, good Lord," I gritted my teeth. "I forgot about that. Things aren't going my way this morning. I'd hate to ask Oda to borrow her auto. She'd make a big fuss over it. I'm not in the mood for her attitude. Besides, she's a suspect. It wouldn't be right to ask her." I leaned against the door jamb, my arms folded. "Well, I'll see if I can borrow Miss Spellman's Packard."

"That's an idea, but she planned to go shopping this morning."

"Then I'll borrow her Model A. I'm working on this case for her, she'd better not argue with me." I know what to do if I have a conflict with a man, knock his block off. When it comes to women, I'm at a loss. "I'll be back in a minute." I grinned at Katy and walked out of the kitchen.

I knew Margaret was up and around the house. I went upstairs and walked toward the front rooms. A door opened and I spotted Cynthia leaving it at the far end of the corridor. "Were you just with Miss Margaret?"

"Good morning, Major," Cynthia answered with a smile. "I just finished dressing her. She's on her way to her sitting room."

"Thanks, what mood is she in?"

"Her usual," she answered with a sigh. "Why, do you need to see her?"

"Yeah, I want to borrow her auto, the Model-A," I said, walking Cynthia down the hall.

"Good luck with that," she responded with a light chuckle. "She's right in here, Major. I'll announce you." She must have noticed the puzzlement on my face, and she explained, "she is easier to deal with if everything is done properly."

I nodded and waited in the hallway. I slipped out a cigar, then remembered Margaret's dislike for the odor. I didn't light it but stuck it in my mouth.

After a few minutes, Cynthia returned. She scurried out of the room, closing the door behind her. "She doesn't wish to speak to you. But—I've got the keys. Miss Margaret wants you to have the automobile back by four this afternoon."

"Oh, that was good of you to go to bat for me. You're an okay gal."

"No problem, Major," Cynthia said. "Ask, and you shall receive. Just be sure to have it back by four."

"It's just after one now. That should give me enough time. What'll Margaret do if I'm late?" I asked with a grin.

"Oh, don't push your luck."

I went to the foyer to collect my overcoat and passed through the kitchen on my way out the back. Cynthia and Katy had sat down for coffee and bagels together.

"Thanks, ladies. Oh, Cynthia, don't forget our meeting tonight at seven in the upstairs parlor."

* * *

The Lajon Bostad was indeed located on the frozen shore of Chippewa Lake, the building designed like a Swiss Chalet with a sloping roof and window boxes bordering the second floor balconies. There were no flowers this time of year but the tall pine trees surrounding the chalet added to the rustic theme.

In my travels with the military, I was never assigned a post in Europe. Gazing at the chalet, I realized that I'd missed out on something grand in my life. I would remedy that missing piece and travel to Europe, as soon as the war ended.

Pulling the exterior double doors outward, I left Ohio

behind and stepped into an alpine retreat. As I walked in, I noticed five lovely girls dressed in Austrian dirndls. They wore the close-fitting, off-the-shoulder bodices and full skirts well.

I walked into the restaurant, observing everything without appearing conspicuous. After all, we weren't sure if this inn had any connection to the case. I needed practice in my sleuthing techniques, so I took a mental note of what might be useful. However, my observations were interrupted by the blonde hostess who offered to show me to a table. I scanned the crowded dining room to see if I recognized anyone. Alas, all were strangers to me. It appeared to be a thriving business with happy customers.

Instead, I decided to pony up to the bar and have a beer. As I walked in that direction, I noticed a waitress who mirrored the hostess. I remember being told twin sisters worked here.

From the bar, I heard an appealing feminine voice ask, "What'll you have, big guy?"

I turned around and came face to face with a Nordic goddess. She was older than the other girls, mid-thirties, with perfectly sculptured features. Her skin appeared baby-soft with a pleasing splash of freckles across her slightly upturned nose. Her glacial blue eyes peered at me from under bangs of strawberry blonde hair. Almost all of her thick mane was tucked into a braid that circled her head. Mesmerized, I missed what she'd said.

She smiled, reading my thoughts. "Did you want to order something?" She had a slight accent.

I attempted to think clearly. "A beer if you don't mind."

"Any preference?"

"Do you happen to have Stroh's Dark?"

"Ah, a man who knows his beers. My father has the Stroh's Beer Company rail in a couple of kegs from the Detroit Lion's Head Brewery. The shipment arrived only the other day. You're one of the first to ask for it," she said with a wink.

I gasped at the name of the brewery. Fortunately, the barmaid didn't notice. What did the name of a brewery have to do with the case? "Your father owns The Lajon Bostad? You'll have to tell him for me what a stunning place this is."

"I am the one you should be complimenting, big guy," she boasted, leaning over the bar and revealing more of her appeal. "Father is somewhat retired now. He left the inn to my younger sisters and me. They're the two girls you were ogling before."

"I wasn't ogling them," I said in my defense. "I was admiring their blue and green outfits. Yours, in red, is quite attractive as well. It enhances your lovely complexion."

Her cheeks glowed as she turned to the row of kegs behind her, placed a large mug under a tap, and pulled. "Here ya go, fresh and tasty." She handed me the large mug. "Where were you stationed in France?"

"I haven't been to France, but if you're referring to my patch, I received this wound in Mexico."

She looked at me, tilting her head like an adorable Irish Setter pup, "When did we go to war with Mexico?"

I had to smile and explain recent history. "It was a good shot at deductive reasoning, my dear. You should be a detective." I changed the subject by asking, "How long have you been here in Medina?"

"I came over at the age of seven. Don't ask me how long ago that was," she said. "My parents came to America from Sweden, settling here. Father always wanted to buy a Swiss chalet in Switzerland, but couldn't afford what was available there. He and my mother opened a sweet shop in downtown Medina. Then they started adding authentic Swedish dishes, and the good Lord led us here."

Her eyes lost their sparkle when she continued. "Our dear mother passed away when I was a teen. I needed to help Father with the inn, so he taught me the business. When my sisters were old enough, I trained them. I'm hoping they will want to take over when I move on."

"Well, whoever runs this business should be set for life. It's a gold mine. There will always be customers for a place like this."

"I hope so," she said. "I'm concerned with all the talk about Prohibition."

"I can understand that, but you seem to be doing well in the dining room." I glanced over my shoulder at the patrons having their lunch.

"I've considered closing the bar and extending the dining room," she said, appearing to be asking my opinion.

"Is that because of the new law, or are you tired of dealing with drunks?" I asked.

She laughed, showing two lovely dimples. "Both, but more so the latter. I don't do much drinking myself and find lushes quite odious. I would rather not offer booze here at all."

"Well, there's your answer," I said, reaching across the bar, patting her hand. "Stick to serving your Swedish meals. It seems to me that people are enjoying it. Come to think of it, I've never had a Swedish dish."

"Well, then, you must try my cuisine. It's all our mother's personal recipes. You're right, we make most of our profits from the food. We are thinking ahead, focusing on the restaurant and providing rooms upstairs for travelers." She nodded toward the staircase I'd passed on the way in.

"You've got a smart head on your shoulders," I said, sipping my beer. "And, a pretty one at that. You didn't tell me your name."

She brightened up with a cheery smile. "I'm Anneka Larsson, pleased to meet you. Our father is Gunner Rosenkranz. My two sisters are Greta, in blue. She's the hostess, and the giddy one in green is Gerda." She glanced out to the restaurant floor. "They're twenty-five, born three years after we moved to America."

I reached across the bar to shake hands, "I'm Major James Mallory."

"Oh, I've heard that name. You're here investigating the death of Henry Spellman, aren't you?"

"Not right now, I'm on my own time. So, you're married?" I asked, glancing for a ring on her left hand.

"Some detective you are. You didn't notice the absence of a ring." She held up her left hand, wiggling her fingers. "I was married, but Lars traveled back to Sweden to visit his family. He was aboard the Lusitania when it was sunk by a German U-boat. His body was never found."

"I'm sorry for you, Anneka."

"It's been over three years now," she said. "Soon after his death, I went to The Palmer School of Chiropractic."

"That's in Davenport, Iowa, isn't it?"

"You've heard of it? Yes, it's in Iowa. Father watched the restaurant for me while I got my degree."

"Good Lord, you're a doctor?" I asked. I have heard of chiropractors or bone crushers, as some call them. "You are just full of surprises. If you have a medical degree, why are you tending bar?"

"First, I have a Certificate in Chiropractic, I can't practice medicine," she explained. "I did open an office here in Medina but had a hard time gaining patients. You know how small towns are."

"Ah, what do these hicks know," I agreed. "So, what did you do?"

"I enlisted my service in the war effort as a nurse. From April to September 1917, I went to France. Father took ill, so I needed to come home."

"Any plans to open another office?"

"I'm not sure what my future holds. But, it's not staying here, pouring beer for big lugs like you," Anneka said, openly flirting now. "Gerda and Greta are more interested in running this place. I'll leave the inn in their lovely hands when I decide where I want to be."

"Good for you. You're a remarkable woman. As for the Spellman crime, my partner and I want to bring the killer to justice. We may need to ask you some questions at a later date. I hope that doesn't bother you?"

"Not at all, Jim—you don't mind me calling you Jim?"

"Not a bit."

"I find the idea of a murder case fascinating," she said. "I love a good mystery."

"Who told you about Garth and me?"

"That would be Cynthia, the quiff of the mansion. She called me this morning to tell me all about the murder."

"Why do you refer to Cynthia as a quiff?"

Anneka shrugged her bare shoulders, gazing around to be sure no one was listening. "It's the way she conducts herself around men. Very forward, I would say. A woman can tell about that sort of thing."

"Can you, now?" A picture of Cynthia in her half-open kimono flashed through my head. "I got that impression myself. She… uh, brushed up against me this morning."

Anneka laughed sweetly. "That sounds like Cynthia."

"Does she come here often?" I asked, finishing my beer.

"You want another beer?"

"Yes, please."

"Maybe once a week," she answered, looking up at the beamed ceiling. "Sometimes alone, but other times with a date. She appears to have a new steady now. Three or four times in the past week, she's come in with the same man. They came in late at night because Cynthia works until eight and then has to sneak out. I don't know who her man is. Would you like to try a Gubbröra with your beer?"

"A what?"

"You've never enjoyed Swedish cuisine, so we'll start with Gubbröra," she replied.

"I'm willing to try a variety of foods, but something called Gubbers …"

"It's Gubbröra," she corrected. "It's a traditional Swedish dish, an egg-anchovy salad. Caviar, parsley, dill, and chives top the scrambled eggs and anchovies. It's all served with a round slice of dark bread. It's delicious."

Clearly, she was proud of her cuisine. I didn't want to offend her, so I placed an order for Gubbe ... whatever she called it.

"You won't be disappointed, Jim."

"I'll get your beer and have the cook prepare your lunch. That'll be a dollar for two beers, The Gubbröra is on me," she replied with a wink.

She returned shortly with my beer and a glass of red wine for herself.

"Do you know any of the other men Cynthia came in

here with?" I asked.

"No," she said, fixing some loose strands of her lovely red hair. "They weren't my type. Not swell guys, like you are. That's enough talking about the case, Jim. Tell me about yourself."

I soon forgot about the murder, the stones, and the Spellman sisters. My attention was on her and it appeared hers was on me. It felt as if we were alone in the hub of the noisy restaurant. "You don't want to hear about my military life, it's a bit brutal," I answered after a quick recap of my early years before the Army.

She touched my arm softly, her face calm. "Okay, Jim, maybe some other time."

Before I responded to her kindness, Gerda came from the kitchen, bearing a plate. "Oh, good," I said, showing little enthusiasm, "I'm ready to try my first taste of Sweden."

"Here's a fork, sweetie, dig in." Anneka watched and waited for my reaction. She then added, "As I said, the recipe belonged to Tilda Rosenkranz, my dear mother."

I'd better like it. I took a nibble. "Not too ghastly," I joked to Anneka, grinning. I tried a bigger mouthful of the salty treat. "Exceptional—in fact, quite delectable." I gazed at Anneka. "This makes two Swedish dishes I find to my liking today."

Anneka had to think a moment, then she blushed and slapped my arm in jest.

As I ate, I kept my eye on Anneka working around the bar. Her walk and body movement seemed familiar.

"What's the matter, Jim? You've got a strange look on your face."

"Have I seen you someplace before?"

Anneka giggled. "I was wondering if you would remember. It was at Craig Rogers' house. You and your friend nearly brushed me off the walkway when I was leaving. Before that, I passed by you at city hall."

"Ah, of course. You were wearing the fur collar up on your green coat. I wasn't able to see your lovely face."

"Well, then, I'll forgive you," she chided.

"What were you doing at Craig Roger's house?" I asked, still enjoying my lunch. "If you don't mind my asking?"

"No, I don't mind. We have a mission to help feed the wounded soldiers from the war," she said, wiping the bar. "A few local men have come home in a bad way. My sisters and I decided to offer a meal to each of the families once a week. Monday is the day I drive over to see Craig's family and make my delivery."

"How wonderful of you all," I said with genuine awe. "I wish more Americans would get involved in that way."

"Just doing our duty," she whispered.

"What do you think of the Rogers family?" I asked, slipping into detective mode.

"Well, he's rather friendly, quite cordial. I spend a great deal of time talking to Craig. Obviously, he doesn't get out much because of the loss of his legs. He's not supposed to drink, but I sneak over a bottle of beer for him."

"What about the other two?"

"Oda isn't home whenever I come by. His mother is an old busybody. Whenever she gets me alone, she talks about her daughter-in-law and what a terrible wife she is."

"Oda is supplying the only income for the household. Lucy should ease up on her."

"I know," Anneka agreed, shaking her head in disgust. "It seems Lucy would do anything to get Craig back to

Canada, but Lucy tells me that his wife won't hear of it."

"I suppose every family has its problems," I said with a shrug. I had finished my lunch and as I wiped my mouth, I nodded toward the empty seats by the fireplace. "Would you like to join me on the sofa?"

Anneka glanced down the bar. There were no customers, and the dining room had nearly cleared, as well. "I'd love to," she responded. She poured another glass of wine for herself and walked around the bar. Standing next to me, I saw that she was tall for a woman, at least six feet. She called out, "Greta, watch the bar for me."

"Okay, maybe I can talk you into a haircut?" she teased, ruffling my shaggy mane as she sat next to me on the Davenport. She sat with her legs crossed, appearing almost queenly. "Do you know what the name of my inn is when translated into English?" she asked, sipping on her wine.

An odd question. "Everything here is European. The decor is Swiss, the food is Swedish, and your dress is Austrian. I thought the name sounded French."

"Father wasn't sure what to name it. He was in London for a short time and enjoyed his time at the Lion's Den Pub. That's what he named our business. Lajon Bostad means lion's den in Swedish."

Lion's Den. I almost dropped my beer. "Maybe that's what Spellman was trying to tell us," I said out loud, forgetting his note in the barn was supposed to be a secret.

"What do you mean?" Anneka asked, fingering my hair at the collar.

"Oh, nothing," I said, glancing away. "I don't mean to leave you in the dark, but, in this case, I must."

She shrugged and stopped playing with my hair. My secrecy seemed to spoil the mood.

I changed the subject. “It must be a hard life to run this place on your own.”

“You mean, for a woman?” she responded, raising her eyebrows.

“No. That’s not how I meant it.” I was making a mess of this. “It would be tough to run a business like this for anyone.”

“Good for you, you saved yourself from a lecture. I happen to be a member of the suffrage movement here in town. You’d better watch your step.” Her eyes twinkled as she laughed.

Our conversation ranged from her family and mine to the war, then to personal feelings. Neither of us realized how much time had passed when the cuckoo clock over the hearth announced the hour.

“Damn it. I have Margaret’s auto, and she wants it back by four.”

“Oh, no. I haven’t been watching the time either,” Anneka said, her eyes glistening. “You’ll be back?”

“Indeed I will,” I stood, reached for her hands, and helped her up. “To discuss the case, or, preferably, to visit you.”

Anneka walked me to the front door. I took her hand and bowed, softly kissing her fingers. We gazed at each other for a moment, then I left the building.

Chapter Sixteen

Garth's Return

Arriving back at the Spellman place quicker than I anticipated, I saw Margaret in the parlor and informed her of her auto's return. Her mouth clenched into a straight line and she said nothing. I left without a word.

Upstairs, I headed for my chambers to think about the name of the inn and what bearing it had on the case. Outside Garth's room, I heard a rustling sound within. Garth was still in Cleveland with Lieutenant Brady and the Pinkertons. Who was meddling in his room? Pulling my Colt from its holster, I barged into the room. To my surprise, there stood Garth, rummaging through a suitcase.

"There you are, Major. Do put away your weapon and help me with this valise."

"I wasn't expecting you back from town so soon,"

I said, explaining the Colt. "Where did you get that?" I asked, pointing to the small black valise in his hands.

"It was in Henry's wardrobe. I remembered it when I returned from Cleveland. This was the bag lost by the New York Central when Spellman came home last month. Remember, they found it and delivered it to Spellman two days before his death."

"What are you searching for?"

"The diamonds, naturally. But all I'm finding is his shaving kit," Garth said, with a sigh. "We'll look again later. What have you been up to?"

"I've only had time to speak to Katy Sparks, the kitchen maid." I realized I was still holding the revolver and slid it back into its holster. "She's an innocent young girl. I don't believe she has anything to do with the murder."

"Nonetheless, Major, I'm sure she had something to say about the others."

"Katy told me Cynthia is a regular gossip. She may well be, but Katy also lets a lot slip unintentionally. She knows the gardener, Joseph, may be carrying on with both Oda and Cynthia."

"How does this sweet girl, Katy, know this?" Garth asked as he sat in his armchair.

"As she put it to me, 'I'm not a kid.'" Garth and I chuckled.

"So, she knows about the birds and the bees?" Garth asked.

"She seems to. Oh, and she told me Joseph borrowed Oda Rogers' car on the night of the murder."

"Indeed." Garth rubbed his chin.

I went through my entire conversation with Katy, finishing by telling him about my meeting on the staircase with Cynthia Browning.

He seemed to give that a lot of thought and conceded that a woman in her position should know how to put herself together before coming down the stairs. "By the way, when in Cleveland, I stopped by your house."

"How are they holding up without me?"

"Just fine. Liz is concerned that you're not getting fed properly," Garth said with a grin.

"Ha, no news there. Let's get on with the investigation. While you were away, I drove out to Lajon Bostad for a look around." I told Garth.

"I was hoping to do that together," he said, his lips pursed. "Did you learn anything?"

"I was there primarily for my own distraction. However, I did learn a few things that may help us."

"What might that be?"

"The tall woman we encountered at Oda Rogers' home is the manager of the inn. She enlightened me about the Rogers family. She also told me Henry Spellman frequented the bar."

"You can tell me all about it later. For now, we may as well go downstairs and find Oda Rogers and Joseph Polletti." Garth led the way to the main staircase.

My mind was whirling with thoughts and ideas as we descended. I heard the sound of furniture moving in the dining room and turned in that direction. Oda was busily arranging chairs after setting the table for dinner. She seemed older than the other two female house staff members. I would assume she was in her early thirties, but the hard labor of keeping this house, as well as her own, added years to her. Still attractive, but the shine of youth had left. Her dark hair, tied in a large bun, held streaks of gray.

"I hardly knew Mr. Spellman. I saw very little of him,

and I mind my own business," she said, in answer to my question, while scurrying around the dining room. "All I know is what I've heard from the sisters as they complained about him. Oh, and what Cynthia jabbers about with Katy in the kitchen."

"What do Margaret and Rachel say about him?"

"Oh, for heaven's sake, I don't remember word for word." She threw her hands up as if pleading to be left alone. She then glared at me with her hands on her hips. "I can tell you one thing, they didn't like him at all. Especially Rachel. Even in her mousy little ways, I heard disdain for him in her voice."

"Both of them spoke ill of him?" Garth persisted.

"Yes. Margaret, because of his wasteful and wanton ways. Rachel seemed to be jealous of his position as the second child." Oda swung the dusting cloth at a side table with a vengeance. "Now, leave me alone."

Garth moved to face her. "I'm sorry to bother you, Oda, but I have a few more questions. The night Henry was murdered, Margaret needed to drive you home. Is that right?"

"Yes."

I saw Garth was in control of the conversation, so I backed away and leaned against the wall to listen.

"You usually drive Joseph the gardener home from work. Why didn't you have your motor car that night?"

"If you must know, I let Joseph use it. He told me he had an important meeting that night."

"Do you generally let others use your vehicle?" Garth asked.

"No, I don't like anyone using my Model-A. But I've learned to trust Joe," she said, starting to fidget from foot to foot. "We have a special relationship."

"Special?" Garth asked.

"None of your business." She glared at Garth, knives of anger coming from her eyes.

"When you drive him home at night, what time do you leave here?" Garth continued to push her.

"Eight o'clock on the dot. I have chores to do at home."

"You never stay later than eight?"

"We may have a cup of tea or something." Oda continued to glower at him, her eyes ablaze, "Hey, what are you trying to get at?"

"Nothing, nothing at all," Garth said, folding his notepad and placing it in his vest pocket. "Thank you for your time."

We both walked toward the hall doorway. Garth abruptly stopped and slowly turned back to Oda, "Oh, one more thing."

"What now?" she asked with her hands on her hips.

"Your husband is Canadian."

"Yes, what of it?"

"Why are you and he in Ohio?"

"For God's sake, man. I'm American and had a hard time finding work in Toronto," she explained. "My mother-in-law worked for the Spellmans years ago and arranged for me to do the same. We'll go back to Canada when the time is right. I've got work to do, leave me to it." She turned her back on us.

I grabbed my overcoat from the hall coat rack and went through the kitchen. Garth followed close behind. I assumed we would be searching for Polletti next. In the rear foyer sat a few sets of boots I had noticed before, lined formally along the back wall. Garth stopped and turned to

Katy, who was sitting at the table, sipping coffee.

"Katy, does everyone leave their boots at the back door?"

"Oh, Mr. Garth, I didn't know you were back so soon," Katy said. "Yes, the staff, as well as Miss Margaret and Miss Rachel. They are lined up according to the importance of the wearer. Miss Margaret is funny about things like that. You can see my dainty little boots are at the far end."

"Is Joseph still in the garage?" I asked her.

"Yes, sir."

We stepped out into the brisk evening air, but before we moved to the garage, Garth grabbed my arm. He squinted at the garage. "I'm going to let you speak to Polletti without me. But, in fact, I'll stand outside the garage door and listen. I want to see how you operate with a male suspect."

"All right by me," I said with confidence.

The door to the garage was around the corner, facing the back of the property. I immediately saw the 1914 Buick B-25 Touring car Margaret and Rachel had used on their visit to Cleveland, along with an assortment of tools, both for auto maintenance and for gardening.

On the far side of the Buick stood a tall, lean man surveying the engine compartment. At my entrance, he stood up and smiled. He was a handsome man with straight, jet-black hair combed back. As I approached, he put his tools down, extended his hand cordially, introducing himself as Joseph Polletti.

"You must be Major Mallory," he said, with a heavy accent. "I have been waiting for you to talk." He pulled a cigarette holder from his overall pocket and placed a cigarette in it.

"Then you must have something of importance to tell

me about the murder. Please continue."

"I am not sure it is important, but I saw a strange man the night of the murder."

"Where was this?"

Polletti leaned against a post in the garage as he continued. "Down the road. I saw a man walking toward town. You see, I left right after dark. It was windy, but I see him standing on the road. I thought, *Who dat man*, and I shrugged. Then I heard about the murder. Poor Mr. Spellman."

"Did you get a good look at him?"

"It was dark and, as I say, it was windy. All I can say is that he was tall and had a big beard."

"Was he a big man?" I asked, thinking about Jackson.

Polletti took a long drag from his cigarette holder and closed his eyes as if forcing a memory to come back. "Yes, I would say so. He seemed to be a big man, I think."

"How were you able to see this man in the dark of night while driving?" I asked.

"I have good eyes. I saw the man well," Joseph said, frowning. "How do you know I was driving? I have no car."

"I was told you were using Oda's motor car. Or am I wrong about that?"

Polletti stared at me blankly as the smoke from his cigarette circled up lazily.

"Tell me, Joe, where did you go that Saturday night?"

"Nowhere," he answered, "I just needed some vino. I went to the Medina Lounge."

I thought of Garth outside, listening. "I suppose there are people who can tell me that they saw you there?"

"I sat alone at a corner table. Hey, have you got da

stolen diamonds yet, Major?" His abruptness startled me. He obviously wanted to change the subject. I allowed him to do so.

"It's odd you would ask," I said.

"You came here to ask me that question, is it not?"

"It was, but Garth and I believe the murder should take priority over the stones."

"Yes, of course, but have you found the stolen diamonds?" he asked again.

"Why do you say they are stolen? We only know them as missing."

"Were they not, as you Americans say, snatched? That is what Rachel has told me." He lost his smile as his lips drew a straight line.

"Was it Rachel or Cynthia, or maybe Oda, who told you they were stolen?" I toyed with him to see which way the conversation would go.

"Ah, you have learned about my friendship with the sola donnas." He smirked as he lit another cigarette. "You American men don't understand how to care for your *donne*. It takes an Italian lover to make them happy." He laughed as if I would join him, then started to cough on his smoke.

"There is gossip around the house about … your friendships. You seem to put yourself in a precarious position by carrying on with two maids at once."

"Don' worry about me, *amico*," he replied. I know how to control my *donne* to my advantage. I make them want me all the more by hinting of others."

"From what I hear from one of the ladies, you don't satisfy her in the least," I retorted. "In fact, she told me that all she can smell on you is garlic and it turns her stomach to be with you."

"Who tol' you such a thing?" he asked, his lower jaw twitching.

"I never talk about what a lady says to me in private," I answered, grinning.

"Well, you tell me," he demanded, jutting out his jaw.

I again grinned and said, "Don't press your luck. Anyone who deserts his country in a time of need certainly doesn't have the guts to face me."

"I no deserter. I was never in the Army, I can't desert."

"Italy declared war on Austria-Hungary in May of 1915. Our records show you entering the United States in June 1915. A coincidence? Besides the Italian government issued a warrant for you. It's on file in Cleveland. No one has acted on it yet. Have a good day, Mr. Polletti."

Chapter Seventeen

Cynthia Browning

Garth and I climbed to the second floor, finding the sitting room Cynthia told me about. It was getting close to seven, and I wondered if Cynthia remembered our engagement. Earlier, when Garth and I searched Henry Spellman's bedroom, my attention was drawn to the connecting door. We were meeting in Henry's private sitting room, I realized now.

"I wonder if Margaret knows the servants are using the room now that Henry is gone?"

"I doubt it," he answered. "Do you think she would tolerate it?"

"This room would definitely make a man feel comfortable," Garth said as he gazed about the room. The walls were covered in forest green wallpaper with cherry wood trim around the ceiling and door frames. The three over-stuffed chairs and ottomans circled the fireplace and matched the green walls. On two of the walls hung paintings with hunting themes. The fireplace, with bookshelves on either side of it, was located on the fourth wall. Next to the entrance sat a sideboard with a gramophone's large ornate cone facing the room.

"Let's give the room a search. Might find something interesting," I suggested.

At first, nothing caught my eye. No tables or hutches with drawers, no books that seemed out of place, and the room had been cleaned recently. Garth peered under the furniture as I walked to the fireplace and glanced into the mirror above it. Rubbing the stubble on my cheek, I thought, I should have shaved this morning. At least I should have trimmed my mustache and goatee. *She's a suspect, James, maybe even a murderer.* I looked down and my eye caught something.

Sitting next to the chair nearest the fireplace stood a small end table. On the bottom shelf was a book. Since all the other books were neatly shelved, it appeared out of place. I picked it up to read the title. *Once on a Time* by A.A. Milne. I smiled as I flipped through the pages. I hadn't read it myself, but I heard that it was a very odd fairytale. Something unusual for Milne to write.

Henry used a telegram as a bookmark. I pulled it out. It was dated February 8th, the day before Spellman was murdered. "This is interesting," I said out loud as I scanned the small page.

"What's interesting?" said a purring voice from the doorway.

Cramming the telegram into my coat pocket, I saw

Cynthia Browning enter the room.

"Oh, nothing of importance," I answered. "Just Henry's reading choices. Fairytales," I scoffed, holding up the book.

Cynthia entered the room, holding a tray with three cups and a silver coffee pot, which she set next to the gramophone on the sideboard. She wore a black dress that fell below her knees. The embroidery was of gold flowers around the hem, sleeves, and neck. It suited her admirably.

"I suppose you're wearing black for Margaret's sake?" I asked, placing the book where I'd found it.

"Katy told me we would have another guest," Cynthia said, handing a cup to Garth.

"Thank you. Yes, I just returned from Cleveland. I'm going to let the Major conduct the interview."

She nodded toward me. "As to your question, yes, Miss Margaret lives by the traditions of the queen," she said, giving a lopsided grin. "Coffee, Major?"

"Yes, thank you, with a touch of cream, please."

"I saw you as a man who prefers everything strong, including his coffee." She winked with a glimmer in her eyes.

"The cream softens the nature of the beast within," I answered.

She turned around and daintily picked up her cup, "Cream and sugar for me, to sweeten my inner beast."

We both laughed at ourselves as I directed her to a soft chair. I sat across from Cynthia and allowed her to get comfortable as she sipped her coffee before I began. Garth continued to stand, glancing across the book covers on the shelves. I was sure he planned to listen to every word that was spoken.

"You must have known Henry Spellman well, to be able to use his sitting room," I said.

"No, I knew little about him, Major. What I knew, I didn't like," she responded, crossing her legs. "I don't like people who talk down to their employees. He was just a nasty man. I tried to avoid him when I was able to. Fortunately, he traveled a lot."

"So, you started using the sitting room after he died?"

"Well, we—all the servants—had been using it when he was away. It's like we're thumbing our noses at him," Cynthia laughed, a deep guttural laugh.

I nodded with a grin. "I can imagine how you felt. There were some generals I would have done that to as well," I said, hoping to make a connection and keep the conversation going. "I noticed that the room is spotless. The four of you keep the room clean."

"Oh, that's Oda. She's a fanatic about keeping things tidy."

"What about the bedroom?" I asked, glancing at the connecting door. "Does anyone use that?"

"Now, Major, that would be telling," she answered, blushing lightly.

"From what I hear, you seem to know a lot about what goes on around the house. Does that include where the stones are?" I made stern eye contact with her.

"Who told you that?" She set her cup on the side table.

"I can't say. However, Miss Margaret tells you about private family matters while you're doing her hair. Is that not true, Cynthia?"

"She does tend to gossip a lot," Cynthia whispered, then shrugged. "I'm a good listener." She opened her small handbag and pulled out a makeup mirror. I watched her examine her full lips and dab a bit of lipstick on them. Cynthia puckered and blotted her lips with a clean hankie. She placed it on the table next to her chair, but it drifted to the floor. I noticed that she held the mirror at an angle, so Garth was in view as he walked around the room.

"What did she tell you about the diamonds?"

"Very little, actually. Miss Margaret isn't sure where they are. She talks about them all the time since her brother returned home. She's as hungry for the gems as he was," Cynthia said, her nose crinkled. "She told me, just the day before the murder, that the greedy bastard most likely carried the stones around with him. Those are her words, not mine."

"Is that what you told Joe?"

"Only what the old bat told me. I didn't know what to believe. I think she was just guessing."

"You don't care for Margaret either, do you?"

"No, she's as despicable as her brother." She squirmed in her chair, nibbling on her lower lip. Again, she held her mirror up to watch Garth.

The squirming and nibbling seemed quite seductive, but then she may have only been trying to sort her thoughts. "Go on, Cynthia. I can see you're hiding something. Something you want to tell me."

Cynthia took a deep breath and continued. "A couple of nights before Henry Spellman was killed, Joseph suggested something repulsive to me."

"What was that?"

"He wanted me to seduce Henry," she said, her jaw clenched at the thought. "His idea was for me to get Henry into bed, rip his clothes off in a frenzy of passion, throw them about the room, and distract him as Joseph went through the clothes searching for the stones."

"I can only imagine what a distraction you are, but did he think that would, in fact, work?" I asked, grinning. "Chances are you both would have lost your employment and would never have found the diamonds."

"I don't find it humorous, Major," she retorted, turning away from me. "I refused, of course. I'm not even sure whether Joseph was serious about it or not. Joe apologized once he realized that he had offended me."

"Have you ever gone out to the clubs in the area?" I asked, switching directions.

"No, Major. I wanted to, but an unescorted female cannot go to such places," she said, sounding almost like Margaret. "I know what you're thinking. You think I've already broken all the rules. But, I get paid well here, and if Miss Margaret knew I went to the clubs alone, she would fire me. So, for the time being, I stay home and bide my time."

"I thought Joseph would escort you."

"He's always too busy. He tells me he wants to go, but then backs out at the last minute. He says he has work to do. I've been thinking about breaking the rules by going out on my own. We'll see."

My impression of Cynthia changed with each statement she made. She appeared confused about her life and where it was heading. "You need to meet other men, Cynthia. Men who'll treat you better than Joseph does," I said, peering into her eyes.

"Do you think so, Major?" she pouted seductively.

"Well, of course, but I have a few more questions," I replied, shaking myself loose from her hypnotic gaze. "What do you think of Rachel?"

"That mousy little thing?" She leaned back in her chair, shifting her eyes up to the ceiling. "She wouldn't know a man if he bit her. You've seen the way she dresses and how she grovels to Margaret, haven't you?"

"To her defense, she is a pretty girl."

"Sure, if she put on some makeup and dressed for the twentieth century. She wears one shade of lipstick. It's a light pink that Margaret picked out for her. The color is no different from the color of her un-rouged lips, so you can't tell she's wearing it. Margaret has her under her control. The poor thing." Cynthia examined her manicured nails on her left hand for a moment, then balled both hands as if hiding them.

"Are you under the control of Miss Margaret as well?" I asked.

"No. She tries, but once I leave her dressing room, I do what I want." Cynthia smirked. "I'm a woman of the twentieth century. I'm free to do as I like."

It appeared to me that she expressed her inner desires, not her reality; she didn't seem to recognize the difference.

She stood up, gliding over to my chair. I remained seated and gulped my coffee. I noticed her eyes seemed to change to emerald green. She tousled her shoulder-length blonde hair as she circled around behind me, lightly swiping her fingertips across my shoulders, "I'm not fooling you, am I, Major?"

"No," I answered. "You are a woman of depth. You are caught between two worlds and don't know which way to turn." I glanced over my shoulder to see what Garth was doing. He seemed to be listening intently as he leaned against the wall.

Cynthia glanced into the mirror above the fireplace,

chewing on her lip once again. This time her eyes filled with tears, and she gently brushed them from her round cheeks. She found her hanky and wiped her eyes then dabbed her lipstick once more. "Joseph was my first and only lover. He charmed his way into my life and my bed." She turned to me, peering down. "Living in this house with four women and abiding by Margaret's strict rules is unbearable. I was so lonely ... but, I know, that's no excuse. I let him use me. I might have said too much to him while we lay in bed together."

Unsure how to deal with a woman's tears, I tried to ignore her emotions. I simply continued the questioning. "Besides telling him that Henry Spellman may be carrying the stones, did you tell Polletti anything more?"

She walked back to her chair and sat down. "Henry's relationship with Karen Bender, 'the little tramp,' as she called her, made Margaret furious. When I told Joseph about Karen, he said, 'Maybe we can use her.' I didn't know what he meant at the time, but now I wonder if I told him something that led to Henry's death."

I thought about the implications of all that. "Are you still in a relationship with Joseph?"

"Heavens, no! Not after I realized he used me to get information. I feel so ashamed, James. May I call you James?"

"Of course, Cynthia. You're right, you can't lead a normal life being cooped up in here. You need to get out and meet others—men and women. You know your conduct was unacceptable, or it wouldn't have produced tears."

"So what do I do?"

"I have an idea. Let me work on it," I said, placing my

cup on the table. "Don't tell anyone what we spoke about, especially not Joseph."

"Of course not, James." She stared at me with a soft glow in her eyes. She reached out, touching my sleeve.

"I'll get back to you later, Cynthia. We have other interviews."

"Miss Browning. It's been a pleasure meeting you," Garth said, standing next to her chair.

Cynthia stood, extending her hand to him. "Yes, Mr. Garth. I hope I've been helpful."

"Indeed, you have been."

When she turned away, he snapped up the hanky she'd discarded and slipped it into his vest pocket. She left the sitting room, returning to her duties.

We also left and walked down to my room; I remembered the telegram I had stuffed into my pocket. I retrieved the piece of paper and read it. It was addressed to the curator of the Chicago Museum of Natural History, a Zachery Hareborn. Henry had made an appointment with the man for this week. He said he had something special to sell the museum and addressed the telegram for the eyes of Doctor Hareborn only. I handed it to Garth and explained where I'd found it.

"I'll have to look into this Hareborn character to see how he fits into the case," he said, shutting my bedroom door. "How much of Cynthia's story did you believe?"

"Her story? You mean she made it up?"

"Of course, a complete fabrication. Cynthia had you wrapped around her little finger, Major," he said, frowning with disappointment. "You can't allow attractive women to use their charms on you."

"What did she lie about?" Garth's attitude was starting

to annoy me. I almost grabbed him by the lapels, but I forced myself to stay in control. He, after all, was trying to help me.

"The use of the sitting room, for one thing. Do you believe Spellman would allow her to lounge about his sitting room, which connects to his bedroom, without restitution? I'd wager that she didn't turn down Polletti's plan. Cynthia kept company with Spellman while Polletti searched through his clothes. She sounded like a pure-hearted school girl trying to explain that away."

"Then why did she bring it up in the first place?" I asked. "I made no mention of it."

"To cast suspicion on Polletti, of course. She had you in her grip; she wanted to use the power over you to steer your suspicions away from her. Cynthia may be at the center of the crime. In that case, she would toss Polletti, or anyone else, to the dogs."

I thought about what Garth said. I had to admit Cynthia had me hooked on her beauty and sex appeal. I felt ashamed of my weakness. "You're right, Garth. I really blundered and made a fool of myself. Maybe I should let you interview the young ladies from now on."

"Nonsense, old man," he said with a slap on my back. "This game is a learning process. Now that you know your weaknesses, you won't make the same mistakes again. Let's go downstairs for something to eat before we hit the town. I'm famished."

Chapter Eighteen

The Sleazy Bar

Medina is a medium-sized country town. Nonetheless, it has its seedier neighborhoods. Billy's Place, we'd been told, sat on a rugged side street, which backed against nearby railroad tracks. A pair of small light bulbs on either side of the door to Billy's Place led us to our destination. I could imagine how the building would shake to the core whenever the train went by.

I parked the Hudson directly in front of the bar, in the low glare of the lights. Other autos sat in unprotected shadows.

Garth and I stepped out of the motor car onto the wooden sidewalk. Rachel called it a gin mill; how right she was. We looked through the grimy windows on either side of the thick door.

I seemed dressed more appropriately for the establishment, with my dark overcoat, tweed jacket, and matching cap. Garth, on the other hand, still wore his gray and white pinstriped day suit. He would stick out like a sore thumb in this place, more like the overseers of the men we were trying to talk to. The working-class men in Billy's would prefer to forget his kind at the bottom of their drinks.

"You look out of place," I told him.

Garth continued to gaze through the windows. His keen eyes seemed drawn to a table next to the window on the right side of the bar's frontage. "If I am out of place, so is he."

I stepped over to the window. Through the dirty pane and tattered curtains, Garth pointed out a man in a dark blue suit sitting with two companions. They were sitting at the table, talking to one of the patrons. We watched as the first patron left, and another took his place.

"Who might that be?" I asked.

"Allen Douglas. I recognize him from the countless newspaper stories about him and Senator Ward. I would assume he has the same thought as we do," Garth said.

"Douglas wants to follow Spellman's trail on his nights out," I said, watching the men inside the bar. "Find someone Spellman confided in, trail him, and shake the gems out of whoever ended up with them."

"He brought along the two Black Hand thugs to stir up a little fear in the men he is questioning," Garth said, squinting as he tried to see their expressions.

"And, to shake them up," I added. "What's your plan, Garth?"

"We need to go in separately," he said. "You first.

The bar is nearly empty. Try to start a conversation with the bartender. See what he knows about who Spellman's friends were. Find out if anyone, besides Douglas, has been asking about Spellman. I'll follow shortly to listen in on Douglas and his friends."

"You think you should do that alone?" My eye was on the two thugs.

"Don't worry, Douglas doesn't want any trouble. He'll keep those two in line," Garth answered. "Besides, Douglas has never seen me before. I'll be as safe as a babe in its mother's arms."

I agreed, then swung open the thick wooden door. The place smelled like a dump, and the door hinge let out a squeak so loud that all the patrons stopped what they were doing and glared up at me. Including the thin, leather-skinned pianist who stopped playing Joplin on the corner piano. All eyes followed me as I sauntered into the small room and up to the bar. Since I made no hostile moves, the customers went back to their drinks. My grizzled hair, mustache, and goatee helped me blend in. Only the eyes of Douglas and his hooligans stayed glued to me.

I stood at the bar, glancing around the room, and took in the sad sight. The dank, dirty barroom reeked of cheap booze, stale beer, and cigar smoke. Depression clung to the walls and hung, like a curtain, over the room. The patrons, indeed, were of the working class. They wore soiled, ragged work clothes; each had grief and hardship etched on his face. A few men stood against the bar as I did, but their heads hung listlessly over their shot glasses and mugs as they waved the bartender to refill them. The six tables behind me held three or four men each. They quietly drank their booze and nursed their empty glasses, in all likelihood, unable to pay for another drink.

I heard no conversation at any of the tables. The veil of exhaustion and fruitless lives hung over the patrons. All, except the table at the front window. Douglas continued to wave over the patrons. He slapped a few coins in their hands and engaged in asking them questions.

"Are you in here to interrogate my customers, like the gent with money over there? Or do you plan to order something?" The tall, bony bartender asked me.

"That's the idea," I answered, turning to stare at the gaunt face of the man behind the bar. "Let's start with a whiskey sour."

"I'll get you a shot of whiskey," he replied. "You'll drink like the rest of these men in here. As to your questions, you're wasting your time. These men ain't gonna say shit to the likes of those thugs, and they ain't gonna talk to you either."

"Because they don't know anything about Henry Spellman?"

"That, and they don't care about who got murdered or who did the murderin'." The bartender spoke with a natural growl in his voice. "These men come in here after a twelve-hour shift. They're working for pennies, so the likes of you can live high on the hog. All they want is a bourbon or a shot of gin to wash away the taste of failure and endless days of working for the men with money."

He sighed heavily, adding, "You want to, you can ask me about that Spellman guy. But, don't ask any of my customers—they won't answer you." He looked me up and down, his gaze taking in my size, my patch, and my steady glare. "I don't want any trouble in my place."

"You allow the three at the window to question—"

"The guy with the expensive suit dropped me some cash to allow him to pester my customers. He can jaw all he wants. They know nothin'. These guys won't tell him shit. But, I've got his money tucked away." The bartender said with a toothless smile.

"What do you know about Spellman?" I asked, staring directly into his eyes.

The bartender's smile vanished, "I know nothin' about the man, 'cept he's dead. Newspapers told me that. His kind doesn't come in here often. I suppose it makes them feel guilty to see these men drink their lives away."

"He *never* came in here?" I pressed for a substantial answer. Out of the corner of my eye, I saw Garth approaching Douglas. The two goons stood, ready to tussle with Garth, but Douglas waved them back into their seats.

"When Spellman came back from Africa last month, he came into the place a couple of times," the bartender said. "I suppose it wasn't to his liking. Look around, big man, you see any women?"

"No," I agreed.

"Yeah, that pampered ass was probably trolling for somethin' sweet to take home with him. He didn't care for my clientele, so he moved on. He'd be better off at the Medina Lounge for those women."

"So, he came in here twice?" I asked, to be sure of the facts.

"That's what I said, didn't I?"

"Yes, you did," I replied, politely, instead of slamming his face into the bar like I wanted to. "You ever talk to him about Africa?"

"I ain't never talked to him about nothin' but the price of whiskey," the lanky man answered.

"How'd you know about his trip to Africa?" I asked, thinking that I'd caught him in a lie.

"Cause the story of his arrival home got plastered all over the local newspaper," he growled. "What, ya think I can't read? What about your whiskey, stranger, you still want it?"

"Sure, why not," I said, tossing some coins on the bar.

He picked up the money. "Or he went to The Lajon Bostad Inn. Not as swanky as the Medina Lounge, but a classy joint, anyhow." The bartender poured me my booze then walked away.

I moved up the bar and stood casually next to Garth, close enough we both could hear Douglas questioning the patrons. The man from DC learned little from the working men. I had expected as much.

The long, boring conversation Douglas had with the drinkers must have annoyed the two Italian ruffians. They were looking impatient. The burly man sitting closest to the bar turned to see Garth eavesdropping on them. "I know you, don' I?" His eyes lit up as he recognized my partner. "Sherwood Garth. You son a' bitch. I know you from New York."

He stood up, facing Garth, who casually sipped his beer. "Yes. I'm surprised you remember me, Stefano Rizzo," Garth said. "But then, I did put your uncle away in the big house, didn't I?"

The Italian's pockmarked face grew red as he sucked in the stale air. "I ought to rip your head off …"

"If you want to get your share of the diamonds, you'll settle down, Rizzo. Now is not the time," Douglas muttered. He turned to Garth. "We had nothing to do with the murder; all I want is my fair share of the gems I worked for. I don't want any trouble."

"I'm glad you're being reasonable," Garth said. "Now try to get your men to see it that way. I would like to speak to you at a later date as well." He glared threateningly at the goons. "Privately."

"Mr. Rizzo and Angelo De Luca will just follow my orders," Douglas said, pulling a thick cigar from his vest pocket. "They don't want to lose a chance of their share of the stones."

"What you tell him everything for?" De Luca asked Douglas, his face flush with anger. "He hears all your talk with these people. I know Mr. Garth too. I no like him." He growled.

Rizzo glared at Douglas. "You talka too much, Mr. Fancypants." He moved dangerously close to Garth, his fists clenched, his face tight with anger.

I quickly threw back my whiskey and stepped forward. The thugs saw my move. De Luca tugged at his partner's jacket sleeve. "We wait. This no time to try anything."

Rizzo, who stood before me, nodded and sat back down. Puzzling. The two of them had a good chance of taking me out. Why did they back off? Douglas must have a tighter hold on them than I'd thought.

"Come on, Garth. Let's get out of here." I said, backing toward the door. "I don't care for the clientele," I added, grinning at the Italians.

"I'm with you." Garth smiled calmly, tipping his hat toward Douglas. We swiftly exited through the squeaky door and approached my Hudson. We looked back, relieved to see there wasn't any pursuit. However, we did observe three faces at the window glaring out at us.

"Start the motor car and get in."

We drove out of the neighborhood, took a deep breath, and headed toward our next destination. "So, what did you learn?" I asked Garth.

"Exactly what I suspected to learn, once I recognized Douglas. He is as anxious to find the diamonds as everyone else. It also seemed that he is no closer to finding them than the rest. Oh, he mentioned that our friend Mr. Jackson had already been there."

"Steven Jackson is in cahoots with Douglas and the Black Hand?" I asked, surprised that Jackson hadn't left Cleveland, especially after the beating I'd given him.

"Not anymore," Garth said. "When he first arrived here, last week, Jackson and Douglas agreed to work together to find Spellman. Then Douglas brought the two thugs into it, and Jackson bowed out."

"How'd you find that out?"

"Before you walked up, one of the patrons told him about Jackson's visit. Once the man left, the Italians and Douglas discussed it."

"It seems Steven Jackson is smarter than we gave him credit for."

"What did the bartender have to say?"

"The only thing I got from him is that Spellman came into the bar twice after he came back from Africa. He wasn't happy with the lack of females in the place and moved on. He suggested the Medina Lounge or The Lajon Bostad Inn."

"And so we shall. Once we get on the better side of town, turn left on the main street." Garth seemed irritated as he shifted in the seat. He appeared annoyed with my simple answers. "Didn't you learn anything more from your conversation? Think, man. What did you derive from your opening statement?"

I glanced over and saw that he was serious. I wasn't sure what he wanted to hear. "I don't know what you mean."

He gritted his teeth, falling back in the seat. "Forgive me, Major. You're new at this," he said with a sigh. "Spellman came in twice when he first got back from Africa. If he were trolling for a piece of tart, as the bartender surmised, one visit would have been enough to see it's a bar that is frequented by down and out working men. He would have moved on to more lucrative places to throw out his line."

"I see." I tilted my head back. "So, he went to Billy's Bar for another reason."

"Excellent, Major. He came to meet someone. Someone who didn't show up the first time but may have the second time."

"How are we going to find out who that would be?"

"I already know, Major," he said with a smile. "One of the patrons whom Douglas talked to mentioned the name of someone Spellman had a drink with two weeks ago. Douglas and his baboons didn't recognize the name, but I did. Jeremy Sweet is one of the curators of the Cuyahoga Museum of History.

Chapter Nineteen

Dancing for Clues

After a short drive over the empty roads of Medina, we reached Tucker Street. This led us through a lovely country neighborhood to the Medina Lounge, located outside of Kelly Park. They designed the lounge as a large woodland cabin, nestled into a crop of fir and pine trees.

The trees engulfed the tavern as the branches hovered over its shingled roof. The streets were better lit than those around Billy's Place, which gave it a more cheerful atmosphere.

I pulled into the well-maintained parking lot that overflowed with expensive and sporty motor vehicles. "Now this is more like it," I said to Garth as I pulled up the brake.

"Yes, in this location, you're the one who seems out of

place. It can't be helped. We'll go in together. They won't throw you out with me by your side."

"Indeed," I said, a bit aggravated. "I don't believe I appear *that* unfashionable."

Garth gave me a slap on the back, grinning cheerfully. "Come on, let's go inside."

We stepped through the double doors and entered a sparkling, bright room with crystal lights hanging from every rafter. It didn't give the illusion of a mountain cabin as the outdoor façade had. Tall mirrors covered the north and west walls of the lounge from floor to ceiling. The windows gave it the appearance of a sunny summer day, not a cold February night.

I looked around and thought that it must be an exciting place for all young people in the area to visit. The crowded dance floor held almost all women, who danced unapologetically with both genders.

A maître d' welcomed us at the entrance, offering us seats. Garth requested a corner table. After being seated, where we could observe the bustle of the crowd, we were served our drinks. Normally, I don't consume much alcohol, but since becoming an investigator with Garth, I'd been indulging a little too much. I ordered a mug of imported Swiss beer. Garth had a shot of bourbon on ice. "The secret is to sip your drink leisurely. Give the impression that you're a heavy drinker, but sip, keeping your wits about you." Garth had an uncanny ability to read my mind.

"How did you know what I was thinking?" I asked, my glare boring into him.

He grinned, a twinkle in his blue eyes, "I've been there. In this business, you spend a lot of time in bars of every sort. If you don't have a drink in front of you, you appear out of place. Now, look about you, learn what you can from the clientele," Garth said. The hat-check girl had taken our overcoats and hats. We comfortably leaned back.

The jazz band stood on the large podium at the opposite side of the room. The band might have been a unit of Buffalo Soldiers that I came across in the west. They were enthusiastically playing an up-tempo piece that got my toe to tapping. The thirty or more young dancers were happily engaged in the camel walk, the foxtrot, or the Maxie, moving to the beat and rhythm energetically.

"Well, I see that the days of prim and proper Victorian lifestyle is gone," I answered to Garth's quizzical gaze. "I don't mean that negatively. I like the free-spirited mindset of our young people."

"Good for you, Major. That course will keep you young at heart," he said, peering in the direction of the dance floor. "What is the average age in here, and what does that tell you?"

I thought for a minute as I watched the dancers, especially the pretty, lithe girls cavorting to the beat of the music. "I would think the area has become the second home to middle-class business people from Cleveland. Or maybe, because of the use of the motor car, that class is moving to the country. The farm towns in the area wouldn't have so many young people with idle time on their hands."

"Excellent observation, Major," Garth said as the band stopped playing *The Sweetest Kisses of All,* and the exhausted dancers retreated to their tables. Garth's gaze circled the room, stopping at a large round table not far from our own. He raised his hand to summon our waiter. "Well, look who's here …"

"Yes, sir?" said the waiter.

"Will you go to that large table and ask Rachel Spellman to join us for a moment?"

The waiter looked in the direction Garth had indicated. "Does she know you, sir?"

"Indeed, she does." He slid a dollar bill across the table.

The waiter picked it up with a smile and walked over to where Rachel sat with two other women and two men. All were huddled together as if telling secrets. Rachel leaned back, trying to see our table. Garth and I leaned forward so we melted into the shadow of the fake tree, which obstructed her view. She hesitantly rose and walked over to us.

Rachel wore a golden gown that fit snugly to her petite form. The straight dresses she wore at home had, unfortunately, concealed her womanly attributes. Her hair, curled in ringlets to her shoulders, bounced merrily as she walked. Ten feet away from our table, she recognized us and cautiously smiled. We rose, offering her a seat.

"Now my secret is out," she said, sitting next to Garth.

"Your personal life doesn't have to be revealed to anyone," Garth said. "Unless it has anything to do with the gems or the murder." He eyed her outfit. "What a metamorphosis."

I decided to allow my partner to carry on with Miss Spellman. Her attraction to him was evident and would surely loosen her tongue.

She squirmed girlishly in her seat, blushing a lovely shade of pink. "Why, thank you, Mr. Garth. I am not always the sheepish girl I appear to be around Margaret."

"Why the secrecy?"

"Can you imagine the brouhaha from Margaret if she knew I had a secret life away from the Spellman mansion?

She would make life unbearable for me." Rachel's face tightened into a frown. "I do nothing that I consider wrong, gentlemen. I drink a little, dance a lot, and have fun with my friends. I feel totally smothered at home, but when I come here, I feel as if chains have dropped from my shoulders. I feel liberated!"

"I understand," Garth said. "Those ringlets are far more attractive on your shoulders than Margaret's chains," he smiled as he moved a strand of her hair off her shoulder. "How do you get out of the house without her knowing?"

"Simple enough," Rachel said. "Margaret's bedroom is at the front of the house. She goes to bed regularly at nine o'clock, and she believes that I follow suit. However, I go to my rooms and dress for a night out on the town. One of my male friends will drive along a path in the cornfield on the back of the property and pick me up. They never pass in front of the house."

"Does anyone else know of this plan of escape?" Garth leaned back in his chair, smiling.

Rachel put a finger against her cheek and raised her eyes in thought. "Maybe Katy. She lives in the servant's quarters in the rear of the house. We get along famously; I don't believe she would tell my sister anything."

"What about Henry? Did he know?"

"Oh, yes. Of course. I forgot about Henry," she said with a start. "Our paths crossed a few times at the club. We rarely spoke of it, except to promise secrecy."

I found it odd, yet telling, that she said, 'I forgot about him.' They'd had a strained relationship, but one doesn't forget a murdered sibling in just a few days.

Garth was following another track. "Did he want anything in exchange for keeping quiet?"

"Did Henry blackmail me like he did everyone else?" Rachel threw back her head, letting loose with a hearty, yet sinister laugh. "What would he get from me? Gracious, Mr. Garth, you know I have nothing he would want."

"Of course, how forgetful of me." He peered into her eyes as the band began to play again. "Would you do me the honor of this dance?"

Rachel's lashes fluttered as she extended her hand to him. Garth led her to the dance floor. To all appearances, they were a well-matched dance couple. They swirled around the floor, moving rhythmically to the music. They were dancing the foxtrot. A two-step variation of the dance allowed small steps, close embraces, and a lot of body movement. I was surprised to see Garth draw her close to him, holding her snugly to his chest as they swirled together.

The surrounding tables diverted my attention from the dance floor. The majority of the young people were gleefully laughing and flirting with each other. Some were drinking, too much for some of them, as they got the giggles. However, two young men at Rachel's table were having none of it. They were similar, average-sized men with dark, slicked-back hair and prominent noses. The slightly heavier of the two, whom I did not recognize, wore a neatly clipped Van Dyke. The other sat brooding with jealousy as he watched Rachel and Garth on the dance floor. A moment after I set an eye on him, I realized why he was familiar to me. Joseph Polletti.

We called it a night after Garth finished his dance with Rachel Spellman. We excused ourselves and went outside. "What was that all about?" I asked, buttoning my tan overcoat. Garth wore the fur-collared coat that I first saw him wear when he moved in. It seemed like a lifetime ago, but he'd been here less than a month.

"You mean the dance?"

"Naturally. You scolded me for trusting women, then you're dancing with them."

"All in a day's work, old man." He opened his coat once again, pointing to a smear of lip rouge on his shirt. "Collecting evidence, my good man." He grinned, but then scanned over my shoulder toward my Hudson. His smile faded. "Someone is standing by your vehicle, Major."

I spun around, slid my hand under my coat, grasping the handle of my Colt. I'd parked the automobile in the shadows of the building. A dark figure stood alone.

"You can put your gun away, Major. It's me, Sergeant Markson," the young policeman called, stepping out from the shadows. "I have an urgent message for you from Lieutenant Brady."

Garth and I walked across the frozen parking lot. "It must be important if he sent you out here on a Friday night," I jested to the young cop. "You should be in the club dancing, not standing in the cold night stalking peaceful citizens."

"I would be, Major, but I'm on duty tonight. Brady has been trying to reach you at the Spellman's place."

"What did Brady want?" Garth asked.

Markson slipped on a pair of gloves, staring Garth square in the eyes. "He has an informant at the ticket counter of The Union Passenger Station. Brady told him to keep an eye out for any of our suspects and to let him know if one of them bought tickets for out-of-town travel."

Garth shifted his feet to keep them warm. "Come,

come, man. Don't keep us in suspense. Who is it?"

"It'll surprise you," Markson answered. Then noticed the frown crossing Garth's forehead. "It's Lucy Rogers, Oda's mother-in-law. She drove into Cleveland and bought two tickets for Toronto by way of Buffalo, New York, early tomorrow morning. What do you think of that?"

"I think it's highly suspicious, considering we just spoke to her early this morning," I said, cupping my hands around my cigar to light it.

"Indeed, it is," Garth said. "Have you been to the Rogers place to ask her about it?"

"I went over after I spoke to Brady. Only Oda was there. She had no idea where the old woman was. She didn't sound too worried, either."

"I would bet she and her son are, at present, on their way," Garth said. "They'll need to stay in the city until their train is ready to leave. Are you going to be there?"

"No, that's why I'm telling you. I have an appointment in Columbus with someone of importance, and I can't miss it. Brady is tied up, as well. He suggested that you get there in time to stop them. Here's a letter of authorization to detain them, if you need it."

"The letter may come in handy. Thank you, Markson." Garth turned to me with a sly gleam in his eyes. "Here we are, doing the work of the police again," he tried to sound annoyed. "Are you up for an early morning rise?"

"Fine by me. You can blow the bugle when needed."

"I suppose you know where the Union Terminal is?"

"Of course. It's right on the lakeside off of West Ninth Street. It's a huge ugly, stone building. It's going to be replaced in a few years," I said, offering some civic news. "The Van Sweringen brothers will be building a complex in Public Square. It'll be the hub for all eastern rail lines."

"Thank you, Markson. We'll get on it," Garth said. "Let's get some rest. We'll take care of this problem in the morning."

Chapter Twenty

On Route to Canada

"Wake up, Mallory, or we're going to miss the train." Sherwood Garth leaned over my bed, shaking the headboard as I slumbered. He was fully dressed and ready to go.

"Good Lord, Garth, why didn't you wake me sooner?"

"I told you we were getting up at five o'clock. Don't you have an alarm clock?"

"Of course." I reached over to the side table and grabbed it. "Damn, I forgot to set it. I'll be up and dressed in five minutes."

"Some military man you turned out to be," Garth mumbled, walking to the hallway.

I was a man of my word. In less than five minutes, I met Garth at the kitchen door. As expected, Oda wasn't working yet; I wondered if she would work at all today under the circumstances. I examined the boots lined up in the foyer and thought about whose boots they were. Then I heard Garth's voice. "Let's go, man, we've got to stop them from getting on the train. If we don't, we have a long trip to Buffalo ahead of us."

I dashed through the back door, cranked up the Hudson while Garth bundled up on the passenger seat, and we were off.

We drove up to this large, stark, but sturdy building. "What time is it, Mallory?"

I pulled out my pocket watch and flipped it open. "It's ten minutes to six. They're sure to be on the six o'clock train east by now."

"There's no time to waste," Garth urgently demanded. "Park the car, I'll get the tickets."

He jumped out, sprinting for the single tower in the center of the north wall. I quickly found a parking space and ran into the building, heading toward the ticket counters. Garth had finished and dashed across the concourse. I intercepted him halfway as he shoved my ticket into my hand, yelling, "Hurry, Major. The train is about to leave."

This is all my fault. If I had set my alarm, we would have been here on time to stop them. Now we have to find a way to persuade them to come back with us.

We reached the platform and, sure enough, the train was moving. We weren't giving up that easily. Garth surprised me with his speed. He ran up to the door of the last car, grabbed the metal handle, and pulled himself onto the steps.

I wasn't about to let him show me up. I sprang ahead, racing alongside the car. Regrettably, I was not as fast as

Garth. I almost lost my footing, but I poured all my energy into my legs and lunged. Reaching out for the railing, I felt Garth's hand grab mine. I jumped and made it to the bottom step of the car.

I stood at the door, my back leaning against the inner wall, gasping for air. Garth was as deprived of oxygen as I was, but we couldn't help but smile at each other. "Now, that was exciting. It was as thrilling as getting on and riding a wild horse when I was a young pony soldier."

Garth laughed, "Major, you never fail to surprise me. I didn't think you had it in you to make that last jump to the step."

"Never underestimate an Army officer, no matter how old he gets. Now what?"

"Now, we find the Rogers'."

We moved from the steps, through the sliding door, and into the presence of the conductor. The short, thin man apparently had seen the struggle we'd had in boarding the train. He held out his hand. "After that spectacular entrance, I certainly hope you have tickets."

"Right you are, my good man," Garth said. "At least I do, I don't know about this vagabond." He gestured toward me.

My smile left my lips when I realized that he'd slipped me my ticket on the run. I'd forgotten what I'd done with it. The conductor leered at me as I rummaged through my pockets. There it was, all crumpled up in my overcoat pocket. "Here you are," I said, thrusting it at the man.

"Excellent, sir. Your compartment is in the next car forward. This, as you can see, is the luggage compartment." He glanced up at Garth, quizzically, "You have no luggage?"

"No, we were in a hurry. Buying the tickets was a last-minute decision. The only seats you had available were in a compartment."

The conductor examined our tickets. "Your compartment is right before the dining car."

"We're looking for an amputee in a wheelchair and an elderly woman pushing him. Have you seen them?" Garth removed his homburg, which he had pushed down tightly while running.

The conductor rubbed his chin a moment before answering. "Well, yes and no. I saw the man in the wheelchair and the woman, but she wasn't the one pushing the chair."

"Really? Was there another with them?" Garth asked.

"Yes, a well-dressed young man. I'd say in his late twenties. He was pushing the chair for the gentleman."

"Did you see where they were seated?"

"I'm afraid not, sir. A porter aided them onto the train and led them forward to other compartments. In the man's condition, he couldn't stay in a sleeper, so I assume they went to a compartment such as yours but farther forward. That was an hour ago. We ask those with needs such as his, to board early."

"Thank you for the information," Garth said, slipping the conductor a dollar bill. "We'll rest in our compartment for a minute."

We crossed over to the next car then into the narrow passageway to Compartment B. We slipped in, pleased to see there were no others assigned to our coach.

"Sit down, Major. We need to think this through before moving on. Have you any idea who the third passenger might be?"

"I was about to ask you the same thing. I'm at a loss.

Markson didn't mention this third party, did he?"

Garth sat back on the brown leather seat opposite me. He tossed his homburg down and thought about the new revelation. "I don't want to charge in half-cocked if they have a bodyguard with them."

"I'll go to their coach and search to see where they are seated," I offered, itching to go into action.

He gazed at the snow-covered fields and nodded, "Okay, find their compartment. If you can identify who's in there, fine, but don't let them see you."

"Right you are, Garth." I leaped up and prepared to find the Rogers family. I left my tan cap and overcoat on with the collar turned up, hoping it might prevent them from recognizing me. I walked, clumsily, because of the lurching of the car, down our corridor. I entered the dining coach, where breakfast was being served. The smell of the bacon reminded me that I hadn't eaten since noon the day before. I would have liked to sit down for breakfast, but I had a job to do.

I walked between the tables, eyeing each passenger, but not finding my quarry. I seemed to be out of place, wearing my overcoat and cap, for all the diners were eyeing me suspiciously as I strolled past them. I crossed over to the next car. At the entrance, I met the porter, a Negro man dressed smartly in his blue uniform.

"Porter, are you the man who escorted the Rogers' to their compartment?"

"I may be, sir. I escorted many people this morning."

"Of course," I said, smiling congenially at the man. "Mr. Rogers is in a wheelchair, and his mother is with him. I was told there was a third party as well."

"Oh, yes, sir." He evidently recollected the group. "I

had a devil of a time getting that wheelchair down this corridor, sir. But, I got the job done. Yes, there is a third party with them, sir. I heard the elderly lady refer to him as Mr. Perkins. He was pushing the wheelchair along when I reached them and offered my assistance."

"You've been very helpful," I said, handing him a dollar tip. "Which compartment are they in?"

"Right down the corridor, sir," he said, still smiling at the dollar bill. "Would you like me to escort you to it and introduce you?"

"No, my good man. Just tell me their compartment number."

"That'll be letter C. I hope you enjoy your trip, sir."

"One more thing … ah, your name?"

"That's Jasper, sir. What else did you need, sir?"

Thank you, Jasper. Go down to letter B in the coach behind the dining car, ask Mr. Sherwood Garth to join me here."

"Right away, sir," Jasper said, a big grin on his face as I handed him an additional fifty-cent piece. "Yes, sir. Right away, sir."

He went into the dining car as I sauntered down the corridor. I didn't want to stand out, but who wouldn't notice a six foot five inch, one-eyed ogre like me? All of the compartments had windows facing the walkway. Many had pulled the curtains closed; I hoped the Rogers family had left theirs open.

I made it to compartment D, which seemed to be occupied by a young couple on their way to Niagara Falls. By the way they were clinging to one another, the curtain should have been closed.

"Stop gawking at the newlyweds, Major. Show me

where the Rogers family are," I heard Garth say from behind me.

"I'm not gawking, Garth," I protested as the young man in D closed the curtains with a tug. "The family is in the next compartment, the man with them is Perkins. Sound familiar?"

"Indeed it does, that would be the elder Longfellow's clerk, Raymond Perkins. Are they all in the compartment?"

I stretched my head to peer through one of the windows and saw that the three were indeed there. Perkins sat on one seat across from Mrs. Lucy Rogers with the wheelchair crammed in between them. "Yes, they're in, what do you want to do?"

"Well, knock on the door," he said, smiling. "They're not criminals, Major. However, Markson asked them to stay in Medina. Let's see if we can persuade them to return."

I shrugged, and knocked on the door. I quickly got an answer. Raymond Perkins stood erect in front of me, about a foot and a half shorter and one hundred pounds lighter than I am. He had a stern look on his bearded face.

"And, who might you be?" he asked, scowling up at me.

"A more congenial way to answer your door would be to say good morning. But since you're a rude little piker, I'm the one who is going to drag you back to Medina."

"Now, now, Major. Let's give the man a chance to make amends," Garth said, sliding past me into the room.

"That's okay, Raymond, you can let them in," Mrs. Rogers said. "I wasn't expecting to be stopped so soon, Mr. Garth. How did you find us?"

Garth smiled at the little lady. Then he nodded for Perkins to sit down. Perkins noticed the unpleasant look on my face and complied. Garth sat down next to Mrs. Rogers as I stood at the door, arms firmly folded.

"I was sent by Sergeant Markson with written authorization to take you back," Garth said, his face stern. Garth knew the 'written authorization' was only suitable for swatting flies. Nonetheless, he waved it around. "Now, tell me why you are running?"

The three looked at each other as if waiting for someone else to speak up. Mrs. Rogers broke the silence. "We aren't *running*. We're moving back to Canada. It's because of Oda and Herbert Longfellow; they've been seeing each other on Saturday afternoons."

"That old degenerate," I declared, my voice rising with anger.

Perkins played with his pocket watch, opening and closing it. "I've known about it since last month when they first met. She visited the old man after work on Saturday evenings instead of paying rent on their house."

"Are you certain that she met him for their rendezvous this past Saturday?" Garth asked.

"Of course. Oda drove that Model-A to our office in downtown Medina," he said, rubbing his Van Dyke. "That was about nine o'clock. Then the two of them used his motor car to drive to his house."

"Longfellow is your landlord?" Garth asked Mrs. Rogers.

"Yes. I don't like the man. Craig had no idea what Oda was doing with the money we gave her to pay the rent."

"Probably hiding it away so she can leave me," Craig said, his face torn with pain. I felt nothing but pity for this abused man. He gave his legs and manhood to his country, finding no compassion from the woman he loved. "I knew about her affair with Henry Spellman as well, but when I found out about this act of prostitution, I had enough."

I viewed Perkins, who again was stroking his beard, and said, "I suppose you told these fine people what was going on."

"Yes, Major, I thought it was my duty. Besides that, I saw the possibility of those two conspiring in the murder and robbery of Spellman."

"So, you decided to leave with the Rogers'?" Garth sounded incredulous.

"The shame and embarrassment on Craig would have been too much for his frail body. I wouldn't just go to the police and tell them about it." Perkins' voice rose, "Just think of the family disgrace. I've known the family since they moved here after Craig left the Canadian Army. I collected the rent myself until last month. That's when Longfellow told me he would assume my duties and collect the rent himself. The cad."

"No more, Raymond," Craig said, holding up a shaky hand. "I don't want to hear any more." The captain turned to Garth and me. "Gentlemen, you can understand why we left. Mother and I were going to the family home in Toronto, leaving all of the sin, pain, and deception behind."

We remained silent for a moment. Garth then spoke quietly, "I'm sorry. I do understand your reasoning. However, Perkins is a material witness, and the two of you are still suspects. We must take you back to Medina."

Lucy Rogers curled her lip. "We can't go back to that …"

Garth put up his hand to stop her words. "You don't have to go back to that house. Major Mallory and I have connections in Cleveland. We can find a place for you to stay there. You won't have to see Oda or Longfellow again. Of course, you need to tell Sergeant Markson your story. He'll travel to the city to hear you out."

"I don't think it's wise to go back," Perkins protested. "It's too painful for Craig, that is."

"Once we have the killer in custody, you can leave for Canada or any other place you like," I added.

Both Perkins and Mrs. Rogers sought Craig's opinion. He nodded in agreement. "I just don't want to see either of those people again," he said, his eyes glistening.

"For now, we stay together," Garth said, rubbing his hands together. "We're on an express train to Buffalo, and it's the first chance to get off, then we can buy tickets for Cleveland. We won't be getting back to Ohio until tomorrow. So, I'll stay in this compartment with Craig and his mother. The Major and Mr. Perkins will use our compartment."

"I think it best that I stay here with the Rogers, Garth," I said, raising my right eyebrow. "I can help move Craig around far more easily than you can." I glanced over to Captain Rogers and added, "Us old soldiers might have a few stories of daring-do to go over."

"Excellent, Major. Now, I haven't had any breakfast, so if you would all like to adjourn to the dining car, the meal is on James Mallory."

Chapter Twenty-One

A Trip to the Museum

We did find a place for the Rogers family. I called on my brother, Phillip, to put them up for a few days. He has a large home in Shaker Heights and plenty of room. His wife, from a society family, was none too thrilled with her husband's hospitality. However, with her haughty nose stuck in the air, she relented. I made up a lie that Lucy Rogers was related to the royal family of England and was visiting from Canada.

"I could understand your sister-in-law's aggravation, Major," Garth said. "Especially, surprising them that way."

"She'll buck up. After all, we've been stuck on that damned train for hours. How do you think I feel?"

"Like we're starting a new day at four in the afternoon," Garth answered with a smirk.

"Now that we've taken care of the Rogers family, what's our next step?" I asked Garth as I pulled away from my brother's palatial home.

"One lead we haven't followed yet is that we learned Spellman met with Jeremy Sweet from the Cuyahoga Museum of History," Garth answered. "I want to see how he fits into this case. I've got the address here for the museum."

"That won't be necessary, Garth," I said, brushing his hand away. "I've been there many times and know the way." I pulled a cigar from my vest pocket and lit it thinking about the gems. I was getting quite astute at driving and lighting my cigar, without sliding into a snow-filled ditch. "I imagine he spoke to him about selling the diamonds. But, why would the curator of a history museum spend the museum's money on diamonds? Unless he knew something we haven't figured out yet."

"One would think a trip to a jeweler would be more likely if it were diamonds," Garth answered. "That's why I want to speak to him."

It took some time to reach downtown Cleveland again. A few horse-drawn carriages from nearby Amish farms clogged the country roads between Shaker Heights and the city. I stopped my Hudson along the curb in front of a gray stone building with four Greek columns in front. The museum gave the impression of a smaller version of the Parthenon. "Well, here we are," I said, leaning to my right to get a better view of the building. "Have you decided what you'll ask Dr. Sweet?"

"I know what I want to ask him," Garth said, opening the door. "I just hope we get the right answers. Come, Major, we have work to do."

We carefully climbed the slippery stone steps, and pulled open the huge wooden double doors, stepping into the foyer. I remembered coming here soon after my retirement and found it fascinating. In fact, I went to every museum in the area to fill my empty life and ward off my boredom of retirement. The first thing I remembered was the echo.

"Follow me," I said to Garth. My voice reverberated throughout the building, even though I spoke just above a whisper. "The offices of the curators are on the second floor."

"Do they have an elevator?"

"Do you trust those things? I feel like I'm in a metal coffin each time I get in one," I said, removing my cap.

Garth laughed heartily, slapping my back, "You're amazing, Major. You can ride into battle with the near certainty of being shot off your horse, but you're afraid of riding in a safe, dependable elevator."

"I'm not afraid of the damned machines, just don't trust them. I'm a little claustrophobic if you have to know."

"Major, you swear too much," Garth said as the elevator door opened.

"The hell I do. Get in the coffin and shut up."

With the sounds of the cables clanging and the motor growling, we made it to the second floor in one piece. I mopped my brow with my handkerchief as I read the wall directory. "Damned fool name for a man, Sweet," I grumbled.

"There you go again, swearing," Garth chided as we walked down the hall.

He took the lead, finding Doctor Sweet's office and entering the small front room. A young man sat at a desk by the door and jumped as we pushed our way through. "Is Jeremy Sweet in the office, young man?"

"Who shall I say is calling?" the secretary asked.

"I'm Sherwood Garth and this is James Mallory," he said politely. "We're on official police business." Garth wasn't lying about the 'police business.' He failed to add that we weren't the police. But it got the same results.

"Oh, my," the young man said. "Is there a problem?"

"No, no, no, we just have a few questions for Doctor Sweet," Garth said, handing the man his card, which contained only his name.

The secretary ran to a back office. In a few minutes, we were standing in front of Sweet's desk. The doctor rose, offering his hand. He was a tall thin man with a mound of disheveled, white hair that matched his walrus mustache, which was bushy enough to cover his mouth as he spoke.

"Have a seat, gentlemen," he offered, resuming his chair. "It is getting late, the museum closes at five. What might I help you with?"

"This is regarding the Henry Spellman murder case," Garth said. "We have reason to believe you can tell us something about it."

Doctor Sweet's mouth began to twitch as soon as he heard the name of Henry Spellman. He leaned forward, turning his head to the door through which we'd arrived. "I don't know the man—why come to me?"

"In a pig's eye, you don't know him," I said, leaning forward, keeping a straight gaze on him.

"We have an extraordinarily busy day ahead of us," Garth said. "My partner hasn't slept well lately. It makes him a bit edgy."

I cracked the knuckles on both my hands as Mr. Sweet

peered my way. "You've been to Billy's Place in Medina lately? You know, that sleazy place off the road a bit?"

Doctor Sweet hung his head, shaking it from side to side. "I suppose if you know that much, you know the rest. Yes, I've met with Spellman. I didn't want to but was talked into it by Karen."

"We were told that you missed the first appointment, then showed up on the next one to talk to him," Garth said. "Let's see if I got this right. You made an appointment to see him and backed out. Then Karen Bender called to persuade you to meet Spellman."

"Yes, well, no, she came to my office in person. Karen can be very persuasive."

Again, the name Karen Bender stirred some faint memory for me, but I had no time to think about it just now.

"Can she? What did you talk about?" Garth asked.

"Look, I don't want any trouble," Sweet said, his white mustache quivering. "I gave him some information and promised not to tell anyone about our meeting. I just wanted out of there. Spellman was a cheat and untrustworthy."

"What did he want?" I said, my voice low. "Did he want to sell the museum a bag of diamonds?"

"Diamonds? Hell no." Sweet seemed acutely surprised when I mentioned diamonds. "He wanted to sell me a box of Greek antiquities. I knew about a theft from the museum in London. Karen told me Spellman had just arrived from England. I put two and two together and assumed they were one and the same. I wanted nothing to do with them."

"Did he show you what they were?" Garth asked.

"No, he said they hadn't arrived yet. I tell you, I didn't

want anything to do with the man. He had an unsavory reputation around town." He leaned back in his swivel chair as if he'd got a load off his mind.

"What else happened?" Garth asked. I hadn't sensed it, but Garth had. Sweet wasn't telling all.

"What do you mean?" Sweet asked, sitting forward again.

"Do you know Zachery Hareborn?"

"Okay, I'll throw my cards on the table," Sweet said. "I only did it for Karen, not for Spellman. I thought she needed a break; she's had a rough life. I told Spellman about Doctor Zachery Hareborn of the Chicago Art History Museum. I don't know for sure, mind you. However, Hareborn is known to buy stolen items. He sells them to big-money clients in Chicago, collectors of rare items."

"That fits into what we know," Garth said, his fingers touching his cheek. "He didn't say what he was selling?"

"He was about to, but I stopped him. I didn't want to know. I didn't want to be involved in anything like that. As I said, I was trying to help Karen." Sweet was wringing his hands by this time.

"It sounds like you care about Karen."

"Yes, I've known her for a few years. Now that Spellman is gone, she'll have a better life. With him alive, she'd stick to him, come hell or high water. Now she has a chance," Sweet said, nodding. "Women are funny that way. They stick to their man no matter how crooked he is."

"Did Spellman contact you after that last meeting at Billy's Place?" Garth asked.

"No, neither of them has contacted me since. I only found out about the murder in the papers. It was shocking."

"Then, we're done here," Garth said, standing. "If

anyone calls you about the murder or the artifacts, let me know. My contact's telephone number is on the back of this card. Tell him you need to see me. He'll know what to do."

"Watch your back," I added, "There are others who have your name but don't know who you are. We hope to clear this up before they do."

Doctor Sweet was visibly shaken after I told him that. He flopped down in his chair as we left his office.

Stepping off the elevator, we headed out into the cold world of Cleveland. Garth asked, "What say we get an early dinner before going to your place? It's too early to go to The Sparrow Club."

"Ah, there's a Polish restaurant down the street. This time it's your treat," I said with a snicker. "I'm hungry."

Chapter Twenty-Two

Karen Bender's Story

Our next stop was to be The Sparrow Club. We planned to meet Karen Bender, the mysterious lady who had been Spellman's companion in Cleveland, as well as in Medina. Hopefully, she would be appearing at the club tonight. However, the Sparrow wouldn't open until later. According to Augie, Karen always came in after nine o'clock, so, we had some time on our hands. We drove over to Sumner Street. Garth called Sergeant Markson and filled him in on what we had learned.

Most importantly, we wanted a policeman watching the Spellman residence. We both worried that the two Black Hand thugs might be planning to visit the Spellman sisters. Markson assigned Officers Leonard and Parks to that detail.

Garth went upstairs to his room after making the call. In half an hour he returned wearing an evening suit. "We have to fit into the crowd at the Sparrow Club, Major," he said strutting down the steps.

"Well, good for you. However, I haven't an evening suit to wear. Remember, I just left the Army. We wore uniforms." I had to admit to myself. Garth looked quite dashing in his black and white tails. He even had a short top hat to add to his charm. "I'll settle for my tweed suit."

Adjourning to my library with coffee, the subject of the female suspects came up again. I was at my desk with my left leg balanced on the corner of it. I lit my cigar, blowing out a procession of smoke rings. "Garth, do you mind if I ask you a personal question?"

"No, go ahead."

"Why are you so adamant about the treachery of women? You seem to distrust them altogether."

Garth was standing at the front windows, squinting at the last of the afternoon sun glistening on the snow-covered headstones in the Erie Cemetery across the street. He turned to me with a sharp grin. "I find faults with everyone equally, Major. However, I find women are far more deceitful than men, using their feminine wiles to cover their lies. The same way that Cynthia used her charm on you last evening," he said, pointing his finger at me as he walked over to the desk.

"I know what you're talking about, Garth. Nonetheless, there seems to be a vendetta in your distrust of the fairer sex. Something you wish to tell me?"

He sat on one of the leather chairs, looking not at me, but at the bookshelves. "The only suspect who ever alluded me, when I served with the NYPD, was a woman.

She outsmarted me at every turn. She used her feminine charms to confound me and, eventually, got away with murder."

"You're saying she was guilty of murder, and you let her escape?" I asked.

"Brenda Forsythe was her name, or still is, unless she's changed it," Garth said, still facing the books. "She was a beautiful debutante from a highly placed family in New York City that was down on their luck financially. I'll omit her maiden name, in case you know the family. They're one of the four hundred. The pretty girls in society have always been snatched up quickly by men with money."

"Yes, that is the way it still works, even today," I agreed.

"Well, Winston Forsythe had money. In this case, Brenda was the pursuer, she used all her attributes to snare the man and his money. A few months after the wedding, the police found Winston bludgeoned to death in front of his fireplace. She was sitting in the next room, covered in blood and sobbing hysterically."

I'd never seen Garth so somber in our short acquaintance. He spoke softly and had a faraway appearance in his blue eyes, remembering the young lady and the crime scene.

"What happened next?"

He abruptly turned to me, "It's a long story of deceit and manipulation," he said. "Brenda wrapped me around her little finger, just as Cynthia was doing to you. I helped exonerate her, and now she and her male friend are living off their ill-gotten gain. I found out later, after the trial, that everything I was told, while we were together, was a lie. She premeditated her husband's murder, made him appear like an abuser. She escaped her rightful fate, making a fool out of me in the process."

"You had feelings for the girl, didn't you?"

Garth turned away and sighed. "Yes, I did. When I learned the truth, I confronted her and her male companion. She laughed at me, the foolish policeman. I walked away, my head low, knowing she got away with murder. My pain ran deep, Major, knowing the feelings she'd expressed toward me were all a lie. I vowed to myself not to trust another woman. The more attractive, the more manipulative they are. In this business, you must clamp your heart in a cage and not let it lead you astray," Garth said, gritting his teeth.

I nodded, as if I understood and would heed his advice, but I pitied him. His attitude could be why he remained single? I didn't know. In a way, his flirting and philandering were just as manipulative, although I realize he does it to bring criminals to justice.

"Well, it's history, Major. Lesson learned." Garth flashed his radiant smile once again.

* * *

Few people were on Ninth Street that evening. After parking my Hudson at the curb, we got out and walked down the sidewalk. A policeman, gingerly swinging his baton, passed us while shopkeepers closed their businesses for the night. Quite a few street urchins ran in and out of alleys, obviously to the dismay of the few motorists on the street.

We arrived at the club to find the dance floor a hubbub of activity. Unlike the sidewalk outside, The Sparrow Club was alive with song, dance, drink, and good cheer. People from the upper crust of Cleveland society came to the

Sparrow to kick up their heels and release the anxiety of the day. The bar was filling up with young gents dressed in the best of evening wear. Their black suits with tails and white bow ties blended well with the shimmering bright colors worn by their lady companions.

Despite my habit of smoking cigars, I coughed, breathing the smoke-filled air. As we pushed our way through the crowd, we found Augie behind the bar, backed by twenty kegs of beer. The short fat man with the jolly face smiled as we approached.

"Well, I haven't seen you in a dog's age, Major," Augie said. "What'll it be, gents? A couple of cold beers?"

"It's only been a few weeks," I said. "We'll take nothing but the best you've got, Augie. This is my partner, Sherwood Garth." I put my hand on Garth's shoulder.

"Glad to meet ya, Mr. Garth."

"Glad to meet you as well. We met your black-bearded bear the other day," Garth said.

Augie placed two beers on the bar and gave me a hard stare. "It appears to have been a head-on collision to me." He and Garth laughed at my expense as I rubbed my bruised jaw.

"We're here to have a chat with Henry Spellman's other companion," I said to ease my embarrassment. "Karen Bender—has she shown up yet?"

"No," Augie said with a squinting stare around the club. "But, never fear, gents, she'll show herself shortly, always does on Friday and Saturday nights. Knows a lot of the men on a first name basis."

Garth scanned the large room, searching for familiar faces, making eye contact with a few, giving them a nod. I saw his gaze land on a few of the attractive young ladies.

He frowned as he saw one dancing with an older man. "Do you know her?" he asked Augie.

"No, not personally. She comes in to find a daddy every once in a while."

"Her father comes in here as well?" I asked.

Garth and Augie both laughed. "No, Major, that's not what he meant."

"You need to pick up on the slang," Garth said. "She is searching for a rich man who can, let's say, support her."

"Oh, I get you," I said, chastened. "Since leaving the Army, I don't spend much time out and about. Does Karen throw bait to *all* the rich men in here?" I asked Augie.

The little man chuckled and coughed. "No," he said, rubbing his chubby cheek. "Karen likes to dance and have a good time, but she always ran back to Henry when he came in."

"The girl on the dance floor with the old guy," Garth said, his attention reverted to the mismatched couple. "She looks like she's doing some fishing. The vamp is throwing out a lot of bait. He dresses like a bit of a dapper, don't you think?"

"Have you seen him before?" Augie asked. "I remember faces, and he's not from this neck of the woods. If you want to talk to him …"

"Don't trouble yourself." Garth smiled, giving Augie a slap on the shoulder. "Just my suspicious nature on alert."

"I've got a house load of thirsty customers. You gents will have to excuse me," Augie said. "There's a clean table in the corner for you. It gives you a good view of the club."

We fought our way through the crowds of well-dressed men and women. It wasn't long ago that it was scandalous for women to drink and smoke in the same room as men.

Now, in the new age, the young people thought nothing of it. The music and dancing had become revolutionary. A young lady on stage with a jazz band sang, *After You're Gone*, a lingering romantic melody. The young couples held each other, swaying in each other's arms. The young singer sang the song as well as Marion Harris did on the recordings I had heard. I sat back, gazing around at the ornate décor as Garth watched the door for our guest.

No sooner had I finished my beer then Augie waved to get our attention. There stood a tall divine woman with curly blond hair bundled on her head and bangs over her forehead. She wore a floor-length gown of cream with long strands of pearls wrapped loosely around her swan-like neck.

I squinted as she walked in, "She looks somewhat familiar."

Garth jumped to his feet, approaching her before any of the young dandies had a chance to move in. In moments, my companion had escorted the lady to our table. Augie came over with her drink of choice.

On closer inspection, Miss Bender appeared to be a woman in her late thirties, still beautiful but not what she must have been ten years prior. Her hazel eyes twinkled provocatively as she gazed at Garth. She stared at me and said, "I understand you and Mr. Garth are investigating the murder of Henry Spellman?"

"Yes," I answered, surprised the word had reached her. "Anything you tell us will be greatly appreciated."

She held her gaze on me as if she knew who I was.

"Have we met?" I asked.

"You don't remember." Her hands were folded softly on the table. "It was a long time ago. You were home on leave; I was visiting your brother Phillip's home near Shaker Heights. You came into the parlor wearing your uniform. You were so dashing and handsome; you gave me the flutters."

"That must have been about five years ago when I was leaving Washington, on my way to Texas to join Pershing." I thought back to those years. My mind at that time was on my career, not on women. "I'm sorry I don't remember you."

"Never you mind—you still are dashing and handsome," she smiled again then seemed to turn her thoughts back to Henry. "I'll tell you everything I know. You see, Henry and I were fond of each other. In fact, we were planning a trip to Illinois when this ugly business occurred. I was supposed to meet him at the very spot you found his body. However, I didn't go to the appointment." Goosebumps rose on her arms and she rubbed them briskly.

"An old barn would be an odd place to meet a lady," Garth said. "Why did he choose it?"

"His sisters don't approve of our relationship. Since we wanted to slip out of town quietly, we didn't want to be seen in public together. If he had lived, he could explain it better."

"So, that's why he was there," Garth said. "Did you tell anyone you wouldn't make it?"

"It wasn't my idea to call off our rendezvous," Karen said, leaning forward. "It was Henry who canceled it. He told me he would explain later. I found it odd that he wanted me to travel to Medina in the first place, then double back to Cleveland to catch a train to Chicago."

"Yes. Strange," I said, glancing over at Garth.

"Had he called to set up the appointment with you?" Garth asked.

"He phoned me at home to set up our meeting. He told me everything was all set for our trip to Chicago. He said, 'the money's in the bank.' It was all a big mystery to me. In truth, I found it exciting," she added, smiling. "Then something happened, and he called off the meeting."

"When was that?" Garth asked.

"The evening of his murder. Henry didn't explain why he canceled."

"What time?"

"He called me here at the club around eight. I was getting ready to leave to meet him when I got the call," Karen said, brushing strands of her blonde, corkscrew hair behind her ears. Karen had a tense stare in her eyes as if trying to understand what happened that night. "I thought that was odd as well. He knows how hard it is to hear on the telephone behind the bar."

"So, you're not positive the voice on the phone was his, are you?" I asked.

She thought for a moment. "As a matter of fact, he sounded different, there was a crinkling noise that altered his voice. However, I am sure that I heard him say not to meet him at the barn and that he would be in touch."

I lit a cigar as I waved for Augie to bring another round to our table. "Have you any idea who would want to kill Henry?"

Miss Bender waited for Augie to leave before answering my question. "He's dead now, so it shouldn't matter anymore," she said. She sighed and sipped her scotch. "Henry was making plenty of money blackmailing two of those partners of his. He had a line on Jackson and Douglas and was sucking them dry or, I should say, he sucked them dry. Douglas stopped paying him some time ago. Jackson told me that he couldn't afford to pay any more. I feared that those sources had dried up."

"We knew Jackson was a victim of blackmail, related to the shooting in Alaska. What did Spellman have on Douglas?" Garth asked.

"It all fits together. Longfellow, the man who died in Alaska, was a good friend of Allen Douglas. Douglas made the mistake of telling young Longfellow too much about why he was being blackmailed. Longfellow naively thought he could talk Henry out of pursuing the payments. Of course, Henry laughed at him. That's what Henry told me. He said he laughed in Longfellow's face. I don't know all that happened out on the tundra, but Longfellow Junior died, and they accused Jackson of it."

"What did Henry have on Douglas?" Garth pushed for more substance in her answers.

Karen's gaze went past us to the bar. Her eyes took on a horrified stare. "I think I may be saying too much," she stuttered. "You'd better leave."

Her change of demeanor surprised us. One minute she was cheerfully telling us whatever we asked, the next she clammed up with fear. I glanced toward the bar. There was no one watching our table. I looked over at Garth, giving him a shrug.

"Miss Bender, what is troubling you?" Garth asked. "If someone is threatening you, let us know. We can help."

"No, just leave, please. I've said enough already."

Garth and I finished our beers and rose to leave. Disappointment was etched on Garth's face. Karen's eyes bore down into her folded hands. She didn't raise her head to see us off.

Chapter Twenty-Three

Suspect in Hiding

We stepped out into the cold night air and leaned against the wall near the club's entrance. People were coming and going, and no one seemed to notice us standing there.

"What was all that about, Garth?"

"Someone scared her," he responded. "Obviously, she wasn't about to give up who it was. That was genuine fear in her eyes."

We began to walk in the direction of my motor car. No sooner had we reached the large window in the front of the bar when I heard Karen's voice calling for us to wait. We turned to see her hurrying in her slippery high heels to catch up with us.

"I'm afraid my conscience won't let you go until I tell

the whole truth," she sighed, wringing her hands together for warmth.

As she said this, I saw, through the window, two figures leaving the club using the back door. Because their fedoras were pulled down and there was a considerable distance from my window, I couldn't see their faces. "What is it that scared you just now, Miss Bender?" I asked, still watching as the dark figures left.

"It was the two men who came to Cleveland the day of the murder," she stuttered. "They have been with Allen Douglas a few times here at The Sparrow Club. I just saw them at the bar without Douglas. They kept turning to watch us. When they caught me watching them, they glared at me with hateful eyes. Then one man drew his hand across his throat. I know what he's telling me."

"They just left. Wait here," I said sternly. "I'm going to see what they're up to."

The street lamp covered the sidewalk with a dim light. I walked quickly, skirting the brick wall until I reached the corner of the building. Garth and Karen were now only shadows on the other side of the light. They appeared miles away. I guardedly peered around the corner toward the back of the club. Only a small, lackluster bulb hung above the rear door, illuminating only some dented trashcans. The rest of the narrow alley was in pitch darkness. I was alone.

I faintly heard voices, so I inched my way down the alley, as quietly as possible. They were speaking Italian.

As I suspected—The Black Hand.

As I stood in the shadows listening, the rear door of the club flung open. A flood of light poured out as an employee stepped out to dump garbage into the trash containers.

"Hey! Whatsa matter you?" the first man yelled, raising his arms toward the employee.

"Don't worry about it, bub," the employee said. "Just dumping the trash."

A short ten seconds, the door was open. The light streamed out, and I recognized the two thugs who'd been with Allen Douglas at Billy's Place the other night.

At the same moment I saw them, they spotted me. Both men scowled at me.

As we made eye contact, I tipped my cap toward them and smiled.

"Hey, you!" the bigger man called.

The light from the club cut off; we were back in utter darkness.

Two bright lights glared from the motor car at the other end of the alley. The lamps grew larger. The engine roared as the thugs drove toward me. I ran.

Garth and Karen stood where I'd left them. I screamed, "Get in the building!"

My companions made it to the door, jumping through, just in time. But not me. Behind me, I heard the engine roar and the gears shifting as the car exploded from the alley onto Ninth Street. It roared down the street, closing in on me. One of the men sat in the back seat, leaning out of the window. His automatic pistol peppered the brick wall of the club with a string of hot lead. Fortunately, I dodged and avoided being hit.

As I stumbled into the entrance of The Sparrow Club, the car raced past the club and sped away.

"What did you do?" Garth demanded to know, as he helped me to my feet.

"What did *I* do?" I was breathing heavily. "I just about

got myself killed."

"Well, be more careful in the future, old man."

"Mr. Garth! Those men just shot at him," Karen said, her face shockingly pale.

"You're right. I didn't mean to treat the situation lightly."

I spoke up. "They were the same two men we saw at Billy's. We need a plan."

We made our way through the throngs of people trying to see what had happened. Our original table was still unoccupied, so the three of us returned to it.

Garth waved to Augie, holding up three fingers. "I think you're going to need another beer after that."

"I've been under fire many times before," I said, tossing my hat on the table. "It causes fear, but I know how to deal with it."

Augie approached with a tray of drinks, "What was the racket out there in the street?"

"I'm afraid your brick wall is covered in pockmarks," Garth answered. "The Major had a run-in with the Black Hand."

"The Black Hand?" Augie said, his voice an octave higher. "I knew those two were no good. I recognized their type right off. You're talking about those pug-uglies in the black coats, right?"

"That's them," I responded, as Karen took her seat.

"Well, I won't let them in my place again."

Garth and I each took a hefty gulp from our beer mugs as Augie walked away.

"They know I'm talking to you," Karen Bender said. "My life isn't worth a plug nickel now. I've seen them before when I was having a late dinner with a friend at Trivoli's."

"What night was that?" Garth asked. I saw his eyes gleaming as he pondered another piece of the puzzle.

"I believe it was last Thursday, the fourteenth. I noticed those two thugs sitting with another man."

"Allen Douglas?" I asked.

"No, James. It was someone else. He had his back to me. All I saw was that he was thin with dark hair." She turned to Garth with tears welling up in her eyes. "What can I do, Mr. Garth? They know I'm talking and will hunt me down."

"Now don't you worry," Garth said. "Those two thugs have no idea where Major Mallory lives. I'm sure he can put you up for a few nights until this gets ironed out."

I glared at Garth with pursed lips. How could he presume that Elizabeth and Frederick would want another visitor without being consulted first?

Karen must have seen my discomfort. "Oh, Mr. Garth, you can't put the Major's family in the middle of this. It may prove dangerous for them," she said, glancing at me. I noticed the fear in her eyes, turning slightly to hope.

"No, my dear," I said. "Garth is right. Frederick is more than capable of taking care of you, and Elizabeth would enjoy the company. The thugs may not be smart enough to know that we are hiding you, but still, I'll give Brady a call and have the house watched."

"In that case, I'll be glad to stay there. Thank you," she said, with a sigh of relief.

"Now that we have that settled," Garth said, "What more have you to tell us?"

"Well, to begin with, Henry was very much at fault in the death of young Longfellow. It was not an accident." Karen stopped long enough to take a gulp from the glass of scotch. She grinned at me and continued to tell the story of the four men's trip to Alaska and the supposed hunting accident.

"Henry used Longfellow's naivete against him, telling him that wearing his parka inside out would keep him camouflaged." Karen giggled as she lifted her glass.

I leaned forward, guiding her hand away. She didn't need any more scotch.

"Henry convinced Jackson he was aiming at a bear," Garth said to clarify what Karen was telling us. "Then poor confused Jackson pulled the trigger and killed Longfellow. Is that right?"

"Yes, that's what happened. Jackson is an idiot," Karen said. "Henry testified in court that it was an accident. After that, he had something to blackmail Jackson with. Henry told him he would change his story if he didn't do his bidding."

Now that Karen had confirmed what we already knew, Garth asked the bigger question. "What did Henry have on Allen Douglas?"

"Some political thing. Before the war started, Sir Chadwick Holdsworth and Douglas conspired to feed false information to Senator Ward. Mind you, this was before our involvement in the war," she said, waving a finger at Garth and me. It was a good thing she'd stopped drinking; she was slurring her words.

"What was going on?" Garth asked.

"It seemed that Mr. Douglas and Sir Holdsworth were scheming to discredit the Germans in the eyes of the American Senate. They were manufacturing false stories of atrocities and barbarism perpetrated by German soldiers, feeding the stories to the senator."

"Senator Ward is an influential and powerful man," I said to Garth. "His word may have steered the country into the European War, which may have been exactly what Holdsworth wanted."

Garth's eyes were fixed on Karen. "Indeed, that is true, but what proof did he have? Was it enough to scare Holdsworth and Douglas into paying him?"

"Oh, he had all the proof he needed. He'd ransacked Douglas' office and found some incriminating letters between Douglas and Holdsworth. There was plenty to prove their deceit," she answered with a malicious glint in her eyes.

"The exposure of which would have put an end to their political careers. Reason enough to kill, I would think," Garth said.

"But where are the papers? Would Spellman run the risk of having those papers found among his belongings?" I suggested. "That would be quite foolish for a man in his position." I leaned toward Garth.

"Excellent point, Major," he said. "Who's to say Douglas doesn't have those papers?"

"I do," said Miss Bender. "Henry kept them in a safe deposit box at the bank. He entrusted the key to me."

"Now, you need to entrust me with the key and location of the safe deposit box. Then we can drive you to the Major's estate for your protection," Garth told her.

Her eyes held a twinkle of seduction as she slipped her fingers beneath the low neckline of her dress and pulled out a small brass key. "Should I trust him with this?" she asked me.

"You can trust him as much as you trust me."

"Why do you keep the key with you?" Garth asked.

"Henry told me to. He said not to trust anyone with it," Karen said, her voice low. "I suppose it doesn't matter now that he's gone."

She slid the key across the table to Garth. "Just a couple more drinks and a dance with you two, then off to the Major's cozy home."

We drew the line on the drinks, but Garth indulged her with a dance after he'd tucked the safe deposit key into his watch pocket.

Chapter Twenty-Four

A Stopover From Douglas

We had planned to return to the Spellman home in Medina to rest up and get a fresh start the next morning. However, first we needed to deliver Karen Bender to Sumner Street, make her feel at home, and to explain the situation to Fred and Liz.

We came in through the kitchen and hung up our overcoats in the wet room. I brushed off my tan corduroy jacket and found Liz busily working on a snack for herself and Fred. The radio newscast about the Great War was to start in the library.

Liz turned to us and announced, "You have a guest waiting for you, Jimmy. You and Mr. Garth, that is." She didn't notice Karen standing behind me.

"Who might that be?"

"Mr. Allen Douglas. He's in the billiards room," she said.

A jolt of concern shot through me, but I tamped it down in front of Liz. "Is that where you usually put our guests? The billiard room?"

"Normally not, but I knew you would be gone some time, so I asked if he played billiards. He has been happily slapping the balls around for the past half hour."

"Excellent, dear lady," Garth said after removing his overcoat. "We have brought a guest for you to care for," he said. He backed away about to introduce Miss Bender.

"Oh, you don't need to introduce Karen Bender to me. How are you, my pet?" Liz asked as she held both of Karen's hands. "Frederick will be so pleased to see you again."

"Mr. Garth–" said Fred coming through the kitchen door. Fred took one look at our guest. "Karen Bender! My little girl," he said. "It's so good to see you again."

Karen's face brightened with a huge smile. "I remember you calling me that all those years ago. I think we'll have fun together again."

I looked from Fred to Liz to Karen. "How do you know Miss Bender? You two don't run in the same crowds, do you?" I asked.

"I imagine you have forgotten, since it was some time ago. And you were still grieving Christina's passing," Liz explained.

Christina—my wife, who died in childbirth while we were stationed in the remote wilderness of Wyoming. I also lost my daughter then. It was a devastating part of my life that haunted me for many years.

"I was disappointed that you didn't recognize me,

James," Karen said. "I had a big crush on you, the handsome young officer," she said, gazing up at me.

"I am sorry to have forgotten you, my dear," I said, thinking back to earlier days, days I had been trying to forget.

"You two would have made a lovely couple," Liz said.

"None of that now," I said. "I was blind to all women back then. I prefer not to discuss it."

"I'm sorry to bring back painful memories for you, James," Karen said. "Forget we spoke of it."

I glanced at both women, "No need to apologize."

Garth broke up the reunion, saying, "I desperately need to speak to Mr. Douglas, but first Miss Bender," he said, turning to Liz and Fred. "She needs to stay in a safe place for a few days. I'm afraid there are men of the criminal element trying to do her harm."

"Oh, my," Liz said, clutching Karen's hands more tightly. "Do they know you're here?"

"No, that's the beauty of it. The two thugs may have an idea where she lives, but, as far as we know, they have no idea who the Major is, or where he lives."

"Of course, she'll stay with us," Fred said. "We're happy to have you, and Liz will keep you well-fed."

Garth put his hands on both of the women's shoulders, smiling fondly. "Please escort Miss Bender upstairs and help her adjust. The Major and I will go see Mr. Douglas. Be sure that Mr. Douglas doesn't discover she is here."

We walked down the hall and entered the billiard room unannounced. Allen Douglas stood by the table, staring at a Frederic Remington original above the mantel. He fingered his handlebar mustache and held a cue stick in the other hand. A stout man in his mid-forties, he had a full head of coal-black hair that matched his mustache. He frowned at us through deep-set, dark eyes as he clutched a thick cigar in his thin lips. His tweed suit appeared rumpled and well worn around the cuffs.

"You wanted to see us?" Garth asked.

"The local constabulary has poured out their wrath on my friend, Herbert Longfellow, so I wanted to speak with you, and here I am," Douglas said. "However, I can't tell you any more than I told Sergeant Markson."

"So the locals have spoken to you, presumably questioning Longfellow's whereabouts more so than yours on that night?" said Garth.

"Indeed, the sergeant did; I would say that he is hounding the poor fellow. Herbert is as innocent of this crime as I am. Especially since we were together the entire evening. Markson is determined to prove Herbert guilty," Douglas said, as he paced the room. "I believe there is the shadow of politics involved."

"How does politics fit into this, Mr. Douglas?" I asked, fearing he was trying to lead us astray.

"Longfellow has money. In the last local election, he financially backed a candidate who ran against the incumbent mayor. The newcomer lost, but only by a slim margin. The mayor took it poorly and threatened to retaliate against Longfellow. Can you think of a better way to get even than to accuse the man of murder?" Douglas said. He coughed on the smoke from his cigar.

"Before we go any further, where are those men you hired?" Garth said, frowning at Douglas. "I don't want them anywhere near this house."

"You don't have to worry about them any longer. I sent the thugs back to New York. I hired them to scare

Spellman into giving up the gems. Since he's dead, they weren't needed. It was a terrible mistake to call them out here."

"Where are they now?" I repeated.

"I dropped them off at the train station myself this past Monday. As far as I know, they're gone," he said, flicking the ash from his cigar onto the floor.

"Well, you're wrong," Garth bellowed. "We just saw them at The Sparrow Club, spying on a witness, nearly running over Major Mallory in their escape."

"The three of you—Rizzo, De Luca, and you—came in from New York on what day?" Garth's assertive voice seemed to worry Douglas.

"That was Saturday morning, the ninth. We shared a compartment and arrived in Cleveland about nine that morning," Douglas replied shakily. "I went straight to Longfellow's home in Medina, arriving around eleven that morning. The murder happened that night, while I was at Herbert's place."

"Where did your friends Rizzo and De Luca go during that time?"

"I checked them into a downtown Cleveland hotel. I told them to stay put until I returned."

"And did they?" Garth continued.

"No, I'm afraid not," Douglas sighed. "They visited Steven Jackson. That's another reason I discharged them. Jackson didn't want any affiliation with the Black Hand and insisted on their leaving."

"Well," I said. "Jackson isn't as stupid as I've been led to believe."

"How did you know this was the Major's home?" Garth asked.

"I- I called Lieutenant Brady," Douglas answered, clearing his throat.

I noticed beads of sweat on his forehead as he glanced at me. We'd check with Brady later on his story.

"I told Brady I wanted to speak to you two. I called ahead. The Major's man, Frederick, said you would be here tonight."

"Did you tell Rizzo and Deluca where we were?" Garth asked, his voice harsh.

"No, no. I told you, I left those two at Union Station on the eleventh. I had no idea they were still in this area." Douglas began to pace the room, looking down at the floor. "Those thugs know about the diamonds. They, for certain, want them for themselves."

Garth shook his head as he walked around the billiard table to face Douglas. "There's something more."

"What is that you say?"

"Come come, man. Let's not waste each other's time. I'm speaking of blackmail." Garth had a smile in his voice. I saw he was using his charm to ease the tension in the room.

"So you know about that," Douglas said solemnly. "Well, I have no shame in it. The payments were of political necessity. What Sir Chadwick Holdsworth and I were doing may not have been totally on the up-and-up. However, it was essential for both of our countries' security."

"I'm not here to debate your political ethics, sir. I'm here to learn to what extent you would go to protect yourself," Garth pressed.

Douglas drew himself up straighter. "I wouldn't go as far as murder, Mr. Garth. Besides, the war is in its fourth year. What we said is irrelevant now. Both Sir Holdsworth and I stopped paying Spellman some time ago. The latest trip to South Africa was to be our last time to collaborate with him. He was a thief and a scoundrel."

"So, you told him it was your last venture together?" Garth asked. "How did he respond?"

Douglas snickered with the cigar clenched in his teeth. "Not well. We always funded his trips, receiving very little from them. I told him I was free from his clutches once the partnership in Africa was over."

"That's when Spellman took off with all the diamonds," Garth said. "Why did Sir Holdsworth go along with him?"

"I have no idea," Douglas said, pointing the stub of his cigar at Garth, "It must have been a last minute decision on his part. I spoke to Holdsworth the night before they ran off with the loot. He was as fed up with Spellman as I was. He told me he was going back to England and would brush Spellman out of his life."

"It appears that it ended up the other way around," Garth said, stepping closer to Douglas.

"The poor bounder should have known better than to trust Henry," Douglas growled.

"So, you believe Spellman killed him?"

"Of course, and kept all the stones for himself. If you want to find the killer, Steven Jackson is a more likely suspect."

"Why do you say that?" I asked.

"He was still being blackmailed by Spellman. Also, he wasn't wise with his money and needed the diamonds more than the other partners. He is a violent man with a terrible temper, Mr. Garth. He is definitely a more likely suspect." Douglas picked up the billiard chalk and began chalking the tip of his cue stick.

"We're watching Jackson, and believe me, Brady is keeping a close eye on him as well," Garth said, leaning on the table.

"His temper is obvious. Be careful if you ever meet him," Douglas continued. "More important, I overheard Jackson threaten Spellman's life on several occasions. There he is, sitting pretty in one of Cleveland's finest hotels. Those are facts you cannot overlook, Mr. Garth."

"Yes, we've experienced Steven Jackson's disposition first hand."

I watched Garth's features sharpen as he thought for a moment. Douglas also watched Garth's face, searching for a reaction to his statements.

"Obvious facts," Garth said deliberately, "can be more deceptive than no facts at all." He added, "You realize that Longfellow was taken into custody?"

"Yes, of course," Douglas replied. "I was there. They let him out later that morning."

"You said a moment ago that you were with Longfellow the entire evening of the ninth. However, Longfellow said nothing about your presence. What's the truth, sir? Were you with Longfellow or not on the night of the murder?" Garth asked sharply.

"Well, we were together part of the evening. I went to my room at Longfellow's house at 8:30 p.m., leaving Herbert alone with a book. I rose again at around 10:00 p.m. to find something to drink. I found him asleep in his chair. He was snoring softly, with his book folded over his chest."

"Then, you returned to your room?"

"Yes, I did. Personally, I don't believe Herbert Longfellow has the killer instinct. The threats you've probably heard about were idle. They meant nothing."

Garth had done an excellent job of baiting the man by lying about Longfellow's statement of his whereabouts. I got the impression Douglas' story was true.

"Did you know where the barn was?" I asked.

"I knew that Longfellow bought a barn, but did not understand the significance of it," he answered. "Nor, had I known that the barn was bought from Spellman's sisters."

Garth rubbed his chin for a moment, staring at Mr. Douglas. "Thank you for your time." Garth then turned to me. "Major, will you show our guest out to his motor car? I'd like to remain behind for a few minutes."

I walked out with Douglas as Garth closed the door behind us. I knew Garth was in a contemplative mood and needed solitude. As we walked down the hall, we heard the clink of billiard balls coming from behind the door.

Chapter Twenty-Five

The Date

I watched as Douglas drove northward, headed back to his hotel in Cleveland, I assumed, since he no longer resided at Longfellow's place.

I walked back into the hallway and decided to drive around the countryside, to contemplate the day's events. I ventured back into the library, finding Garth shuffling through a pile of papers and photographs on the desk. "Garth, I'm going out for a drive. I'll leave you to your studies."

"Enjoy yourself. When I'm done with these bills, I plan to call Toronto. I'm sure Liz will be happy with the phone bill."

"Toronto? What on earth for?"

"Just a few questions that need my attention. I'll tell

you about it later."

I gave him a quick wave and grabbed my overcoat and cap. Jumping into my Hudson, I took off.

I headed east, toward the palatial neighborhoods of Shaker Heights. The scenery is not as beautiful in the winter as in spring or summer, but the area does have its own particular attraction. The full moon brightened the road for me and the crisp breeze rejuvenated me.

As I drove, my mind was on Anneka. I couldn't help myself. I was under her spell and couldn't shake it. Or was it that I didn't want to shake it? I turned the Hudson around and drove to Medina.

* * *

I headed for The Lajon Bostad Inn. It was relatively late when I pulled into the parking lot. There were only a few autos in the lot, which was encouraging. I parked close to the restaurant's front entrance. Pulling my coat snugly around me. I thought to myself, *this is the moment.* Then I forged ahead into the restaurant.

The fetching Anneka caught my eye as she worked behind the bar. The last few customers were seated at tables. I strode past her sisters and employees, stopping at the bar.

Anneka looked up and smiled. "Hi there, did you want …"

"I want you to leave the rest of the work to your sisters and the staff," I stood with my hands firmly planted on the polished pinewood bar. "I'm taking you out."

"I've got work …"

"Leave it," I pressed, leaning forward.

She took a deep breath and let it out. "Well …"

I reached out my left hand to take hers.

"Okay, Jim. Let's go." A sparkling grin crossed her face as she ripped off her apron, darted around the bar, and fell into my arms. She shouted instructions to the staff as I whisked her through the front door.

Outside, she slipped on her fur-collared overcoat and I helped her into the Hudson. "Where are we going?" she asked.

"I don't know," I answered, driving out of the lot. "Anyplace we can be alone. You have any suggestions?"

"Do you want to go to Cleveland?"

"Anyplace your heart desires," I offered, sitting next to the lady I'd decided to marry, whether she knew it or not.

"There's a small restaurant tucked away in West Park," she said. "They stay open late for the night shift factory workers." She settled into a comfortable position.

"Well, then. That's where we go." I pushed down on the accelerator, driving northwest to the growing community of West Park.

As we cautiously drove over the twisting roads in the dark, she asked me, "What's all the tough-guy business back there, sweeping me away? Are you trying to impress me?"

I grinned sheepishly as I glanced at her. "I guess I was. Did it work?"

Anneka laughed, shaking her head. All her red curls danced in the moonlight, swirling around her face and shoulders. The unkempt look was sensuous to me.

"No, Jim. It didn't impress me. I already know you're a tough guy," she said softly. "Now, I want to see the gentleman in you."

She guided me into the western neighborhoods, to an area called Kamm's Korner. On Lorain Avenue, there was a small restaurant set back from the street. I would have missed it if she hadn't pointed it out.

"Is this secluded enough?"

"Looks cozy enough for us," I answered as I helped her out of the auto.

We walked up to the dimly lit patio leading to the front door. Inside, it felt like walking into somebody's home. At the sound of the bell over the door, a big motherly woman greeted us. She led us to a table in the rear corner. By the twinkle in her eyes, she'd guessed we wanted romantic seclusion.

"Wait until you see how much she feeds you," Anneka murmured.

"Wonderful. I just realized I've eaten very little today," I replied. Anneka was right; Edith, the owner, waitress, and cook, came out with the daily special. Two plates brimming with meatloaf, carrots, broccoli, and potatoes, all covered in a thick gravy. She set a teapot on the table with two cups and saucers.

"Now you two lovebirds enjoy your dinner," Edith said, grinning. "I'll be back later."

We sat in silence for a moment after Edith left us. I gazed across at Anneka, "I want to know all about you." I picked up the teapot and poured two cups of hot tea.

"You mean above and beyond what I've told you?" She picked up her fork and tasted the potatoes.

"Yes. Were you as pretty a little girl growing up? Were you happy? Have you ever been in love?"

She laughed, "Yes, I was a cute girl, running around in the snow of Sweden, my hair in long braids, swinging as I ran. I loved to be outdoors to run and play. I had a happy childhood. Then, our parents decided to move to America. I was scared to death at the thought of coming to a place where I was a total stranger."

I found myself enjoying the meatloaf as I listened to her happy memories.

"You weren't happy to come to America?"

"Not at first. I grew to enjoy life here once I learned the language and made friends. And then…"

"Then your mother died," I helped. "That must have been a traumatic experience for a young girl."

"Yes. I loved her dearly," Anneka said, her head bowing slightly. "But Mother left me with two special prizes."

"I suppose raising your two little sisters interfered with your life."

"I honestly didn't mind. When I was younger, I didn't go out with any boys. When I grew older, my father arranged a marriage with Lars." She got quiet.

"Did you love him?" I tried to ask gently.

"No," she said abruptly. I heard the anger in her words. "Lars treated me like a hired hand around the restaurant. That's how I learned to manage the business. Lars kept me on a short leash that I constantly pulled on. I wouldn't have been able to attend school if I'd remained married to Lars."

"Now, you're free to choose your own future. I remember you telling me about your certificate in chiropractic. Have you given thought of opening an office somewhere?"

"You made me think about that," she answered, tugging at her earlobe. "I talked to our father about it. He said he would sell the restaurant to help finance my practice and open another inn for the twins."

I reached across the table to grasp her arm, "That's wonderful. I hope it works out for you."

"It's not easy for a woman to start a practice like that. Society still condemns any woman with aspirations to move into a man's world," she said, holding her head up.

"If anyone can do it, it's you, Anneka. You're a strong woman."

"What about you, Jim? Are you ready to tell me about your past life?" she asked, moving her chair around the small round table, so she was right next to me. I smelled the fragrance of perfume in her soft red hair.

I opened my heart to her. I spoke of the battles I'd fought in, how I overcame the fear of combat and the associated regrets. I also told her about Christina and the baby's death. The words seemed to flow from me quickly and easily. She listened intently as I poured out my inner feelings, my misgivings, and my dreams. All throughout, I thought I would start afresh with Anneka. But, now was not the time to tell her that.

Anneka reciprocated, divulging some of the secrets of her past life. The trust between us grew as we spoke openly. I felt the warmth of her presence.

"What are you doing here?" a gruff, unfriendly voice said.

I looked up to see Steven Jackson's surly mug peering down at me. "I might ask the same of you, Jackson. Did you follow us here?"

"Funny man," he growled. "I can go where I please. You must have been told I come here, so you and this vamp of yours are trying to catch me with something."

I pushed my chair back and stood nose to nose with

him. My eye glared at Jackson. "You've insulted someone very dear to me. You're not leaving this place until you apologize to the lady."

Jackson seldom dealt with someone his size. I saw by his expression that I intimidated him by my aggressiveness. He shuffled his feet as his eyes looked away from mine. "You ran away from me at the hotel. You ain't so much."

"My partner and I had reasons to leave, reasons that are none of your business," I told him slowly, so the buffoon understood. "Right now, I have no reason to leave. You do. Now apologize and get out of here."

Undeterred by his size and strength, I had the upper hand. There was no way he would intimidate me. Not in front of Anneka. "So, what's it gonna be, tough guy, you do the right thing, or do we go outside?"

We stood in silence, toe-to-toe. Anneka remained silent, knowing this was not the time to interfere. Finally, Jackson flinched. "I apologize, ma'am." He gave me one more snarl then walked away. I watched him as he stomped out the door.

I sat back down, a little shaken, and a little embarrassed by the whole affair. Anneka's eyes were wide with admiration. "Thank you," she said. "Who was that monster of a man?"

"Steven Jackson. He was one of Henry Spellman's partners in Africa and Alaska. Long story." I wiped my forehead with a napkin and smiled at Anneka. "He ruined our time together. I didn't want to talk about Spellman or any of those involved. I only want this time with you."

"You're sweet, Jim," she said, taking my hand, holding it tightly. "Let's make-believe he never entered the restaurant."

"Good. Tell me more about what you have planned for the future," I said. The night went on. We sat at the small round table until three in the morning, just chatting. It was the most delightful night of my life.

Chapter Twenty-Six

Markson's Visit

The next day of the investigation brought a disappointment. Using the small key Karen Bender had provided, we stopped at the bank, where the safe deposit box proved to be empty. So much for our hope of finding the diamonds there. Next, we headed for the Spellman home, where Katy prepared flapjacks for us after learning we'd not had breakfast before leaving Sumner Street. We were just finishing them when the maid showed Sergeant Jack Markson into the dining room.

Instead of the usual introductions, Oda said, "I need to clean this room next. Be quick about your business."

"Why certainly, dear lady," Garth said, bowing his head. "Would it suit you if we adjourned to the trophy room instead of staying here?"

"Suit yourselves," she responded with a shrug. "I don't get to that room until after the noon hour."

Taking our cups, we exited to the corridor. I saw that the coffee pot was almost empty and hightailed it to the kitchen to refill it while Garth and the Sergeant waited in the hallway.

Katy had cleared our breakfast dishes, and when I followed her into the kitchen, I noticed Cynthia sitting at the table, sipping coffee. This time she wore an appropriate morning dress. I stood at the kitchen door and watched her, wondering how much of her story the other day was fabricated. My visit to Anneka's place contradicted a lot of what Cynthia had told me that evening. She was obviously a liar, only God knew what else she was hiding.

She turned when she caught a whiff of my cigar smoke and said, "The Spellman sisters are up, Major. It gave me a chance to dress early," as if reading my mind. She used her seductive smile on me to seal her subterfuge. Cynthia then explained that Margaret was up and bathing. She would be going upstairs in a moment to lay out her morning outfit.

I went to the stove and found the coffee, filled the pot, and began to leave the ladies. A thought came to me. "Has Miss Margaret said anything about funeral arrangements for her brother, Cynthia?"

"Yes, the coroner just released his body for burial. Miss Margaret was livid that it took so long," Cynthia said with a crooked smile. "She wants to get the whole thing over with. Mr. David Wilkes-Hadley, the funeral director, was here yesterday and started making arrangements."

"I assume there won't be any Christian services for him," I said.

"Good guess, Major," she said as she picked at her

nails. "Mr. Spellman's feet arc sure to be dangling in lava by now—what's a service going to do for him? The funeral is scheduled for this coming Tuesday, the nineteenth."

I thought her statement was rather callous. Katy, who was listening, glanced at me and held her nose. It made me laugh as I left the kitchen.

* * *

I joined Garth and Markson in the hallway. "Sorry it took so long," I said as we headed for the trophy room at the rear of the house. We were about to pass the room Edger Spellman had used as a study when I noticed a light coming from the partially open door. "Garth," I called out. He stopped at the sound of his name.

He gave me a puzzled look and backtracked. "What is it?"

I nodded to the open door. "Isn't this door usually closed?"

Markson said, "To end all the mystery, Major, open the door all the way and see who's in there if you must."

I did so and stepped into the room. No one was there, so I took a look around.

It was decidedly a man's room. The mahogany desk in the center of the room was twice the size of mine, and appeared to me a disorganized mess. I noticed a large painting on the west wall. "Look at this, Garth," I said. "This must be a painting of Edger Spellman."

Markson joined us and agreed. "I've seen a photograph of him in his youth. This is the patriarch of the Spellman family."

"It's a huge painting," Garth observed. "He thought

very highly of himself, don't you think, gentlemen?"

"Yes," I said. "The man in the portrait seems familiar. I've seen that face before, but I can't place it." He appeared to be a domineering man with a scowling glare, muttonchops, and a receding hairline.

"I see what you mean," Garth said, standing directly in front of the portrait, rubbing his chin. "It could be one of the sisters. There are similarities." We both chuckled.

"In any case, since there's no one here," Markson said. "Let's get down to the trophy room for our little chat."

We entered the room and I closed the door behind us.

"A cup of that coffee you brought in would do me some good. It's blasted cold out there." Markson made himself comfortable in a dark blue easy chair. "I like this room," he commented as his eyes scanned the animals placed on the walls.

To the rear of the room sat several chairs with pillows; all offered a good view through the French doors to the gardens. In the spring and summer months, the landscaping would have been spectacular with the flowers and trees in full bloom. Today, it looked drab with dull, gray skies and the garden overrun with colorless plants.

I poured coffee for Markson and placed the coffee pot on the table as Markson brought up the subject on his mind. "I'm sure you remember the clue Spellman left."

"You mean, the lion's head?" I asked.

"Of course," he said, sitting tall in his chair. "Haven't you searched the head on the wall yet?" Markson was shocked that we would neglect such an obvious clue.

"We noticed it," Garth said, stretching his arms, almost in a yawn.

"Well?"

"Well, what, Sergeant?" I asked, a smirk on my face.

"Have you looked?" His brow was tightening with each vague answer we gave.

"Certainly not," Garth answered.

"Why the hell not?" Now, the policeman was getting angry. He apparently didn't believe that we were sitting ten feet away from an unmistakable hiding place and had ignored it.

"Well, sir," Garth replied, pouring another coffee for himself, "We're just pulling your leg. Of course, we did. The other night, when we arrived late, we came in and pulled the head off the wall."

"What did you find?" Markson asked, leaning forward.

"A lot of dust but nothing else," I answered him. "It appears that the clue points elsewhere."

"I see," Markson said, falling back into his chair. His face showed disappointment, but he seemed to trust our instincts. "Garth told me that you would be interviewing the staff. How did that go?"

"I understand the staff a lot better," I said, brushing cigar ash from my tan jacket. "Cynthia has a reputation for being a gossip. However, I found that Katy, in the kitchen, is a wealth of information. Her innocence blinds her to how much she reveals. She seems to know every move made by the people in the house."

We spent the next few minutes in the trophy room filling Markson in on what we'd learned from the interviews with the four staff members. He tended to agree with Garth's assumption that Cynthia was lying about everything. He put her at the top of the list of suspects and planned on talking to her once more.

There was no doubt that Joseph Polletti was as big

a cad as Henry Spellman himself. However, one cannot arrest somebody for being a lecher. Markson found it hard to believe the story about Polletti coercing Cynthia into bedding down with Spellman. He laughed at the image of Polletti crawling around the floor while the other two were playing man and wife on the bed just feet away from him.

Garth said little about what he learned on his trip to Cleveland. He did say that Lieutenant Brady used his police position to ensure access to the New York Central passenger lists and schedules for the past few weeks.

Markson finished his coffee, said he had duties elsewhere, and rose to leave.

I stopped him. "I just spoke to Cynthia in the kitchen. I asked her about the funeral services for Henry."

"The coroner just released the body," the sergeant said. "I was wondering when they planned to plant the guy."

"Crudely put, but what did she tell you?" Garth asked, grinning at Markson's comment.

"It's going to be this coming Tuesday, only four days away," I told them, stubbing out my cigar. "They should have hired a taxidermist to stuff the scoundrel and place him in this room with all his trophies."

"It would be fitting, wouldn't it, Major," Markson said, giving a bitter laugh.

"I also learned that there will be no Christian services. They plan on a simple graveside service and maybe a reception afterward," I said.

"I'll learn more once I speak to Margaret," Garth said, shaking his head. "I'll insist on them being at the reception. I want everyone there."

"How do you plan on getting all of Spellman's enemies to come?" Markson asked with a quizzical frown on his forehead.

"Simple enough," Garth said. "You and your men can round up those in Medina. Brady and the Cleveland PD can bring the people in Cleveland down here. We'll all be meeting in the Spellman dining room for a luncheon."

"Do you think Margaret will approve of this get together?" I asked.

"She'd better, if she wants the diamonds returned. I've spoken to Lieutenant Brady. He approved of the plan."

Markson brought up a new subject. "I just remembered. Since Polletti was driving Oda's car that night, I want to search it."

"Be our guests," Garth said. "We looked it over and found it had been cleaned on the inside passenger side and the rear seat of the motor car."

"Not on the driver's side?" the sergeant asked. "How odd."

"We thought so too," I added. "It's the Model-A parked behind the garage. Margaret doesn't allow her to park in the garage with her Packard."

Markson made a huffing sound, shook his head, and left by way of the rear French doors.

This left Garth and me alone in the trophy room. We both sipped at our cups of coffee, contemplating what our next step would be.

"Garth?" I said, placing my coffee cup down. "It has little bearing on the case; nonetheless, I spent the evening with Anneka Larson last night."

"You did? Well, you're right. It has little to do with the case." Garth rolled his eyes to the ceiling and added, "Thank you for telling me, friend. Is something serious coming from this encounter?"

"May very well be," I answered, smiling. "If nothing

else, Anneka has helped mend my soul. I believe I can move on."

"Well done, Major," he said, grinning like the Cheshire cat. "Now, try to concentrate on the case."

Chapter Twenty-Seven

Assault of the Black Hand

Garth and I left the trophy room, heading to the front of the house. Walking past old man Spellman's study, Garth noticed the door to the room was ajar again. He pushed it open and peered in.

"Oh, Mr. Garth," Rachel Spellman said, putting her hand to her chest. She wore the same drab dress she'd worn the previous day. She'd tied her hair back in a small, tight bun. Her appearance was entirely altered from the vivacious woman at the Medina Lounge a few nights before. She sat at the desk, an open ledger in front of her.

"I didn't know you used your father's study," Garth said. "I assumed Margaret would handle the finances for the family."

"I can see why you would come to that conclusion,"

she answered. "But, Margaret doesn't like dealing with the household budget, so she allows me that privilege."

"Then you know more about the expenses than we thought," Garth said, stepping into the room.

Besides the painting of Edger Spellman, I noticed a display of *La Vie Parisienne* magazine prints that covered the walls. I wasn't sure who had put them up. I spotted the dates—between 1916 and 1918. Edger Spellman had been gone long before that. The prints depicted some very provocative themes. I decided Margaret to be too prudish to hang such artwork, so it had to be Henry Spellman or Rachel. However, if it had been Henry, he would have hung them in his sitting room.

"Yes, Major?" Rachel said, watching me admire the artwork. "I can see your wheels turning. Who hung the artwork?"

"I was giving it some thought," I said, surprised at how well she read my thoughts.

"It's mine. The art expresses what I'm feeling. Margaret never comes in here, so she can't ruin my fantasies. The office is my way of getting away from all the others and be myself."

"It might be best to keep the door locked," I suggested. "I can only imagine your sister's reaction to the prints."

"I know, the old prude. I was just about finished balancing the books," she said, standing with a pleasant smile. She closed the ledger and locked it away in a drawer of the desk. I was surprised by her demeanor. There was no blush on her cheeks or any indication of embarrassment concerning the sleazy artwork.

Rachel walked up to Garth and took his arm, "I could use a cup of coffee about now. Won't you gentlemen join me?"

"We have work ahead of us, Rachel. I'll take a rain check on the coffee," Garth answered.

We stepped back into the corridor, but before leaving, Rachel locked the door. She again held Garth's arm as we continued to the front hallway.

"I need a word with Oda," Rachel said to Garth. "I'll only be a minute."

I glanced into the kitchen and saw Katy sitting alone, with a book in front of her. "Where did Cynthia go?" I asked.

"Miss Margaret was ready to have her hair done," Katy answered, her eyes lifted off the book.

I nodded and excused myself. My partner stood alone in the hallway. "What have we planned for the day, Garth?"

He turned around to be sure no one was listening. "I thought it would be profitable to do a little bar hopping today."

"Bar hopping?"

"We still need to cover The Lajon Bostad Inn, Major. I'd like to stop there for lunch if you're up to it?" Before I answered, someone pounded on the front door. Rachel, who had gone to the dining room to speak to Oda, followed the maid to the hallway. Rachel stopped next to Garth, giving him a seductive smile, and put her arm through his.

Oda mumbled something about Grand Central station as she reached the front door and turned the knob. Straightaway, the heavy, oak door flew open, knocking Oda from her feet, slamming her into the wall.

"Stefano Rizzo," I heard Garth murmur. He guided Rachel to stand behind him.

The dark monster of a man grabbed Oda roughly by the shoulders and shoved her into the hallway with his left hand, as he held a .45 in his right. Rizzo aimed the weapon at Garth and me.

Just then, Katy screamed from the kitchen. Apparently, the two Black Hand goons had timed their entrances perfectly. Angelo De Luca, the other brute, had lifted Katy off her feet, carrying her into the hallway. He also carried a .45 in his waistband.

"Drop the girl," Rizzo growled. "See who is upstairs and bring them down here." His black eyes glanced up the staircase. De Luca did precisely as he was told. Poor little Katy fell hard on the tiled floor. He ran up the stairs.

"Hey! There's no reason to treat her that way," I said, stepping forward.

I felt Garth's hand on my sleeve, but it was too late, "You shut up your mouth, Mr. Policeman," Rizzo said, glaring at me murderously. "You always in our way. I shoulda' run you over last night and squashed you like a bug."

"I'm not a policeman," I growled back. "What is it you want here?"

"Don't be stupid. You know what we want," the mobster said, grinning with stained teeth. "We talk to the old lady."

Looking through the kitchen, I could see to the back door. I nodded to Garth, and he looked as well. Sergeant Markson was outside, gazing in. He pointed toward the rear of the house and held up his handgun. I understood immediately what he wanted us to do.

Yelling and screaming erupted from upstairs. De Luca, holding his .45, was pushing Margaret down the stairs, one step at a time. She stubbornly clung to the banister, trying to fight him off, but his strength made that impossible.

I'd never heard such foul language coming from someone who claimed to be a lady. Margaret's face was flushed with rage as she screamed insults at the big brute.

Cynthia was little trouble for De Luca. With his left hand twisting her arm up behind her back, she stumbled down the stairs. At the bottom, De Luca shoved Margaret into the foyer and pushed Cynthia to the floor.

"We got a warm, soft one here," De Luca said, nodding at the shaking girl at his feet.

Cynthia crawled away from him on all fours and ran to me. She began to sob into my chest. I felt her whole body shuddering.

To De Luca's lewd remark, Rizzo said, "We're not here for that. Keep your paws to yourself." He glared down at Margaret, gasping for air, sitting on the bottom step of the staircase. "We're here for the stones."

De Luca stepped forward, waving his .45 wildly toward all of us. "I wanna you all stand at the wall," he said. "You move without being tol', I shoot you."

We all complied. Rachel clasped Garth's arm; Cynthia clung to me. De Luca held the gun on us, enjoying the ladies' fear.

Rizzo concentrated on Margaret. He leaned over her, glaring down with icy black eyes. "You know where the diamonds are."

"I-I- don't," she stammered.

"You no lie to me!" he yelled, yanking her hair so he could see her face.

For the first time since my arrival at the mansion, I saw fear in her eyes. Margaret's arrogant stare crumpled as a pool of tears welled up in her eyes, ready to overflow. Rizzo held tightly to a handful of her hair, twisting it tightly.

Margaret screamed from the pain, fear contorting her face.

"You lie, lady! I know. Someone tell me you had them." Rizzo released her hair and slapped her viciously across the face.

Tears streamed down her red cheeks. She held her hand up, expecting another blow. I caught sight of Oda, staring at De Luca. There was no room in her hate-filled eyes for fear. Next to her, Katy trembled but kept her composure. Her eyes darted around the hallway, searching for a way out.

Rachel stood on the other side of Garth, clinging to his hand and quaking with fear. Her eyes were wide as she chewed her lower lip. If Rizzo failed to get what he wanted from Margaret, Rachel would be the next target of his wrath.

Rizzo shouted at Margaret, "We not stupid! You tell us where the diamonds are, or we kill someone."

"Please—I don't know," she pleaded. Her once-domineering voice shook uncontrollably. "I hired these two men to find the diamonds," she pointed her trembling finger at us. "If they had found them, they wouldn't be here any longer." Margaret tried to reason with Rizzo, but the only answer he gave was another hard slap.

De Luca blurted, "Those two policemen are here to find the killer of your brother. They no here for the diamonds. Now you tell me, or I kill someone."

Rizzo looked at De Luca and snapped his fingers. The smirking big man glared at the six of us, reached out, and grabbed Katy by the arm, pulling her away from the wall. "We start with the pretty little one," he sneered.

I instinctively moved forward again. This time, I shouted, "You don't need to do that."

De Luca shoved Katy away and came at me, his semi-automatic weapon slashing across my head. "How many times I need to say shut up?"

The gun struck my temple, sending searing pain through my skull. For a second, I feared I would black out, but I struggled to stay on my feet.

"Maybe we make *you* first one to die," he sneered, aiming his gun at my forehead.

"No, don't," Cynthia called out.

Rizzo turned to De Luca, "Stop playin' with them. Bring the little one over here."

Katy tried to pull away, but De Luca's strength was too much for her. He shoved her, whimpering with fear, to Rizzo's feet.

"You no want me to carve the pretty little girl up, do you?" Rizzo said, pulling a stiletto knife from his pocket, flipping the blade out with his thumb.

"No, but …" Margaret stuttered.

"She's telling the truth, Rizzo," Garth said.

"Why you say that?"

"You don't need to hurt anyone," Garth said. "I may know where the diamonds are."

"Why you not say so?" Rizzo asked with a crooked grin.

"No one asked me," Garth said, offering his cheeky smile.

If Garth was trying to charm these two psychos, he had a tough job ahead of him.

"The diamonds are just down the hallway, in the trophy room, gentlemen," he said with a soothing tone, hoping to keep the Italians calm.

"Get up," Rizzo yelled at Margaret, whose tears

continued to stream down her cheeks, making tracks through the face powder Cynthia had recently applied. He glared at Garth. "Diamonds better be there."

Garth, with Rachel still clinging to his arm, led the way down the corridor. De Luca forced the rest of us to follow, holding Katy by her arm, keeping his .45 aimed at our backs. I kept my eye on Garth, up at the front, waiting for a signal. Yet, none came. He seemed to be encumbered by Rachel, but he was too much the gentleman to shrug her off.

He was taking a big chance. We both knew the diamonds weren't stashed in the hollow of the lion's head. What if we miscalculated what Markson had in mind? I prayed the sergeant was ready to help.

In the trophy room, DeLuca pushed us against the wall facing the French doors to the garden. Rizzo glowered around the room. He turned to Garth and demanded, "Okay, Mr. Policeman, where are my diamonds?"

"You're standing in front of them," Garth answered calmly.

Rizzo saw the lion's head on the wall. "Ah. Mr. Policeman, you take the head down."

My gaze went to the doors. Sergeant Markson was crouched behind an evergreen. The French doors were open a crack. Markson was watching us, holding a long-barreled revolver. I caught his attention and tilted my head toward Rizzo. He nodded back. De Luca was rubbing the barrel of his .45 against Katy's cheek, smiling as she shivered and tears ran down her face. I focused on Markson again, signaling my message. He nodded, understanding.

"It should be rather easy to pry these screws from the board holding the head to the wall," Garth was saying to

Rizzo. "May I borrow your knife for a moment?"

"I no give you my stiletto," Rizzo said, almost laughing.

"Never mind then, I have something that'll do the trick," Garth said with a sigh. He reached into his pocket, bringing out a tool with a folding screwdriver head, and went to work on the screws. I noticed he was taking his time with them.

Rizzo became impatient and called to his partner, "Give me the girl."

De Luca yanked Katy toward Rizzo.

"Hurry it up or I give the pretty girl a bloody necklace." Rizzo placed his stiletto dangerously close to Katy's throat.

Her eyes bulged with fear. "Please, don't hurt me," she pleaded.

I felt anger boil inside me, but I had to trust the plan. Markson rose, taking aim through the glass door at Rizzo. Garth looked at me then let the lion's head hit the floor. He yelled, "Now!"

Markson's bullet ripped into the back of Rizzo's head. The stiletto dropped as Rizzo crumpled to the floor.

De Luca froze for a split second then turned his gun on Garth.

I was faster. In one motion, I shoved Cynthia and Oda aside, reached under my jacket, and drew my Colt. I pulled the trigger and saw De Luca stagger back. Blood spilled out onto his jacket. He looked at me in utter surprise and tried to lift his weapon. But, my second bullet went straight into his heart. He was dead before he hit the floor.

Markson swung open the broken door and rushed in. The deathly silence in the room erupted into mayhem as the hostages realized it was over.

Katy broke down in sobs and Oda went to comfort her.

Rachel hugged them both. I knew better than to interfere, mainly because I wouldn't know what to say. I'd spoken to soldiers after the heat of battle, but this was different.

Margaret was staring off into space, unable to process what had happened.

What really surprised me was Cynthia's reaction. She stood over the two dead men, cursing them and kicking their bodies. "How dare you invade our home and threaten us? You stupid Wops! You filthy pigs, you can't–" She stopped when I grabbed her arm and pulled her away.

The anger drained from her instantly. "At least we have the killers of poor Henry."

"We'll see, I said. She clasped my arm. "Please take me out of here, James."

Markson would handle the aftermath. I put my arm around Cynthia's waist, leading her toward the hallway. "Ladies," I called to Oda and Katie, "you don't need to stay in this room. Please come with us." I held out my free hand, and the two of them ran to me.

Garth was ahead of us as he escorted Rachel to her father's study, her place of refuge. He left her there and returned to the trophy room.

I escorted Cynthia, Oda, and Katy down the hallway, telling Garth I would take them to the parlor. Settling them on the settee, I poured each a glass of whiskey. Even young Katy needed a shot of fortification. The three women were comforting each other as I walked out.

I rejoined Garth at the staircase and saw that Markson had just hung up the telephone under the staircase.

"I called the office and arranged to clean this up," he said. "There'll be an investigation, Mr. Garth, but we did the right thing. They would have started killing the women."

"Where did you learn to shoot like that, Markson?" I asked. "That was one hell of a shot."

"I had taken some firearm instructions," he answered quietly. "I just got lucky, I suppose. Thank you both for backing me up. What about the diamonds?"

"We knew they weren't in the lion's head," I answered. "We still have to find them."

I noticed Margaret, staring into a wall mirror. She was patting her face with a handkerchief and seemed to be more composed. "Miss Spellman, are you all right?" I asked.

"I will be, Major. I need a cup of something to drink. I'll send for Cynthia." Margaret turned to face me. "What made you think the diamonds were in the stuffed lion's head?"

"This is still an open case," I answered. "The evidence needs to be guarded."

"But, these two hooligans are Henry's killers, right?"

Garth stepped up to answer for me. "I don't believe they are. There are too many unanswered questions. Indulge us a little longer. I want to get to the bottom of this as much as you do."

Chapter Twenty-Eight

The Lajon Bostad Inn

The drive to The Lajon Bostad Inn had become familiar to me. I'd been there twice before; this time I brought Garth with me. Plus, I eagerly anticipated another visit with Anneka and unwinding after this afternoon's dramatic showdown. I drove my Hudson into the parking lot and left the motor running. Turning to Garth, I asked, "What's the plan?"

"Similar to the other establishments we've been to," he answered. "You've been here before, so go in first. Find your new friend, Anneka, see what additional information she may have. I'll follow and talk to some of the patrons."

"That shouldn't be a problem," I said. "I'll go through the back door; it's closer to the bar. We can share information later."

"Good thinking. Get a move on."

The evening wasn't as cold as the past few. Garth enjoyed wearing the finest of evening wear. Tonight, he slipped on a three-piece, dark gray striped suit. He had recently bought a pair of two-toned shoes and a walking stick. His black homburg completed the outfit. I felt underdressed in my tan tweed jacket and a matching cap. Well, that was his way, and he looked perfectly dapper.

I turned off the ignition and stepped out into the darkness. I threw my overcoat on the back seat, turning to Garth as he walked around the front of the Hudson. "Do you think he left the diamonds here at the club?" I asked.

"They weren't in the stuffed head in Spellman's trophy room," he answered. "The clue has to mean something. It might be pointing here," Garth said, nodding at the inn.

I circled the inn, glancing up into the starry sky above Lake Chippewa, and breathed in the fresh, clear air. It reminded me of my stay in Wyoming at the beginning of the century. The bright lights streaming from inside the lounge, reflecting off the lake, added to the beauty. To my left, on the lakeshore, sat a rustic cabin. A light flickered through the windows. I assumed Anneka's father was sitting in the warmth of his fireplace.

I walked in, taking a quiet corridor toward the front. It passed the staircase to the upstairs. Glancing around, my gaze landed on the cuckoo clocks and prints of winter-themed artwork covering the walls around the restaurant. On the north wall sat the massive fireplace where Anneka and I sat a few days ago, the first night we met. At the time, it held a warm, crackling fire. Tonight, the flames were low; the embers gave little light. Two young couples sat in its glow. I took a seat at the bar and admired the exposed beams above me. They made the room appear larger, more welcoming, and, with the dark furniture, cozy.

I removed my jacket and cap and settled into my seat. Anneka's sisters and several other waitresses in brown and white dirndls were bustling about, chatting and laughing with the guests.

"What'll it be, big guy?" Anneka greeted me from behind the bar. What a gorgeous woman, I thought. Her strawberry blonde hair hung freely to her shoulders tonight instead of being up in a braid.

"Did you want a Stroh's?" She looked into my eyes and whispered, "I missed you."

"Me too," I said in a low tone. Then louder, for the other patrons' benefit, "Yup, a Stroh's will do. One for you too."

A few moments later, she was back with two beers. "How's the case going? Have you caught the killer yet?"

I glanced around to be sure no one was listening. "Not yet. It seems to take more than a few days to figure these things out. I'm learning it's just like a military campaign. You've got to collect all the facts before you go over the top with a decision. Margaret believes the killers were the thugs who accosted us this morning. Garth and I think otherwise."

"What do you mean? Who accosted you?" she asked.

"Oh, I'm sorry. The news hasn't traveled very fast." I explained what had happened. Anneka's mouth dropped open, and her hand covered it as I gave her the gory details.

"Good Lord, Jim. Please be careful, I don't want to … never mind. Just be careful." She took a deep breath and leaned toward me. "I was thinking about the women at the Spellman place. Whenever Rachel comes in, she's the life of the party. She can drink you under the table," Anneka said, her smile returning. "Cynthia calls Rachel a dead-head because of the way she acts around Margaret. She knows nothing about Rachel's social life. Rachel's such a good actress. She has everyone in the Spellman household fooled, including her sister."

"You talk to both Cynthia and Rachel?"

"Not together—the two of them never come in on the same day, Anneka said. "I have a way of getting people to talk. I learned that talent while my patients were on the table. It's part of being a chiropractor."

"Why don't they ever come in together? Does Rachel think Cynthia is beneath her?"

"I don't think it's that. After all, Rachel comes in with that Italian gardener, so she doesn't mind socializing with the help. There's a chance Rachel is jealous of Cynthia."

"You mean Polletti?"

"That's him. He comes in here on Tuesdays with Cynthia hanging all over him. So, it may be Polletti who decided where they go in the evenings."

"Judging by what I've told you and what you've seen, would you consider Rachel as being a part of the plot to kill Henry?" I asked.

"I don't know—maybe." Anneka shrugged her creamy shoulders.

"It would move Rachel one step closer to an inheritance," I conceded.

"Your partner seems to be working the case as well," Anneka said, nodding toward the restaurant.

"How do you know that?"

"I can spot an outsider easily. Your partner is at one of the tables hobnobbing with Gerda."

I looked out into the crowd and saw Garth at a table with a couple of gents, talking to one of Anneka's sisters. "You recognized him? From where?"

"From the Rogers' house. Even if I hadn't seen him before, I put two and two together and inferred that he was Sherwood Garth, your partner," Anneka said, a grin on her face. "He's a stranger to my place, yet he's chatting everyone up as if he were an old friend."

"Garth would be impressed by your deductive reasoning," I said, lighting one of my cigars. "What is it you deduce from my visit?" I asked.

"I deduce that you are deceiving me."

"Oh? In what way is that?"

"You told me you're here on official business," she said, her voice low. "Yet, you are wearing a wonderful cologne, and you've trimmed your mustache and beard. I think you're here to get closer to a lady who finds you adorable."

I retorted with a wink, "Go get that man, whom you adore, another beer before the scent wears off, my dear." If she were on my side of the bar, I would have reached out to touch her.

After her return, I said, "I need to know about Henry Spellman. Did he come in here often?"

"Oh, yes. Greta always waited on them," she answered, placing another frothy mug in front of me. "Let me bring her over here."

Greta was the mirror image of the sister who was flirting with Garth. She seemed to have a thoughtful, astute gleam in her eyes when I asked how well she knew Spellman.

She glanced around to be sure she wasn't overheard. "I don't like talking about my customers. But since it's you asking … Anneka told Gerda and me all about your detective work, Major Mallory." She smiled toward Anneka. "As to Spellman, before he left for Africa, he and Karen Bender would come in maybe two or three times a week. Lately, more like once a week. Henry always asked for my table." She blushed slightly.

"He flirted with you?"

"One could say that. Even when they left me proper tips, I didn't bite, I'm no floozy. Once they understood that, we became friends. They told me they liked to get away from the big city places."

"Hold on, Greta," Anneka said. "I've got customers down the bar. I'll be back in a minute." She scurried off to do her duty.

"They also spoke of leaving town, never returning," Greta went on, although her sister Anneka requested she wait. "They would be going to Chicago; from there, they would disappear. Oh, did Gerda tell Anneka about the box they left with her?"

"A box?" I digested the revelation for a moment. Garth should hear about this.

I left the bar and interrupted his dinner conversation, practically dragging him with me to the bar. Greta, meanwhile, fetched her twin.

"Gerda, what's this about a box?" I asked.

She looked toward her older sister. "I almost forgot to tell you, Anneka. Henry asked me to hide something for him. Now that he's dead and these two detectives are here, it would be a good time to bring it out."

"What are you talking about?" Anneka said, pressing her lips together. "Bring what out?"

"Go to the register and push down on the 'no sale'

key," Gerda instructed.

Anneka's eyes held a quizzical gleam but followed her sister's directions.

"Now, reach into the rear of the drawer, and you'll find a small flat box," Gerda said.

I saw her eyes widen as she pulled out a small wooden box that had been out of sight. It was about ten inches long and three inches wide and quite flat, just two inches in height, with tape wrapped around it. "What in the world …"

"I'm sorry I didn't tell you earlier, but I forgot." She glanced down at her feet. "Henry Spellman left it here the afternoon he was murdered. He came in alone for lunch. He had a club sandwich and a bowl of chicken soup. He didn't even finish the sand—"

"Let's get to the box, Gerda," my partner said, touching her hand softly.

"Oh, that's right, the box. Yes, when Henry paid the bill, he handed it to me. He said not to open it. He asked me to keep it in a safe place and to give it to no one 'cept Karen Fender, I think it was."

Anneka shook her head, "Gerda, Gerda, Gerda, what am I going to do with you?" Anneka handed the box to Garth, then turned to Gerda. "That's Bender, you nit."

"It looks like Greta is falling behind," Gerda said. "I have customers to take care of." She scurried off but turned to give Garth a wink.

"If that's evidence, I'll leave you two alone to discuss it." She leaned over the bar and said, "Let me know if you need anything, Jim." Her voice fluttering so close I felt her warm breath on my ear.

"Anything?"

I let out a sigh as she walked away. Garth and I huddled over the box. He pulled the tape from it and lifted the lid. The first thing I noticed was a note. Garth unfolded it and read:

"*My dearest Karen,*

If anything should happen to me, take these to a man named Dr. Zachery Hareborn at the Chicago History Museum. Don't take anything less than $70,000. They are worth twice that on the open market. Then leave Chicago, go to any place you want. But not Cleveland or anywhere nearby. It's too dangerous. Use the assumed names we talked about. Be safe, be happy, I love you, Henry."

Garth opened the box, and we saw the answer. "I thought so. Let us say goodbye to the ladies and be off. This is the answer to all our questions."

Chapter Twenty-Nine

Another Attack

With a plan in place to see Anneka again Monday afternoon, I returned with Garth to the Spellman residence. Everything was quiet and dark as we climbed the staircase. I assumed Margaret and young Katy had tucked away in bed for the night. However, it would be highly speculative as to whether Rachel was home and what of Cynthia? The only way to be sure was by knocking on their doors, and I wasn't about to do that.

Garth suggested that we talk about the case as we headed for the library. He threw his overcoat and hat across a chair and sat behind the desk. "I'm staying up, Major. I think I've got this thing solved." He opened the box he had pulled from his pocket and revealed the items within, eight nickel-colored metal disks. "These certainly answer the question about the message in blood."

"Coins? Henry clearly had us guessing." I stood leaning on the doorjamb, still wearing my overcoat. "But, about that message in blood, how do you interpret that?"

"What do you mean?" Garth looked up from the items, his eyes gleaming with curiosity.

"I believe Spellman expected Karen Bender to meet him at the barn. So, he left the message for her. She was the only one who would have understood the meaning. He certainly didn't leave it for the police."

"Good point, it may have been a pre-arranged password only she would understand. If that's the case, she knew about the contents of the box all along," Garth said.

"And, didn't tell us about them at The Sparrow Club," I said. "That half-shot woman lied to us. We need to talk to her in the morning. I want to find out why she didn't tell us about the code."

"More than likely because of the Black Hand pursuing her," Garth said. "Then we put her in custody at the Sumner Street house where Fred and Liz stuck to her like glue."

"Until the two thugs were killed," I said, stroking my goatee. "*We* know they didn't kill Spellman, but Karen doesn't know. I called Fred and told him that the thugs were dead. He probably passed it on to her. She may think the investigation is over."

"We'll have to call and warn them that it's not over." He placed the lid back on the box and turned back to a list he'd started. "By eliminating those who could not have done it, our list of murder suspects dwindles."

"Contrary to what Margaret believes, the Black Hand thugs are off the list. I alibi Jackson, and Longfellow and

Allen Douglas alibi each other," I said.

"Remember, it took two to kill Spellman, Major. And, those two gentlemen both have strong motives."

"Yes, revenge on Longfellow's part, and greed on Douglas'. What about … oh, I'm getting a headache. Look at the time Garth, it's after midnight. I'm tuckered out and need to bunk down."

Garth squinted at me. "You indeed need a lot of sleep, Major. Goodnight. By the way, when are you getting together with Anneka?"

"As soon as the case is closed and we know that she had no part in it," I lied, and left the room, wanting to prevent any disharmony between us. But then I was flooded with guilt. Still, we should have this solved by Monday, so I hadn't really lied, right?

As I walked past the telephone under the staircase, it began to ring. Who on earth would be calling at this time of night? I was the only one besides Garth up at that hour, so I answered it. "Spellman residence."

"Is that you, Major?"

"Yes, Fred, what's going on?"

"Thank God. I've been trying to reach you all night. No one was answering the phone." His voice was shaky; I sensed something was wrong.

Garth walked up behind me as I asked Fred, "What is it?"

"Miss Bender is gone, sir."

"Where did she go?"

"I'm not sure. She told Liz she needed to go to the grocer for something and said she would be right back. She borrowed my model-A and left."

"How long ago?"

"It's been almost four hours. I assumed Karen may have gone to The Sparrow Club. I called Augie and he hasn't seen her," Fred continued. "I tried her apartment telephone and it rang with no answer. I then called the telephone operator, who said it was off the hook. Liz and I were terribly worried. We are responsible for her safety. We thought after the two Black Hand members were dead, she'd be safe. Could you …?"

"Garth and I will check into it. We'll let you know what we find." I hung the receiver on the cradle and turned to Garth. "Karen's missing."

"Call Brady and tell him what you know. Tell him to meet us at Miss Bender's apartment. You have the address, right?"

"Yes, I'm right on it."

"I'll get my overcoat," Garth said, trotting down the hallway. "I'll meet you at the Hudson."

Within minutes we were bundled up in my auto and heading north. Karen lived on the west side of Cleveland, in an apartment building off Clark Avenue. "We'll swing around the downtown roads of the city. It'll get us there faster," I said, as we traveled at an unsafe speed. As far as we knew, she could be hurt, or worse.

"Did you get Brady?" Garth asked.

"Yes, he was not very happy about being awakened at one in the morning."

"That's the life of a police detective," Garth said, dryly. "That was foolish of Fred and Liz to let her go out alone. He at least should have taken her to the grocer."

"They're not the police, Garth. They have little experience in police work. Everyone assumed the Black Hand thugs were the killers, so Fred and Liz thought the danger was over and let their guard down."

He glanced at me as I gripped the steering wheel and guided the car around a few curves in the road. "I'm sorry, you're right. They didn't know the game I was playing to draw out the real killers. But take heart— she may not be in any danger whatsoever."

Garth gripped the dashboard and peered out onto the dark road ahead of us. On the country road, without street lamps, the night fell over us like a black fog.

Finally, we reached a paved road again and both of us sighed with relief as street lamps appeared. I slowed down and peered out, but there were few street signs. The city could only afford to put them on the busier roads. However, I remembered Karen's description of her apartment building.

"Ah, there it is, Garth," I said, pointing to the left side of the road. "Twenty-Third Street." The night closed in on us as we cautiously turned down a narrow, unlit alley and pulled up at the rear of the run-down building. I saw the lights of Brady's car pulling up behind us.

"Where have you been?" Garth asked Brady.

"I have to get dressed, don't I?" he answered, his voice like gravel. "I had to pick up Cecil, the beat cop, on the way. We may need him." He nodded to the big, brawny, colored man in blue who stepped from the passenger side of the patrol car. "I hope he isn't necessary, Mr. Garth."

"I hope so too. It may be a wild-goose chase," Garth said. "Karen Bender thinks she's safe because the two Black Hand members are dead."

"And, she's not?"

"Not at all. The Black Hand thugs didn't kill Spellman. We know that by the train schedule."

The four of us knew that the Black Hand members were passing through Pittsburgh on a train at the time Spellman was being murdered. Garth, Brady, Markson, and I had kept that information to ourselves. I wondered now if that was wise.

We walked through the entrance of the apartment building to the mailboxes. Hers was number 281. "The second floor, let's move it." I led the way up the wide staircase to the second floor with my Colt gripped tightly in my hand.

Charging down the hallway, we reached apartment 281. The door was partially ajar. Brady grabbed me by the arm and pulled me back. "This is police business, Major. Stand aside." He nudged the door open and called in, "Police! Is somebody in the apartment?"

At first, all was silent. Time seemed to stand still as we strained our ears. Then a whimper, which expanded to a sorrowful cry, and then the voice of Karen calling, "Help me. Please, help me."

Brady led us into the dingy, untidy apartment. I followed him with Garth and Cecil trailing us. We found Karen lying on a couch, her clothes torn, blood smeared down her arms and chest. "He just ran out the back," she stammered. "There's a back staircase from the kitchen to the alley," she whispered. "I think he went down there."

"See what you can do for her, Major," Brady said. He dashed into the kitchen with Garth following him.

I holstered my Colt and knelt beside Karen. There were stab wounds in several places about her torso, but most were superficial. I turned to Cecil. "Call for an ambulance." He grabbed the telephone on the side table; evidently, there was no service. He dropped the instrument and ran from the room.

I found towels in the kitchen and scurried back to her. Fear glowed in her eyes. Her lips trembled as I pressed the towel to the most severe wound. "You'll be all right, my dear girl. I've seen wounds like this in combat. They're painful but will eventually heal. Don't worry, an ambulance is on the way."

"Am I really going to be all right?"

"Steady on there, girl." I tenderly ran my free hand over her forehead. "I'm an officer and a gentleman. Would I lie to you?"

She flinched in pain as I compressed the towel, but I could tell she trusted me. Tears ran down her cheeks into her tangled hair. "It looked like that Italian who works at the Spellman place. He's a little coward. He was shaking more than I was and crying as he slashed at me."

"Major," Garth called, running back into the room. "We've got our man on the run. I need you."

"I can't leave her for God's sake. This wound is bleeding."

"I'll take care of her," Cecil, the beat cop, said, "I've helped others in Europe during the war. The ambulance will be here in minutes."

"Go, James, I'll be fine. Get that coward for me," Karen said, her lips quivering.

She would be fine. I left Cecil to take over and went with Garth. "Which way?"

"Down in the alley. Brady has him cornered," Garth said, moving down the back steps, with me close behind. We barged through the wooden door into the alley. It was black as pitch.

"Brady! Brady, where are you?" Garth called. No answer. I saw my Hudson, a few feet away. I tapped Garth on the shoulder and nodded to the auto. We ran to it, I jumped behind the wheel as he turned the crank. The auto sputtered to a roar.

We were halted by a bright beam of light from Brady's flashlight. "Over here! He's started an auto and is moving toward the back gate. After him!" He ran to his police car and followed us.

I maneuvered around crates, barrels, and trashcans until we found an open gate leading to another street. We drove through the gate and saw an old model Locomobile speeding onto Twenty-First Street. Its top was down, and I saw the back of Joseph Polletti's dark head.

"We can catch him in my Hudson," I yelled. Brady was already on our tail in his squad car. Our adrenaline pumped full force as we took off after Polletti. In the distance, the siren of the ambulance wailed as we jumped on the trail of our quarry.

I seemed to know the city streets better than Polletti, for we caught up with him as he swerved from the road into an alley and back out again. The Locomobile was not made for racing and Polletti was unsure of himself behind the wheel. He drove through the inky black alleys as fast as the auto would allow with Garth and me, and Brady, locked on his tail, keeping him in sight.

The Hudson took corners on two wheels, beautifully. Forty miles per hour was dangerous, but I didn't care. I wanted that Italian in my grips for what he'd done to Karen.

Gears ground noisily. Polletti spun around to see us closing in, swerving off the road, into front yards, barely staying in control. Brady drove well, staying right with me on the hard packed, icy road. A frigid wind blew through the windows.

The Locomobile sharply turned onto a narrow side road, skidding sideways on a patch of ice in the dark. Polletti frantically wrenched his steering wheel. It was too late. With a crash of metal and glass, the Locomobile landed against the solid trunk of a large oak.

I violently geared down and put all my weight on the brake. Garth and I lurched in our seats, inches from hitting the windshield.

Brady managed to miss us by inches. He jumped from his vehicle and ran toward the ruined Locomobile and the victimized oak tree. Garth and I were right behind him.

Polletti slumped over the steering wheel, blood streaming from his head, nose, and mouth. Miraculously, he still breathed. He was shaking intensely, his hands curled into fists.

Garth pulled him back into the seat and shouted, "Why? Why, man, would you attack Miss Bender?"

"She made me do it." Polletti's voice trembled, the words almost inaudible. He gave a hideous gasp and clutched his chest. His eyes rolled back as he collapsed across the passenger seat.

Lieutenant Brady rushed over and pulled him up, but it was too late. He felt for a pulse and found none. Polletti was dead.

I leaned over the crumpled mass that used to be Joseph Polletti and tried to feel sorry for him, but I couldn't. It's not for me to judge, but it seemed he received his just rewards.

"She made me do it?" I said out loud. "What do you think he meant?"

Brady and Garth both shook their heads in silence. Then Garth spoke, "Can we keep this to ourselves?"

"You mean the attack on Bender, the chase, or his death?" Brady asked.

"We probably can't keep the press from Karen's assault, since she is, at this moment, at the hospital. I'm just saying … in New York City, the police covered up certain things. Temporarily, that is."

"Yes, of course," Brady said, pulling his black cap snugly on his bald head. "We'll call for the wagon and take his body to the morgue as a John Doe. Do you think there's someone else involved, besides this man?"

"As he said," Garth responded, his jaw tight. "*She* made me do it."

Chapter Thirty

A Visit to the Hospital

The motorcar accident and death of Joseph Polletti had occurred in the early morning hours of Saturday. Garth and I spent Sunday in different ways. He locked himself away in the trophy room, sitting at the French door, staring out at the cold world beyond the frosted windows. He insisted he needed to think things through on his own, without interruption.

I obliged his request and gave some thought to attending church services. I changed my mind when I realized that I knew of no sanctuaries in Medina. Chuckling to myself, the irony came to me—I knew all the bars in town, but no churches.

My date with Anneka wasn't until tomorrow, so I decided to go for a short drive around town. I had returned to the kitchen for my coat when I heard the doorbell chime. In a few minutes, Oda came into the kitchen and told me, in her less than charming way, "You have a visitor."

"Who might that be?" I asked, thinking of Markson or Brady.

"See for yourself," she answered.

I brushed off my compulsion to address her rudeness and walked past her into the front foyer. Standing there in the long green overcoat I'd seen her wearing at the Rogers' home, was Anneka Larsson. This time she wore a wide-brimmed, white hat with green feathers protruding from the brim. Green was an excellent color for her, bringing out the soft red hues of her long, wavy hair.

"What a pleasant surprise," I said as I reached out for her hands. "What brings you out on this cold day?"

"Well, you brought me out, Jim," she said, her cheeks pink from the cold. "I heard about what happened last night. I'll admit, I feared the worst. Are you all right?"

"I'm more than all right, now that you're here," I responded. "I was about to go for a drive. Now we can go into the city."

"Yes, we can," she beamed. "Get your coat, and we'll be off."

We walked out the front door, arm in arm, and found Anneka's Model-N Hupmobile parked behind my auto. Her one-seat auto with the canvas top would be dandy for a summer drive. It was far from suitable for a winter road trip. I escorted her to my Hudson and opened the passenger door for her. "You'll be far more comfortable in my auto. It's a bit warmer."

She glanced at the small Hupmobile and said, "You're probably right, Jim. I hope my father doesn't notice it's missing from the parking lot."

"I'll cover for you, my dear. I'll tell him we're on official business." I drove away from the curb and turned toward the route to Cleveland.

"A penny for your thoughts, Jim," Anneka said, noticing the deep frown on my face.

"I was thinking about the poor girl who was stabbed last night."

"You mean Karen Bender, Spellman's girl?"

"Yes. She was caught up in a web of deceit and violence that I don't believe she understood. I blame myself for her predicament."

"Why on earth do you blame yourself? You barely knew the girl," Anneka asked, her eyes wide, her mouth slightly parted.

"No, as a matter of fact, I knew her from years past," I said, glancing at Anneka. "A few years after my wife passed away, I met her at a cocktail party at my brother's home. I was a widowed soldier at the time, and my family thought me ready to remarry. They were wrong. Karen was a beautiful debutante who became infatuated with me. Because I was still in grief over the loss of my wife and child, I gave her no thought."

"That's understandable," Anneka said, reaching over to touch my arm. "I'm sure, if she was that lovely, there were other men who would have taken your place."

"That's what I thought. I went back to Washington and returned to my duties. I gave her no second thought," I went on. "Unbeknownst to me, she retained a longing for me." I sighed, visualizing poor Karen in her hospital bed.

"She fell into the lifestyle of a merry femme fatale. That's what the papers are saying about her." Anneka shook her head. "You're not responsible for the life she adopted."

"Logically, I know you're right. But, I still feel damned guilty. If only ..."

"You can't change the past, you big lunk. Nor should you sulk about it," she said, almost scolding me. I saw her face mellow into a smile. "You're such a soft-hearted man, Jim. That's what makes me care for you so much."

I smiled broadly at her confession of feelings for me. I reached over and took her gloved hand and kissed it.

"You still need a haircut, though," she said, laughing sweetly. "If you'd like to, we might visit her in the hospital." Her offer surprised me.

"You wouldn't mind?"

"Of course not. If visiting Miss Bender clears up your feelings of guilt, let's do it. We have the time and she should be able to have visitors. That's the least we can do." Anneka was proving to be more than a beautiful woman. We headed for Cleveland's west side.

* * *

St. John's Hospital had sat on Detroit Avenue since 1880 and was managed by Catholic nuns. Within an hour, we were walking through the doors of the hospital. It was deathly quiet in the front hallway. I removed my cap and brushed my bushy hair back. We must have appeared lost as we scanned the halls.

A sister of the Saint Francis Order approached us. She was an elderly woman wearing a floor-length black habit. She knew about Karen being admitted last night and offered to escort us to her room.

We walked silently down the hall to Karen's room and were met by a Nurse Hillary.

Karen appeared to be asleep, her eyes closed, her breathing shallow. She was covered by a white sheet, which failed to cover the bandages on her wounds well. I glanced back at Hillary and asked, "How is she doing?"

"Quite well, actually. The majority of the wounds were minor." Nurse Hillary looked over at the bed and sighed. "There were two that punctured her lung. Those will take time to heal. However, the doctor is confident that she'll rehabilitate to full health."

"I'm glad he thinks so," Karen said from her bed, her voice low and crackling. "I feel like I've been run over by a horse and carriage."

"You're awake?" I asked. "I hope we're not disturbing you."

"Not at all," she said, trying to sit up.

"Now, you stay down," Hillary demanded. "You're not ready to sit up yet."

"But, the Major's here. He's the hero who saved my life."

"For goodness sake, Karen. Cecil and I kept you alive until the ambulance came," I said, walking up to the bed. I gazed at her and said, "You're still lovely even with all the bandages and lack of rouge on your cheeks and lips."

Karen looked at the nurse and managed a smile. "See why he's my hero? He saves my life and then lies to me."

Nurse Hillary rearranged Karen's sheet. "I'll leave you three alone. Call me if you need anything." She gave me a smile and scurried from the room.

"And, who is this you brought with you?" Karen asked.

"I'm sorry. I nearly forgot," I said.

"The big oaf would forget his own name," Anneka said with a wink at me. "I'm Anneka Larsson. You may remember me as the barmaid at Lajon Bostad."

"Oh, yes," Karen's eyes widened in recognition. "Of course, I remember you. You and your sisters. Did you bring me a beer?" she asked with a slim smile.

"I tried, but your nurse Hillary took it and is drinking it right now," Anneka joked.

"How do you know one another?" Karen asked.

"I was investigating all these crimes," I said. "Anneka attracted my attention. But, we're here to check on you. The nurse says you're getting better."

"Yes, I am, James. I'm feeling quite chipper," she said. "Except it hurts when I breathe."

"Well, I won't suggest you stop breathing. But try not to run in the Boston Marathon." We all laughed. Regrettably, Karen winced in pain.

"No more jokes, Jim," Anneka said.

I remembered what Garth intended to ask her. "Karen, why didn't you tell us about the prearranged code words you and Henry had for each other?"

Karen glared at me oddly, her left eye squinting. "What code words? I don't know what you mean."

"When we found Henry's body in the barn, he had written 'Lion's Head' on the floor," I explained. "He was expecting you to visit him, so Garth and I thought it was a prearranged message for you."

"No, I know nothing about a code word, James. We planned on going to The Lajon Bostad before leaving town. I don't know why he would leave that message."

"Don't worry about it, dear girl. It means nothing."

She nodded and said, "I heard that you and Mr. Garth apprehended the man who attacked me."

I wasn't sure if I should keep the truth from her about Polletti's death. So I said, "He won't bother you or anyone else for a long time."

"Good. Who is the creep?"

"Joseph Polletti, the Spellman's chauffeur, and gardener," I said, my eye narrowed. "Don't you remember him talking to the Black Hand killers?"

She forced a smile and lay ominously still. "You mean at Trivoli's restaurant?"

"Yes, of course. You said that you saw Polletti…"

"No, James. The man who tried to kill me *wasn't* the same as the man I saw at Trivoli's. The man at Trivoli's was similar in shape and size, except that he had a beard."

Anneka moved up to the other side of the bed and said, "That means the killer is still on the loose." She gazed at Karen and spoke in hushed tones, "You still may be in danger, sweetie."

I felt a jolt. "Good Lord! You're right, Anneka. I need to get to Garth." I stood and squeezed Karen's hand as I kissed her forehead. "I'll contact Lieutenant Brady and have a man watching over you."

"I don't understand why anyone wants to kill me, James. What have I done?"

"It's not what you've done, my dear. Someone thinks you know something."

"We've got to find a phone, Jim," Anneka said. "I'll stay with her while you call."

In less than ten minutes, Brady had one of the local officers by Karen's side.

Anneka and I left for Medina. While driving south on Twenty-Fifth Street, Anneka asked, "Do you think she'll be all right?"

"I hope so," I answered. The streets were empty of

delivery trucks and autos. A quiet Sunday afternoon.

"Have you ever thought about moving out west?" Anneka asked out of the blue.

I kept my attention on the icy road and thought about her question. "My life is all topsy-turvy right now. I'm not sure what I plan on doing. Why do you ask?" The auto bumped along the rut-covered road.

"My sisters and I have discussed it," she said, as she rearranged her wide-brimmed hat. "Since Father retired, we've been considering a change," she said, smiling at me. "There's a lot of money being made in Southern California, and I bet the people there don't have a Swedish restaurant to spend it at."

"They may need a chiropractor there as well. That's something to think about," I said. Was she hinting that I join her? At the moment I couldn't contemplate anything. To change the subject, I asked, "The funeral for Henry Spellman is Tuesday morning. Would you like to go with me?"

"Aren't you the romantic one," she said, reaching over for my hand. "A date at the hospital, and our next one at a funeral. Where do you plan on taking me after that? The execution of poor Henry's killer?"

"It does sound a bit morbid, doesn't it? Well, are you coming with me?" I asked, my eye on the icy road.

"I wouldn't miss it for the world," she said with a jovial laugh. "Where is it going to be?"

"Shaw Cemetery," I said. "No formal services, just Reverend Wilkes-Hadley speaking a few words at the graveside. Afterward, the guests will adjourn to the Spellman mansion for a luncheon."

"So, what are 'we' going to do?"

"We'll be investigating," I said, driving along a well-worn country road. "You, me, and Garth will be standing away from the other mourners and watching to see who's there, who's not there, and how they react to the proceedings."

"Shaw Cemetery is minutes away from Chippewa Lake. I know the place well," Anneka said.

"Then, I'll meet you there."

"I'm afraid not, Father doesn't think women should drive themselves around, unescorted," she said, twisting her fingers together. "He didn't know that I drove to the Spellman place this morning."

"I see," I said. "Then Garth and I will pick you up at ten.

"It's a date."

Chapter Thirty-One

Henry's Funeral

The plot Margaret had chosen was far from the cemetery entrance. It lay along a wooded area next to a gully. Garth, Anneka, and I stood on a small rise above the site, all of us dressed in traditional funeral black. We were not too far away as to appear disrespectful, yet a reasonable distance to be able to scan the proceedings.

"I'm not surprised Miss Spellman chose this plot for her brother," Anneka said softly as she pulled her coat close around her, snuggling into her fur collar to ward off the chilly breeze. "She's as cheap as Rachel and Cynthia told me she was."

We three viewed the early arrivals. I mentioned the frozen ground the gravediggers needed to hack through and hoped they got extra pay for it.

"As tight as Margaret is with the dollar? I doubt it," Garth replied. "Did you contact Brady to see that Steven Jackson was invited to the services?"

"I sure did," I answered. "Brady thought it best that Jackson skips the funeral and be taken directly to the Spellman house for the luncheon. I can't, for the life of me, see why you want him at the funeral or the luncheon."

"Yes, on second thought, Brady's arrangement is safer," Garth responded, rubbing his gloved hands together. "As to Jackson's presence at the luncheon, you'll learn more in time."

The horse-drawn hearse backed up to the gravesite, and workers moved to extract the casket from the rear. Margaret again showed her frugality in her choice of the coffin. It wasn't much more than an old pine box, similar to the caskets we used in the Army for transporting fallen soldiers to their loved ones.

As we were speaking, Margaret's Buick limousine pulled up. Because of Polletti's death, Markson arranged for Officer Jack Leonard to drive the Spellman sisters and servants to Shaw Cemetery. After helping Margaret and Rachel from the back seat, Leonard ran around to the front passenger seat, extending his arm for Cynthia Browning. Oda Rogers followed the Buick in her Model A Ford. Katy Sparks was with her.

"So the entire household is with us," I said to both my companions.

"Seems Cynthia has found a replacement for Polletti already," Garth said, clicking his tongue and frowning.

"Oh, it hasn't been just since Joseph's death, Mr. Garth," Anneka said. "Jack and Cynthia have been at my place four times since they met last week."

"Leonard had better watch his ass," I said, chuckling. "She's an unpredictable woman, to say the least."

"Who are you talking about, Major?"

I spun around and saw Sergeant Markson stepping up the hill toward us. A large black overcoat bundled around him, opened at the neck, revealing a black suit with a red cravat. A black fedora was perched on his head with the forward brim rakishly tilted down.

"Ah, Sergeant. It's good of you to join us. I introduced him to Anneka, and he remembered her from the inn. "Lieutenant Brady will have Jackson and the Rogers clan at the Spellman place after the services here," he told Garth.

"What are you two talking about?" I asked, looking from one to the other. "What's happening after the services?"

"Well, old man. While you were spooning about with Mrs. Larsson yesterday, I came up with the answers regarding the diamonds and, above all, the killer. Your call yesterday, about Karen Bender's attacker, proved to be quite helpful in my thought process."

"Then we better get over to the house," Anneka said.

Chapter Thirty-Two

A Crowded Dining Room

We arrived at the house before the guests. Since Henry Spellman proved to be such a nefarious character, only those brought against their will by the police, and those who felt obligated to be there showed up.

The luncheon was served by a catering service that the funeral director, David Wilkes-Hadley, hired. I must say he did an excellent job of putting things together for the Spellman family. If Margaret had planned the luncheon, we'd have had ham sandwiches and tea. She would dismiss us as soon as we finished. I had to chuckle to myself as I imagined the woman trying to pull a crude stunt like that.

My empty stomach gurgled as I saw the platters full of a variety of sliced meats. A half dozen salads, plates with cheese, condiments, and fruit were spread out for the guests.

"Major," I heard Garth call as he stopped at the door into the dining room. "I want you to be the front man for our little gathering. Stay at the door and make sure all take their designated seats."

He pulled out two pieces of lined paper and handed them to me. "Here's a clumsy but accurate diagram of where I want everyone seated," he said. He pointed to the only other exit, the door to the kitchen. "Officer Padua will be stationed there. See to it that he has this diagram. Other officers will be posted around the room. It's important that no one leaves."

I had my doubts about how enforceable the request was but agreed to do my best.

"I knew I could count on you; now, I need to prepare the evidence," he said, nodding to a table in the southeast corner of the room.

Markson came into the dining room, still decked out in the mourning clothes he'd worn at the funeral. His sandy-colored hair and boyish features went well with the black suit. "Well, Major, your friend Garth told me the room is all mapped out, and you would tell me where to sit."

"Yes, he has something planned," I showed Markson his seat, situated between Longfellow and Jackson, who still wore that silly, ill-fitted derby. We both knew of the animosity between the two men. "That's why I have two of Cleveland's finest against the wall behind you." I pointed to the diagram.

Padua took his copy of the diagram as I explained our duties. He was more than happy to deal with any disturbance. One after the other, the other guests arrived.

Raymond Perkins and Herbert Longfellow came in and apparently assumed they would be seated together.

However, I showed Raymond Perkins his seat on the south side of the table. He was not at all thrilled to be taken away from his employer and seated next to Lieutenant Brady. Perkins pulled out a cigarette holder and jammed a pre-rolled cigarette into it. Brady had Lucy Rogers at his other side, with Craig in his wheelchair next to her.

Lucy and Craig glared across at Longfellow on the opposite corner of the table. I quickly spotted Garth's pattern of seating enemies within sight of each other.

Margaret and Rachel Spellman arrived as the hors d'oeuvres were being served. Margaret, as usual, had a snide remark. "You couldn't wait for the hostess to arrive? How unbecoming." She was wearing her 1880's mourning dress with a wide-brimmed hat holding several black-dyed ostrich feathers in its ribbon. Rachel, on the other hand, wore one of her evening dresses, a bright orange, fringed dress reaching to her calves. She'd adorned herself with a long pearl necklace and had applied makeup. Quite out of place for the occasion. Margaret was not amused.

The final guest, Allen Douglas, strutted in wearing an elegant blue pinstriped suit, his head held high. I sent him to the foot of the table. He faced the Spellman sisters who were sitting at the head.

Garth, seeing that all had arrived, began speaking in his resonant voice. "I'd like to thank all of you for coming this afternoon." He stepped past me to circle the table, examining the guests as he did so. The fireplace, across the room, was ablaze with a fire to warm the occupants. "I'd like to thank the Spellman sisters for allowing us to use this somber moment to reveal the culprits in these crimes," he said, nodding at the sisters. "I thought it best to use a large comfortable room and include all concerned."

Garth studied the scornful faces and must have seen their distaste at using a funeral luncheon to speak of the unfortunate happenings. "Now, don't let my inquiry stop you from enjoying the meal we've prepared."

Despite this, no one touched the food.

Cynthia, Katy, and Oda sat on chairs from the parlor, now arranged along one wall. Near them, Anneka sat in a comfortable lounge chair with her legs crossed at the ankles, her fingers clutched on her lap. Her eyes twinkled as she watched me, her lips parted in a smile. Of all the room's occupants, she seemed the only one amused by all this.

On my right, stood a very anxious Eddie Bennett. We needed the bartender there to identify the man he'd seen at Trivoli's Restaurant. I wished Karen Bender could have been present. She would have corroborated with Eddie's story, but unfortunately, was still in the hospital.

"Get on with it!" Longfellow shouted. "I have work to do." He wore an old-style black suit with heavily starched cuffs and collar. The coat made his white beard and hair look like freshly fallen snow.

"We'll get on with it, old-timer," Sergeant Jack Markson said. "You'll get your work done. Just have some patience."

Garth had circled the room, watching for signs of nerves or guilt among the guests. Now, finally, he spoke "As you can see, two of our suspects are not with us. Joseph Polletti and Karen Bender are resting, and hopefully, healing in the hospital. I found it imperative that I bring you all together. I'd like to thank Markson and Brady for delivering the invitations."

I watched for reactions to the lie about Polletti being in the hospital, but my attention was drawn to an angry voice.

"I don't remember receiving an invitation, Pink," Jackson said, using the insulting tag for a Pinkerton man.

"Certainly, you did," Garth said. "It was attached to the handcuffs Lieutenant Brady and three of Cleveland's finest threatened to slap on you."

"You're not funny," Jackson growled, stroking his beard. "You know I didn't kill Spellman. What do you want with me here?"

"A little cooperation," Garth said. "Yes, you are right, we know you didn't kill Spellman. Major Mallory, my partner, is your alibi."

"Then, why am I here?"

"Two reasons, sir. You may be interested in knowing where the diamonds are. And, you and Mr. Longfellow may have a few words of reconciliation."

Jackson glanced down the table to the elderly Realtor. Longfellow stared back and, with misty eyes, nodded. "We'll speak of it later."

"Now onto a more likely suspect," Garth said, walking toward Allen Douglas, who had not removed his hat, in anticipation of a short meeting.

Douglas' eyes went to the ceiling with a sigh, "I thought we were all through with this, Mr. Garth."

From the other side of the table, came the voice of Longfellow. "He's not your man, Mr. Garth. I told you he was with me that night."

"Ah, yes," Garth said, turning to face Longfellow. "Douglas also told me you were together at the time. But, he also said he got out of bed at ten to get something to drink. You were cozily snoring with a book on your chest in your favorite lounge chair."

"Yes, that's right," Douglas said, leaning back in his

chair, now arrogantly chewing a cigar butt. "I couldn't be involved."

"You might have crept out of the house when you saw him sleeping," Lucy Rogers said, beginning to take an interest in the conversation. "The barn is but a few minutes away. You brought those—those *killers* from New York here to steal the gems. How do we know you didn't meet them and take them to the barn to kill Spellman?"

"I told you, Mr. Garth, that the Black Hand hoods were the killers," Margaret said. "Why are we going through all this? You're wasting our time."

Rachel crossed her legs and put her hand to her mouth. I noticed her stifling a grin, but I don't believe anyone else had. Rachel gazed up at me and caught my eye. She winked, then turned away. "No, Ma'am, I am not wasting your time," Garth said. "Rizzo and De Luca were not guilty. Although they had motive, the evidence shows they were nowhere near the barn the night Henry was killed."

"That's right," Douglas shouted. "I fired them the day after they arrived in Cleveland. I took them to the train station myself Friday night. It was the day before the murder."

"Yes, and Lieutenant Brady went to Union Station on Ninth Street and verified what you told us. After the three of you met with Jackson at the Hollenden Hotel, you had a falling-out."

"Yeah," Jackson growled. "I came to Cleveland a week earlier than Douglas did. We left England on January twentieth and docked in New York on the twenty-eighth. I was to go to the Hollenden Hotel and wait for him. He told me he had friends who would help us get the diamonds back. So, I sat in the hotel for a week and drank up my money in the bars waiting for him. When he got there with the two hoods, I knew what they were as soon as I saw them. The broken noses and bulges in their jackets told me all. I got pissed off at Douglas and told him I wanted nothin' to do with 'em."

"Good for you, Mr. Jackson," Brady said. "Unfortunately, Mr. Douglas didn't know full well what they were like."

"I sent them packing that very night."

"We have a witness at an Italian restaurant who saw you talking with them late on the eighth."

Douglas began to sweat.

Garth leaned on the dining room table and stared down on him. "Is that the last time you saw them?"

"That's it, Mr. Garth," Douglas answered, his swagger returning. "I know what you're getting at. You think I had something to do with them attacking you here in this house. Well, I didn't. I had no idea they were back in town, and I certainly was not involved in that fiasco."

"After Mr. Douglas dropped the thugs off at the train station, he checked out of his hotel and moved in with me," Longfellow added.

"Yes, we had a man watching Longfellow's house, and he didn't see the hoods coming or going." Garth walked away from Douglas and crossed the room. "The attack at the Spellman house happened while you were staying at Longfellow's. The ticket clerk verified the Italians got off the eastbound train in Pittsburgh Friday night and bought tickets for Cleveland. They would have arrived the next morning."

"See, they *were* here in the area," Margaret stated. "You keep avoiding the truth and wasting time. Those hoods killed my Henry."

"Relax, Miss Spellman," Garth said, smiling at her. "We

have physical evidence that rules them out."

Margaret pushed herself up from her seat and huffed in disbelief. "What evidence? You keep talking about evidence but produce none of it."

Garth directed her to the side table. He stepped behind it as Margaret walked up. "Take a gander at these," he said, placing several photographs on the table. "This particular one is quite impressive." Garth carried it around the table for all to view.

"As you see, there are two sets of boot prints in the snow. Meaning two killers, not one. One of them was wearing boots with a plain flat surface. It is a man's size ten. The female who was with him wore a size eight with a ridged sole. The woman walked in the footprints of the male. It gives the impression of one perpetrator until you survey the picture closely."

Garth turned to Margaret. "Who wore the woman's size eight, Rizzo or De Luca?"

"Not amusing, Mr. Garth. What other evidence do you have? Her voice rose as she took her seat. Do you know who the killer is? If so, tell me."

"Oh, yes, we know who the killers are," Garth said.

I sensed a shift in the atmosphere. My Colt was holstered safely under my black jacket, in case the policemen needed my assistance. "Go on, Garth, tell them the rest."

"Yes, Mr. Garth," Markson said, nodding toward Lieutenant Brady. "We've given you a lot of leeway in this investigation. Fill in the blanks for us."

Chapter Thirty-Three

The Revelation

I'm getting to it, Sergeant." Garth walked back to the evidence then changed his mind and eyed young Raymond Perkins. I shifted to the right to get a better view of Longfellow's clerk.

"Please tell me why you lied the other day about Oda?"

Perkins pushed his chair back, but I stopped him with a hand on his shoulder. I bent and growled into his ear, "Answer the man's question."

Perkins' eyes circled the table, stopping at Mr. Longfellow's frown. "Yes, Perkins, answer the question," the old man said.

"I told no lies, sir. I just told them what I saw."

"Come now, Perkins," Garth said. "You told Craig Rogers and his mother that his wife had spent Saturday night at Mr. Longfellow's home, paying the rent on her back."

"What!" Longfellow shouted.

A gasp of disbelief came from Oda as she put her hand to her mouth. Cynthia put her arm around the maid's shoulder.

Garth put up his hand to silence the hubbub. "I already knew, when you told the story, it was a lie. You kept staring at your boots as you spoke, a sure sign of lying. Saturday was the night of the murder. Oda had worked her regular shift, but since she loaned her auto to Polletti, Margaret drove her home We have witnesses. Now, again, tell me why you lied."

Perkins searched for help from Lucy Rogers, who turned away. "I have nothing to say," he answered.

"Well, then, I'll tell you. You orchestrated the plan to alter suspicion from you and your partners onto Oda Rogers. You convinced them that Oda wasn't much more than a prostitute. She had been spending time with Polletti, who, in turn, hinted it was more than a ride home he received. Then you made up the story about Mr. Longfellow. The heartbreak you caused in Craig Rogers prompted him to leave for Canada. You even went to the extent of accompanying them to make sure they left."

"How could you, Raymond?" Lucy Rogers said, sitting rigidly in her chair. "We trusted you."

"As I did," Longfellow added. "What an unbearable scoundrel you are."

Douglas spoke up. "Oda Rogers never stepped foot in Longfellow's home that night or any other night while I was there."

"Thank you, Mr. Douglas," Garth said.

"All right, so I lied," Perkins shouted. "But it was only to protect—"

"Protect whom?" Margaret interrupted.

"Protect himself," Garth said. "He thought he knew where the diamonds were hidden. So he needed to get Mrs. Rogers out of town, to have them for himself."

Lucy Rogers laughed, but it was joyless, almost maniacal. I stepped closer to her and gazed into her eyes. Her blue eyes had faded to gray and stared off into emptiness. "I wanted my boy to get what he deserved. We needed to go to Canada and leave Oda behind. I had to do something to drag him away from the clutches of that she-wolf." Suddenly, her eyes flashed and she stared spears of hatred toward Oda and nailed her against the wall. "Craig and I needed to leave."

Next, she turned on Perkins, her eyes burning with hostility. "Go ahead and tell them how Polletti, the weakling, broke down." I laid a hand on her shoulder, fearing she would jump up and attack.

"You don't have to, Mr. Perkins. I know most of it."

"Get on with it," Allen Douglas said. "I want to get back to Washington and forget this ever happened."

Garth walked back to the side table and lifted two bags from under it, pulling out the contents of one bag. "This is one of many cigarette butts we found at the murder scene. If you look closely, you can see a tiny slit on the end of the cigarette butt. Polletti used a holder that leaves the same slit. So, we were convinced he was the murderer."

"But, it turned out that we were mistaken," I said, interrupting Garth.

"Go ahead, Major."

"Once we spent time with Lucy and Craig Rogers and

Perkins on the return train trip, we discovered Perkins uses the same type of cigarette holder that makes the same small slit on the cigarette. Besides, he wears a size ten boot, Polletti wore a twelve."

"Joseph Polletti isn't the killer?" Cynthia asked.

"Miss Browning, Polletti was only using you to get information from Margaret. You told me about all the questions he asked during the interludes of your passion."

"Yes," Cynthia admitted.

"What did you tell him?" Garth questioned.

"Just that Margaret said Henry carried the diamonds with him at all times," Cynthia replied. "I certainly had no idea—" She shook as she spoke.

"Who was it that told Polletti to use Cynthia? Answer that, Mrs. Rogers?"

"I told him to get whatever he wanted from you, you stupid girl." Lucy shifted her gaze back on Garth and said, "Joseph was a deserter from the Italian Army, so I threatened to turn him in if he didn't do as I wished." Lucy giggled under her breath, like a naughty child. "I just wanted those diamonds."

"How did you get involved in the murder?" Garth asked Perkins.

Perkins sighed, realizing he'd better come clean. "It was the real estate, the ten acres that the barn stood on was the third sale Margaret made to Mr. Longfellow. I delivered the money to the Spellman place each time and found Rachel alone. We discussed the loss of a total of forty-five acres, and if it continued, all she would have left was the house when her siblings passed away. She might even have lost the house. For Rachel's sake and my own, I needed to stop the bleeding of the Spellman fortune. Margaret had wasted the money from the sales by financing all of Henry's excursions around the world. Alaska and South Africa were only two of his travels."

"You were romantically involved with Rachel as well," Garth said, grinning. "I saw that when I danced with Rachel at the Medina Lounge. You were filled with jealousy, weren't you?"

"We struck up a romantic friendship when I came to the mansion on business," Raymond Perkins said in hushed tones. "She had nothing to do with the murders, believe me."

Garth walked back to the side table. "Actually, I do believe you. I have evidence. He held up a small, silver tray with hankies and, in his other hand, his shirt from the other night.

"What do you have there?" Margaret demanded.

"Samples of lip rouge," Garth replied. "I have a sampling of every female in the Spellman and the Rogers' household. Some of the cigarette butts left at the murder scene are covered in, what the salesperson at the Medina Fashion store told me is, 'cherry red.' Cynthia wears tango red, which is a bit lighter. Oda's lip rouge is raspberry, dark, but not dark enough. Rachel is ruled out by her softshell pink color."

"I wear a light pink color so I can wipe it off easily if Margaret happens by," Rachel said, grinning. "So who is the winner of your lip rouge contest, Mr. Garth?"

"Rachel," Margaret admonished. "This is serious business."

"Shut your mouth, big sister," Rachel yelled. "I'll do as—"

"That'll be enough of that," Brady said, standing.

"We'll have no more outbursts from you two."

"Thank you, lieutenant," Garth said, walking over to the seat Brady vacated. "As I was about to say, the 'cherry red' lip rouge belongs to Lucy Rogers. What have you to say to that?"

Lucy gave a heavy sigh. "All I wanted was my boy to get what he deserved. Didn't Polletti tell you?" Lucy asked.

"We want to hear it from you. You not only wanted Henry dead but Margaret as well, right?"

Lucy writhed around on the chair. I saw her face twitching, and saliva drooled from her lips. "I killed Henry. Raymond didn't have the guts to do it," she yelled. "The coward couldn't even slit the bastard's throat."

"The small cuts on Henry's throat— that was Perkins' doing?"

"Yes, Henry almost got away. I grabbed the stiletto from Raymond and plunged the blade under Henry's ribs. I did it over and over again. It made me giddy when I saw the pain in Henry's eyes. So, I pushed it deeper into him. I almost peed my undies in excitement as I twisted the blade."

Everyone sat, stunned, as she relayed her perverted story. It was hard to understand how a middle-aged lady would do such a thing. However, it appeared to me that the words were coming from an insane woman.

"What about Margaret—you were going to kill her, too?" Douglas called out, after gulping down a glass of water.

"We had that worked out, didn't we, Raymond?" Lucy asked, still grinning. "Since everyone was convinced that the Black Hand killed Henry, we hired them to kill Margaret. It wasn't our original plan, but it seemed providential."

"Good Lord, the woman is raving mad," Margaret said, waving a black hankie before her face.

Perkins slumped in his chair. I saw that he now fully understood that the game was over, and he had lost.

"What did you offer the two men, Perkins?"

"We were certain Margaret had the diamonds. The two thugs would have kept them if they had killed her during the attack," Perkins admitted. "They were delighted to go along with it."

"What part in the murder of Henry Spellman did Polletti play?" I asked Perkins.

"He was the driver of the getaway car. He was to meet us either at the entrance of the barn or along the road. It all depended on which way we had to escape. He must have seen the police cruiser driving up to the barn, because he circled around, parked along the road, and watched for us."

"It worked out fine," Lucy said, rubbing her hands together. "He dropped me off at the house then took Perkins home. It's a shame we couldn't celebrate together after the kill." Lucy's shoulders shook as if she was cold and she started laughing again.

"These two were willing to give up the diamonds to the Black Hand, so there was a deeper, final motive for killing both Henry and Margaret Spellman," Garth said, glancing at Markson and then at me. "Do you remember the portrait of Edger Spellman in his study, Markson?"

"Yes, you and Mallory said you both saw a resemblance to someone," Markson answered. "Did you remember who it was?"

"Indeed, we did," I said. "We had just visited the Rogers' home earlier in the week. The painting was the spitting image of Craig Rogers."

"That got me thinking of a motive that would tie all this together." Garth walked over to Margaret and spoke to her. "You don't remember a pretty little maid who worked for your father when you were young. You were around ten years old at the time."

"We had many maids over the years, Mr. Garth. I can't remember them all."

"I imagine not," Garth responded. "That's why I had to search for the information. Your father kept good records, despite the clutter. I managed to find a list of servants from the year 1888. A maid by the name of Lucy Richards worked here for two years. Your father abruptly discharged her in October of that year."

"So what?" Margaret said, not understanding what was happening. "I imagine you're insinuating that Lucy Rogers is that same girl."

"I am, and I also checked the birth records in Toronto. Three months after leaving Medina and returning to Toronto, Lucy Richards delivered a boy named Craig."

"Are you saying—"

"Yes, Margaret, the birth certificate lists the name of the father as Edger Spellman of Medina, Ohio. With that information, she planned on seeking Craig's share of the Spellman fortune. Craig is older than Rachel but younger than you and Henry. Once you two were done away with, Lucy would introduce the true heir to the Spellman fortune."

"Where did the Rogers name come from?" Jackson asked.

"Lucy married Edward Rogers in Toronto and gave his name to Craig when he adopted the boy," Garth answered.

"I would have fought her in court," Margaret said, her

chin held high. "That Canadian wouldn't have gotten a cent."

"That's why they needed you and Henry dead. They waited for Henry to come back from Africa." Garth turned to all those in the room. "As Perkins said, Margaret sold off a good part of the property, so they needed to work fast. Polletti found out from Cynthia that Henry and Karen Bender were leaving for Chicago. They used that information to set Henry up in the barn for an easy kill."

Craig Rogers sat rigidly in his wheelchair listening to all that Garth said. His face was pale, his lips trembling, "Mother, tell me this isn't true. You aren't capable of—"

"Of course I am, darling boy," she said, holding his hand tight. "I needed to get you away from Oda and her deceitful ways and then claim the Spellman fortune for you. We would have lived in this big house and been waited on by servants. When I was ready, I would do away with Rachel and Perkins too. We would have everything."

"You're mad, mother." Craig turned to Markson and pleaded, "Can't you see she's mad, sergeant?"

"Yes, Mr. Rogers, but I'm not a judge," Markson answered, letting out a harsh breath. "Your mother needs a good lawyer, Craig."

"Wait," Rachel said. "You said you had more evidence. What is it?"

"Something small, but it places Lucy at the murder scene as well." Garth walked back to the side table, reached under it, and pulled out a pair of boots. "They match perfectly to the indentations in the snow behind the barn. I found them in her bedroom, where I also found the sample of lip rouge."

"Sergeant, you need to take these two into custody," Garth said.

"My pleasure," Markson replied, rising from his seat and waving for Officer Beltran.

Officer Parks walked up and grabbed Perkins by the arm. "Let's go, buddy. We have a dark, cold cell waiting for you."

Perkins stared at Rachel with pleading eyes, "Please help me, I did this so we could be together."

"You fool, you were fun to dance with. What made you think I would marry you? You certainly misread my intentions. The truth about you killing my brother would come out someday. What did you think I would do, shrug it off?"

Garth wasn't finished with Perkins, "Officer, hold on a minute. Raymond, why did you have Polletti try to kill Karen Bender?"

"She knew too much. She saw Rachel and me together a few times. Karen also found out about my meeting with the Black Hand. Lucy and I feared that she was smart enough to put it all together," Perkins said. "If Polletti got caught killing Bender, he would get pinned for the murder of Henry as well. No one would believe Lucy or I would kill anyone. Not until you showed up, Mr. Garth."

Lucy, already standing, pointed her crooked finger at Anneka and yelled, "You were next to go, sweetie. You asked too many questions when you visited us with your baskets of food." Officer Beltran slapped the cuffs on the woman and began to escort her out as she laughed hysterically. Markson, standing at the door, said, "Be easy with her, Beltran. She's as crazy as a loon."

"Oh, what a polite man you are, Sergeant Markson," she said, "And so handsome too. What about Joe, will he be joining us?"

"I'm afraid Joseph Polletti is dead. He was killed in an auto mishap," Markson responded.

"Oh, the poor dear," she said, "I suppose that's the chances you take. Let's go, Sergeant. All this talk of murder is tiresome."

Chapter Thirty-Four

The Stones

Parks and Beltran have left with the prisoners," Markson told us. "I need to head over there as soon as possible."

"Okay. We have one issue to deal with," Garth said, walking back to the side table.

I heard Markson sigh. The high-strung, impatient man wanted this to be over.

"Yes, you're right, Markson. Let's finish this," Garth replied. He looked around the room. "I believe most of you can leave."

The household staff quickly rose from their seats and scurried out of the room.

"What about the diamonds?" Steven Jackson asked, rising from his chair. Officer Leonard placed his hands on his shoulders to keep him seated. "I got a right to know," he growled. His face, what I saw of it, turned a crimson red.

"You certainly do, Mr. Jackson," Garth said, gazing around the room. "Why don't you, Mr. Douglas, and the Spellman sisters join us in the study where we will have a little more privacy. Markson and Brady will join us."

I offered my arm to Anneka and we followed the procession down the hall. I noticed Margaret, staring off into space. Her lips trembled as she wrung her hands, appearing to be on the verge of a nervous breakdown. She blinked firmly after being seated and shouted out, "Well, do you have the diamonds or not?"

"No, but I know where they are," Garth admitted.

"Then get them!" she shouted even louder.

"That would be rather hard to do, dear lady," Garth said, bowing his head slightly. "Please allow me to explain."

"Be quick about it," Douglas said, his arms crossed and the half-smoked cigar rolling between his lips.

"To start with," Garth said. "Spellman and Sir Chadwick Holdsworth stole the diamonds and left for London intending to sell them."

"That much we know," Douglas said, still scowling at Garth.

"The two of them went to the British Museum of Antiquities and made a deal with Rupert Shepperson, an unscrupulous employee at the museum. My sources told me that they traded the diamonds for something of even more value."

He revealed the black valise. "At the time, I didn't see this compartment in it." He turned the end of the valise toward the table and popped open a small door on the bottom of it.

"It's empty," Markson said.

"It is now," Garth responded. "Let me reveal a secret clue we had found at the murder scene."

"Go ahead, we have our killers." Markson allowed.

"In the stall of the barn where Spellman met his maker, we discovered words etched on the stall floor. With his own dying blood, he wrote, 'Lion's Head.' He thought Karen would be on her way to meet him. He didn't know that Perkins called the bar in Cleveland and imitated his voice. Perkins told Karen not to come. She would have understood the message in the stall if she had seen it. You see, when Karen visited Henry, they would go to The Lajon Bostad Inn or in English, The Lion's Den Inn. It was their favorite place in town."

"So, this Karen Bender has our stuff?" Jackson said, drumming his fingers on the table.

"No. Hear me out," Garth said, appearing frustrated with the interruptions.

"Anneka Larsson is the manager of The Lajon Bostad Inn," I said as introduction. She stepped forward to add what she knew.

"On February eighth, Henry Spellman came into our restaurant," she said. "He handed my sister, Gerda, a box and asked her to hide it for him and release it only to Karen Bender."

"What did she do with the box?" Douglas called out.

"She placed it in the rear compartment of our cash register. Gerda is a bit absent minded and forgot to tell me it was there," Anneka answered. She pulled the box from her large handbag and handed it to Markson.

"Markson, open the box and show the contents to the others."

"What you see here is a group of rare Greek coins. There are only eight of them in existence," Garth said. "They were minted in the city of Mytilene between 521 and 478 BC. The obverse of the coin is the head of a roaring lion, and the reverse is that of a calf. The coins are worth far more than the diamonds Spellman gave up for them," Garth explained.

"Spellman planned on a trip to Chicago to sell these to the museum." Markson held up one of the coins to the light as the others bent over the table to examine them. Some of the guests reached to pick up the coins, however, I stopped them. There's no telling whose pocket they would have slipped into.

"Of course, we can't keep them. The coins are stolen property," Garth said. "Handle them delicately, Markson. There's a reward for them. The Major and I will be sharing it with the Rosenkranz sisters."

"Oh my, I didn't know that," Anneka said to me, excitedly clinging to my arm. She then turned to Garth. "How much is the reward?"

"Converting pounds to dollars, the reward is around twenty-five thousand dollars," Garth said. "Split five ways that's five thousand each, a good sum to walk away with."

Anneka's grip tightened on my arm when she heard the amount. "Oh my, we have to celebrate this good fortune," she said, beaming. "The girls and I closed the restaurant for the day. It sounds like a wise decision on my part."

"Let's not jump ahead," I warned. "We have to deliver these coins to the British Museum before we get the reward."

"Wait just a damned second," Jackson said, scowling at Anneka, who was smiling gleefully. "What about us? Are we left with nothing?"

"Heaven forbid," Garth said. "No, you'll still have the diamonds. I received a wire yesterday from Scotland Yard, and they have Rupert Shepperson and the stones. They'll send them to the three of you once the trial is over."

"Which will take how long?" Margaret asked.

"I have no idea. But Mr. Douglas is still on the staff of Senator Ward. Douglas might ask him to intercede for you," Garth said, glancing at the heavy-set man. He received a nod of assurance.

Douglas said, "I'll speak to him when I return to Washington."

"If you re-box the coins, Markson, please pass them over to Lieutenant Brady. He has the connections to get them back to London and have the reward wired to us."

"Very good, Mr. Garth, I'll get right on it," Brady responded. "It seems like the clue that Henry Spellman left was the key to the return of the diamonds."

"What will happen to Lucy and Perkins?" Garth asked.

"I'm no judge," Brady said, shaking his head. "But it appears as if she may be off her rocker. She'll probably end up in an asylum. Perkins, on the other hand, may face the hangman."

"Unless his lawyer can show that he never killed anyone," I said.

"Either way, he's in jail now," Brady said with a wave.

Garth, Anneka, and I walked into the hallway and found Oda and Craig waiting for us.

"Mr. Rogers," Garth exclaimed. "I'm glad you hadn't left yet. Garth handed Craig the papers from Toronto and said, "These may help you gain your share in the Spellman fortune."

"As well as legal issues we need to deal with," Oda added. "I've been in the study thousands of times to clean and never once noticed the resemblance between Craig and the old Spellman man."

Anneka stood close by my side listening to the conversations around her. She tugged at my jacket sleeve and led me away from the crowd.

"I told you the restaurant is closed for the day." Her hand lovingly caressed my cheek. "Tonight would be an excellent time for the fondue I promised you."

My mind darted to Christina for a mere second, but without further hesitation, I pulled Anneka close and smiled. "That's a marvelous idea. You get it ready, and we'll be there tonight."

"Just you and I?"

"I thought, for tonight only, I'd bring Garth and Markson." Seeing her disappointment, I added, "We'll have many nights alone in our future."

"Mmm, I'm sure we will." Anneka leaned up and kissed me, bringing on a hoot and holler from around the room.

Chapter Thirty-Five

Fondue at The Lajon Bostad

The parking lot sat eerily empty when we arrived at The Lajon Bostad Inn. Because the girls had closed the restaurant to the public, no one was here to upset our gathering. We watched the flickering light from the vast fireplace dancing on the windowpanes as I drove my Hudson over the rutty driveway to the inn. Garth sat next to me. Jack Markson, who'd eagerly accepted my invitation, sat in the rear.

"I've only been here a few times," Markson said. "But, when I have, I've always had a good time." He wore a black evening jacket with gray slacks, white bowtie, and a low top hat. "I should have worn something more appropriate for the weather, but an overcoat would have been in my way."

"You look fine," Garth assured him. Garth wore his

pinstripe suit and homburg. "In fact, we may be overdressed for the occasion. I believe it will be just the three of us and the three sisters."

I agreed with Garth. They were overdressed for a private party. Of course, I seemed underdressed. I had discarded the black mourning suit in my room at the Spellman place, and worn my tweed jacket and cap. Since leaving the military, I rarely dressed to-the-nines as the young people call it. I prefer to be comfortable and not try to be showy. Besides, Anneka likes me the way I am.

We left the auto and stepped up to the front entrance. Before we had the chance to knock on the door, it swung open. Anneka's voluptuous figure stood in the entrance to the hall. The flames from the fire behind enveloped her, giving her a passionate glow. She had braided her strawberry-blonde hair and swirled it around her head, with tall white feathers on the right side. I stared, in awe of her beauty. She wore a beaded, crepe party dress, which made me feel all the more ill-dressed for the occasion.

"You look just fabulous, my dear," I said, passing through the door.

"Thank you, Jim. Please come in, everyone. We have everything ready for you," she said, taking my arm and leading me in. Garth and Markson followed into the spacious, near-empty restaurant. Greta and Gerda were sitting on the sofas surrounding a low table with a fondue pot and six skewers upon it. The three half-sofas formed a U shape, with the fourth side facing the hearth.

Gerda jumped to her feet, sauntered up to Garth, and grabbed him by his arm. "Oh, Mr. Garth, how wonderful to see you again."

Garth seemed pleased by her greeting. "You, as well,

Gerda. You're perfectly charming in your violet dress, my dear. How did you ever know that was my favorite color?"

"Oh, how funny, it must be karman, Mr. Garth," Gerda said, giggling. "Calling you Mr. Garth is somewhat awkward. What is your first name?"

"My first name is just as awkward, itself. But it is my mother's last name, Sherwood." He answered, returning her smile. "And it's *karma*, my dear."

"That's why I simply call him Garth," I said from the sofa across from them.

"Well, if your name is Sherwood, who's karma?"

"I'll explain it later," Greta said, her eyes on the ceiling.

"How about if you call me Woodie," Garth responded, leaning close to her ear.

"Mmm, Woodie, I love it." She smiled coyly as she led him to the sofa nearest the fire.

"*Woodie*, what a cute name," I chided him and laughed.

"Not you, old man," he said, his eyes gleaming with mischief. "You are only allowed to call me Garth."

"I'll remember that, Woodie." My comment made Anneka laugh. I then noticed Markson standing behind the third sofa, facing the fire. "I am sorry, Sergeant, I forgot you haven't been introduced to the ladies." I stood and made formal introductions and returned to my seat next to Anneka and scooted over to be close to her.

"Forget Sergeant. I'm off duty, it's Jack," he said to Greta, then glancing at the far wall of the restaurant. "I see you have a gramophone, and you're dressed for a dance. Would you like to kick up your heels?"

Greta wore the latest fashion, a short crème-colored dress with the hem reaching just below the knees. "I'd love to dance, Jack. But I haven't had the chance in some time.

I might trip if I *kicked up my heels*." A concerned gleam in her eyes.

"If you trip, I'll be right there to catch you." Jack smiled, showing a set of straight white teeth.

"Come on over and pick a recording you like," she said, pulling him by the hand over to the gramophone. "But no kicking." She waved her fingers at Jack.

"I promise not to kick," he said, smiling broadly.

She seemed to prance over to the back wall with a wiggle in her step and the beads on her dress swinging with her movements.

I'd thought Jack and Greta would hit it off, and judging by their silly flirtation, I appeared to be a real matchmaker.

"Well, Woodie, aren't you going to ask me to dance as well?" Gerda said, leaning into Garth. "I like to dance—it makes my ears tingle."

"But, of course. I am waiting to see what Jack is going to play. I certainly want to see your ears tingle as well."

"Help me move the table and chairs, so we have a dance floor," Gerda said, pulling Garth off the sofa.

I felt like the odd man out. Anneka sat close and stared into the fireplace, lost in thought.

"Don't worry about me, Jim. I'm not much for dancing. Let the young people exhaust themselves on the dance floor."

"I'm glad you said that. I'm a bit of a rube when it comes to dancing the new steps," I said, genuinely relieved. "In the Army, I learned to dance formally. As an officer, the Army required me to attend certain affairs."

"That's what civilians think officers do all the time," Anneka said. "One hears so much about the galas of the generals and politicians."

"In some cases, yes, it was part of our duties. Especially when in Washington," I answered, putting my arm around the back of the sofa behind her. "I avoided them as much as possible. Hated the formality of it. I preferred being a hardened cavalry officer in the field of action."

"What about your time in Washington? What did you do?" she asked, turning to face me fully.

"I helped my old friend, Teddy Roosevelt. I spent a few years in his administration, working on modernizing the Army."

"It's a good thing you did so, Jim," she said, laying her hand on mine. "Did he know this horrible war was coming?"

"You might call it a knowledgeable premonition. TR saw the war clouds rising, as many others had. But, let us not talk of war. It's a very unpleasant topic."

"I understand," she agreed. "It sounds like the youngsters found some music to dance to."

"Isn't that The Original Dixieland Band they're listening to?" I asked.

"Yes, and they have a recording of The American Quartet and Bill Murray's song *Pretty Baby* and others. They'll be working up an appetite, for sure."

"I happen to enjoy *Let Me Call You, Sweetheart.* It's easy to dance to, and I like the lyrics as well as the melody," I said.

"Oh, Jim, yes, you may call me sweetheart." She laughed and put her head on my shoulder.

I started to say that I'd only been referring to the song, but something stopped me.

I love this woman. Maybe … I don't know. I overthink things.

She saw the confusion on my face and nervously

laughed. "I was just teasing, Jim. Listen, they're playing it right now."

Our eyes met and I took her hand, leading her to the edge of the dance floor. It felt completely natural, my arms around her, although I had none of Garth's finesse and we danced only until the end of the one song.

"Let's get some of this fondue before the others come back," I suggested as we returned to the sofa.

She joined me and picked up one of the fondue forks and stabbed at a carrot. "It must be fascinating to put all the clues together and come to a logical conclusion," she said, examining the cheese pot.

I was chewing on a piece of sausage dripping in cheese sauce as I thought about her statement. "Well, it was a complicated mess. Garth and I thought, from the beginning, that the whole thing revolved around Rachel Spellman. It seemed that she had control over a couple of saps, two men who were lusting after her."

"Cynthia had said she was a mousy little thing, but I saw that wasn't always the case when she would come to our place."

"Garth and I saw her at the Medina Lounge, away from her sister," I said. "She was a real quiff and had men doing cartwheels for her."

"It's as if Rachel had two personalities. She wasn't always that wild. When she was with Perkins, she was all the lady."

"Well, she had nothing directly to do with the murders," I said. "However, if she hadn't led Perkins and Polletti on, as she did, her brother might still be alive."

"It was all about the box Gerda had in the register?" Anneka asked.

"For the greater part. But the murder came about by Craig's relationship with the family. Lucy Rogers would have had Margaret Spellman killed and taken the spoils of the Spellman fortune. I think it runs deeper in a family of malcontents who hated one another."

"How sad." Anneka's face fell. "Little did she know that the fortune had dwindled down to an old house and a thousand acres of land."

"After seeing you and your sisters interact, I can see why you would feel that way," I said, letting my arm slide from the sofa to her shoulders. "There's a lot of love in your family."

She nodded as she moved closer and snuggled. The music continued. It was a slow piece and I watched the two couples dancing closely. I pulled Anneka close to me. Leaning down toward her full pink lips, I kissed her. She gave no resistance and parted her lips for me.

We didn't notice that the music had stopped until the others returned to the sofas.

"You two enjoying yourselves?" Markson asked with a smile.

"Knock it off," I grumbled. "Sit down and have some fondue."

The four of them had raided the bar and each held a glass of wine. Markson glanced from me to Garth and said, "Unfortunately, I have something to say that will take the air out of your balloon."

"Uh oh," Garth said. "Markson lost his position and needs to move in with us."

"Well, you're trying to be funny, but you're close."

"All right, now you've got our attention," I said. "What's the big news?"

"First of all, my name isn't Jack Markson. I'm not a sergeant for the Medina PD."

"I figured that out the day of the murder," Garth said. "The real sergeant is Padua, isn't it?"

"Oh, you're so smart, how did you know that, Woodie?" Gerda asked, holding his arm tightly.

"Padua's blue uniform was faded every place but on his sleeves, where the stripes had been removed. It was because either he was reprimanded or he took them off himself," Garth explained. "I checked his records, and he was asked to take them off temporarily and pose as a patrol officer."

"Very good, Mr. Garth," Markson said. "You're right. Padua is the sergeant. Lieutenant Brady and I arranged for him to step aside for the occasion."

"All right," I said, a bit gruffly. "Who the hell are you, and what's your game?"

"My real name is Jack Collins. I was with the United States Secret Service. Former President Roosevelt then hired me as his personal bodyguard. My game, as you say, is to watch you two and determine if you are up to the standards of Mr. Roosevelt. He has a job open for you."

"Up to his standards?" I said. "TR knows me, he knows what my standards are. What utter balderdash."

"Yes, Major," Collins said, putting up his hands. "I may have worded that wrong. He knows you quite well. He has quite a lot of admiration for you. He doesn't know Garth personally but has followed his career since he was a detective for the New York P.D. He is quite impressed with you."

"Then, what are you spying on us for?" Garth asked.

"Spying is a harsh word, Garth. However, I suppose that's what Brady and I were doing. We were asked by

Theodore Roosevelt to see how well you worked together."

"You mean Roosevelt had Pinkerton transfer me to Cleveland so you could watch us?" Garth asked. "And how did he arrange a murder to suit his fancy?"

"Oh, that was sheer coincidence, Garth. The Spellman sisters calling on you was not part of the plan. However, it worked out well since TR will need your services shortly. If it weren't for the Spellman case, we would have waited for something else to come along."

"What if we're not interested in this project?" Garth asked, still put off by the subterfuge.

"I'm not sure I want to leave," I said, my gaze fixed on Anneka. "Granted, he is my old comrade in arms … I just don't know."

"I want to hear more before I commit myself," Garth said.

"I must add that I'll be going on this journey with you if you decide to go." Jack Collins stood behind the sofa leaning on it and made firm eye contact with both of us. "He didn't mean to offend you; he holds you both in the highest esteem in your fields. I have determined that you can work together, admirably, and with me, as well. I said as much in my last report to the former president."

"Well, then, what is it we need to do to find out about the mission?" I asked.

The room became quiet. Even the gramophone stopped playing.

"You don't want to miss this opportunity, Jim," Anneka said, leaning over to me. "You were telling me how much you missed the action. Now's your chance to get back into the fray. You can always come back to me when you're finished." She smiled and batted her long lashes alluringly.

"Garth and I do work well together," I said, agreeing with Collins' assessment. "That's why I think I'll turn it down. He and I have all the tools to become a detective agency. More important, I've been without the love of a good woman far too long to chance losing her."

I leaned forward and questioned Garth. "Well, what do you say, Garth?"

"I'm always up for an adventure, old man." He turned to Collins. "I was in the Secret Service from 1912 to 1914, I don't remember meeting you."

"That's because I had previously left. Mr. Roosevelt hired me away from the service in 1912 when he was running for president as the Bull Moose candidate."

"Well, I'm with the Major on this," Garth said, "Mallory and I have discussed other plans. We may open our own detective agency—Garth and Mallory"

"Or Mallory and Garth," I added.

Garth put his arm around Gerda and led her to the dance floor. Collins escorted Greta over to the bar to round up more drinks, which left Anneka and me alone in front of the dying fire.

"What do you think?" I asked Anneka. "With no prying ears about, did you want me to leave?"

Her eyes stared at her hands in her lap, her fingers intertwined. "No, I don't want you to leave. In fact, my heart jumped when Collins made the offer."

"I don't need to follow him or Roosevelt to find adventure," I said somberly. "You and I both know where that lies."

"Yes, running a restaurant," she said, smiling.

"Oh, get Gerda and Greta to do that," I said, grumbling under my breath. "I want you by my side."

"I can help you with your detective work," she offered.

"I'm sure Garth would love that," I said, watching Garth on the dance floor, spinning Gerda around. "Ah, the hell with what Garth wants. He's got his own ghosts to deal with," I said, turning to face the woman who belonged to me. "I want to spend the rest of my life with you."

Anneka softly gazed into my eye, her lower lip trembled. She said nothing.

"Do you understand what I'm asking?"

Anneka threw her arms around my neck and pulled me close. Her kisses melted every fiber of my body. She pulled away, her eyes boring into mine, "What do you think? Yes, I'll marry you, big guy."

Our lips met again, longer and softer than before. Nobody was around to interrupt us. After the long kiss, Anneka backed away and gazed into my eye. "You honestly want to go on this adventure, don't you?"

My head bowed as I thought about it. "Maybe I will just go to Sagamore Hill to hear the president out. I owe him that much."

"What about Garth?" she asked. "I believe he turned it down because of me."

"I'll convince him to go have a listen, as well," I said, "That shouldn't be hard."

"I'll be here, waiting for you," Anneka said. "No matter what you decide."

* * *

Thank you for taking the time to read *The Greek Coins Affair*. It's my first novel and of course I hope to build a following of loyal readers for the next ten books, which I have planned for this series. If you enjoyed this one please tell your friends, and I would be so grateful if you would consider posting a review. Word of mouth is an author's best friend, and very much appreciated.

Thank you,

Rick Adelmann

What's next for our MG&M detectives?

On the eve of his wedding, Major James Mallory receives an invitation to attend a reunion of his old Army comrades, to be held at the Wyoming ranch home of his former commander, Colonel Isaiah Johnston. James and Anneka decide the trip to Wyoming will suffice as a honeymoon, for now, until the couple relocates to their new home in California.

Hilltop Ranch is remote and secluded, and by the second day, the dozen guests, their wives, and the household staff are snowbound. And that's when the murders begin.

With no other law enforcement at hand, Mallory, Garth, and Mallory search out the evidence and put together the clues in this devious and complex puzzle.

Check out all the books in this series:

The Greek Coins Affair

The Hilltop Ranch Affair

The Blue Sky Affair

The San Carlos Business Guild Affair

The Forgotten Murder Affair

The Irish Manor House Affair

Visit Rick's website: rickadelmann.com

Facebook: https://www.facebook.com/rick.adelmann.752

Twitter: https://twitter.com/RickAwriter

Pinterest: https://www.pinterest.com/rickcnbike/

Instagram: https://www.instagram.com/ricksmysteries/

The writer of this story is a heck of a guy. Rick Adelmann has been around the hill and has fallen off a few ridges. Always a writer, He started at the age of twelve. His little sister asked him to write a play for her and her friends to perform for their parents. It was a smash hit!

He spent a couple of years with the Cleveland PD, enlisted in the Air Force, worked at a Medina, Ohio radio station, then headed out to California to make his fortune. And, forty-five years later, he's still trying to make it.

At least he's prepared himself. Rick kept writing as he worked for a BA degree in History, taught school, acted in a couple of movies, repossessed cars, sold real estate, work in security, and manned the cord boards at the phone company.

All this experience gave him ideas for plots and characters. When not writing, he spends time with his lovely wife Gayle, greets people at his church, putters in his garden, watches baseball, and plays with his dachshund, Cookie.